Wonder

A SOUL SAVERS COLLECTION OF
HOLIDAY SHORT STORIES & RECIPES

KRISTIE COOK

Published by
Ang'dora Productions, LLC
24123 Peachland Blvd C4
#148
Port Charlotte, FL 33954

Ang'dora Productions and associated logos are trademarks and/or registered trademarks of Ang'dora Productions, LLC

ISBN 978-1-939859-17-4

Printed in the United States of America

To all of the strong women in the world and the men
who love and respect them

Acknowledgements

Appreciation always goes first and foremost to the reason for the season (and the reason for everything, really)—my Maker and my Savior.

Next, I thank the members of Kristie's Warriors who were so kind to contribute their recipes: Heather Brandt, Stacey Nixon, Debbie Poole, Charlotte Wilcoxson, Kelly Victorine, Susan VanNort, Felicia Semmler, Heather Wakefield, Michele Luker, Jessie de Schepper, Katherine Murphy, Claire Downes, Chrissi Jackson, Jill Cruz, Zee Hayat, Wendy Jahnke, Christina Silcox, and Tammi Swartz. Thank you, as well, to my mother-in-law Wanita Cook, who allowed me to share our family recipes. Thank you to the rest of the Warriors for all of your help in telling the world about *Wonder* and the rest of my books.

Thank you to Kristen Yard for helping me pull this all together. Thank you again to Chrissi Jackson for all that you did with the original *Wonder* stories. This bundle obviously couldn't have happened without your work last year.

Most of all, thank you, reader, for purchasing my books, reading them, and, I hope, enjoying them. I would write anyway because I can't *not* write, but you make it so much more fun and interesting. *You* are a very special gift to me during the holidays and every day of the year.

Halloween Stories & Recipes

Possession

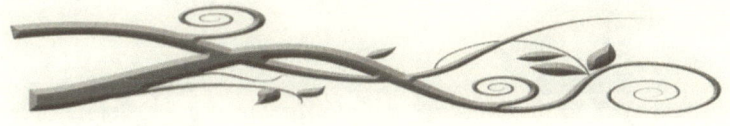

This story first appeared a few years ago on A Life Bound by Books blog for their Haunted Halloween feature. I spruced it up a bit and posted it on my blog in 2013, and I thought it would be a great addition to include in this collection. Please note that this doesn't really fit anywhere specific in the actual story because it's made up. If you must try to stick it somewhere, it would basically fit in right after Devotion, when they're all still on the Amadis Island. Of course, if you've read that book and read this, you know that doesn't work either. Really, it's just a tiny little story for fun.

I placed the last candle in Tristan's birthday cake before my eyes swept over the banana-gasm goodness Blossom had prepared on my behalf. When I deemed the job perfect, I turned to face Owen.

"So are you going to tell me where he is or not?" I demanded.

Owen leaned back against the counter, crossed his arms over his chest, and shook his head. "You know he wants nothing to do with this day."

"Yeah, yeah. He doesn't like to be reminded of how old he is, which reminds him of his previous life. But I'm glad he's here in my life now so—" I shut my mouth at the peculiar look Owen was giving me. "What?"

He pushed his hand through his blond hair, making it stand up like a scarecrow's. Thus his nickname. "That's, uh, not the real reason he doesn't like this day."

"What do you mean?"

"It's not just his birthday. It's Halloween, too."

I rolled my eyes. "I think I've brought him around to liking it."

"I doubt it. Have you ever even spent his birthday with him?"

"Well . . . I didn't know it was his birthday at the time. When we first started dating. But we did Halloween stuff together and he had fun."

"But were you with him at midnight?"

I tried to think back. "It was a long time ago. I don't remember the exact time he brought me home."

"It had to have been early. Because at midnight . . . " Owen's voice trailed off. His sapphire blue eyes lit up, and his mouth twitched with excitement.

The anticipation was killing me. "What?"

"Well . . . it's not just Tristan's birthday, and it's not just Halloween. This also happens to be the day—" He paused for effect. "—Jordan died."

I cocked my head and squinted my eyes. "Jordan? As in—"

"As in the Daemoni, the first of Tristan's kind. And since Halloween's when the veil between our world and the Otherworld is thinnest—"

"Wait. Do the Amadis believe in that?"

Owen shrugged. "I just know it seems to be true because that's when . . . well . . . " He cleared his throat, again building up the suspense. "That's when Jordan's spirit takes possession of Tristan's body so he can roam the earth again and search for his sister, if just for a few hours."

I burst out laughing so hard I nearly hit my head on the counter's edge.

"Ha! Nice spooky story, Owen. Hilarious!" I cut off the guffaws and glared at him with all seriousness. "Now tell me where he is."

He stood up to his full height and lifted his hands out in emphasis. "Alexis, I'm serious. And since you look so much like Cassandra, Jordan's prey, you should probably stay far, far away from Tristan tonight."

"Now that's absurd. Fine. Be that way. I'll find him myself."

"Alexis, please—"

I didn't listen for his plea, but I thought I heard a sigh of frustration just before I flashed. I appeared in the place where we'd all been earlier this morning—an ancient stone house in the Greek countryside. Tristan and Owen wanted to check it out, but I felt edgy as we explored the ruins. Ready to leave long before they were, I'd left them here and went back to help Blossom with Tristan's cake. Tristan hadn't come home with Owen, and since Scarecrow wouldn't spill where else he might be, this was my best guess.

The sun had set already and the moon hid behind a heavy blanket of clouds. Darkness filled the dilapidated house, making it even spookier than earlier. Although in remarkable condition considering its age, the house was losing its shape, some walls nothing more than piles of rubble. A breeze blew through holes where stones had crumbled away and through windows with no glass, ruffling my hair. I tried not to think of the cobwebs in the corners or of the spiders and other creatures that made this place home, but I couldn't help it. The hairs on my arms rose and a hint of fear traveled down my spine. Soft light briefly filled the room, and I looked up through a hole in the roof to see the moon disappearing again behind a thick cloud. Complete darkness consumed the house and me, and my breath caught in my lungs. *Maybe I should go.*

Then lightning flashed and showed the silhouette of a large figure standing by the window. I breathed a sigh of relief.

"Tristan!" I hurried toward him, toward the safety of his muscular arms and his powerful body. Of course, I could have probably taken on whatever would attack me, but there was no comparison to the security I felt when in my husband's arms. Nothing would harm me when he was by my side.

But before I took more than a step, a strong gust of wind blew up around me and whipped my hair at my face. A raspy voice hissed, filling the air around me with "Caaaa-sssssannn-ddddrrrraaaa. . . "

I froze. The hairs all over my body stood on end, and my heart raced. What the hell was going on? And then I remembered a stray bit of today's conversation between Owen and Tristan—something about this being Jordan's house. *Son of a witch!* How had I missed that earlier? The story of Jordan and Cassandra and the different paths they chose ran through my mind. We were right on Jordan and his witch's old stomping grounds! And on Halloween, no less.

Had Owen been serious? Was this the real reason Tristan had come here today? My whole body began to tremble.

"T-t-tristan?" I said again, my voice small and shaky now. I could barely make out the figure at the window, but I sensed the movement as it turned. Lightning flashed again, illuminating his beautiful face. And although it looked very much like Tristan, the deep blue eyes and white-blond hair definitely weren't his.

I opened my mouth to scream. The figure suddenly stood next to me, silencing any noise that tried to make its way out. My mouth slammed shut as I stared up at the menacing form.

Lightning flashed. Tristan's face right before me. Then Jordan's. Hazel eyes. Blue. Sublime face. Twisted with malice.

His hands clamped onto my shoulders and squeezed. I swung my arms and bucked my body. He tightened his grip on me, holding me still.

"Hello, little sister," he whispered in my ear. Definitely not Tristan's lovely voice. This one resonated with something sinister, full of horror and threats. "Nice of you to come play. I've been waiting for this for a long, long time."

I closed my eyes and screamed.

Again, no sound came out. My body thrashed, and I tried to kick my legs, but something wrapped around them. Eris's magic tangling me up? Had Jordan brought his evil witch with him? Well, I had my own power. I began to gather the electricity within me, growing the force into a strong current. My lids popped open to glare the revolting demon-man in the eyes before I fried his soul out of my husband's body.

Except bright daylight blinded me.

I flew up to a sitting position and gasped as I found myself on the couch at home. Owen and Tristan, standing in the kitchen and holding plates full of birthday cake, turned to look at me.

"You slept through Halloween," Tristan said. He held up his plate. "But thanks for the cake."

"Bad dream?" Owen asked.

I nodded, still unable to speak. A sharp pain shot from the base of my neck to the front of my skull. I winced. They exchanged a knowing glance, and I remembered when I'd felt a similar pain—as though someone had jabbed around inside my brain while I slept.

Another time I supposedly had a bad dream only to learn differently later.

"Um . . . " My voice came out roughly, as though sandpaper made up my vocal chords. I cleared my throat. "What happened last night?"

Tristan raised an eyebrow and studied me with sparkling hazel eyes. "We took Dorian trick-or-treating, came home, and you passed out on the couch. You don't remember?"

Dorian bounded into the room then. "You shouldn't have eaten so much of my candy, Mom. It made you sick and probably gave you nightmares."

I blinked, trying to clear the cobwebs from my mind. Of course. What else could it be? Tristan doesn't really become possessed on Halloween. I peered at Tristan—my soul mate, my true love—and he gave me my favorite grin. But something flashed in his eyes and not the usual gold sparkles.

Was that a hint of blue . . . or just my imagination?

Endings

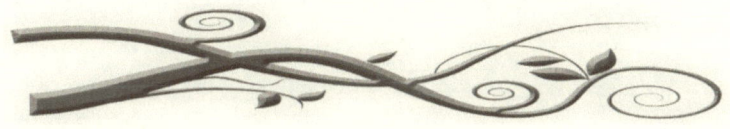

Did you ever read those choose-your-own-adventure stories when you were young? If you loved those, you might enjoy this story immensely because you get to choose the ending for the main character. These are all new characters living in the Soul Savers world and have nothing to do with the main series. I hope you enjoy this. And don't worry if you cheat and check out all the endings. I won't tell.

Chapter 1

The cool night air blasted into my face the moment my friends and I stepped out of the fraternity house, a frigid contrast to the heated party inside. I pulled my jacket tighter around my skimpy costume, but it did little to warm me up. The earthy smell of burning wood and leaves wafted in the air, and I wished I were wherever it came from, sitting next to a bonfire under the stars. It surely would have been a better way to spend Halloween night than at a frat party, especially since my boyfriend didn't show up—maybe because he didn't know he was my boyfriend. Yet. I just had to get him to notice me, and I thought this costume would have done it, but alas, maybe it wasn't meant to be. I'd have to resign myself to staring at him in our history lecture every Thursday.

"Ah! It feels so good out here," Corey said as he pulled off his mask, his voice unusually throaty. It got that way when he'd been drinking, and he'd had plenty to drink tonight. His black hair was damp with sweat and smooshed to his head. He ran his fingers through it and gave his head a shake, spraying us with droplets of sweat.

"Ew! Corey!" Whitney squealed, jumping away from him before smoothing her hand over her straight blond hair, and then wiping her palm on her skirt.

"You're so gross," Maria added, knocking into me as she, too, hopped away. We both stumbled—a result of heels and a few too many shots—and giggled as we used each other to stay upright.

Mike, the only other guy in our group, laughed at his roommate's antics, making Corey grin.

"You think they purposely made it hot as Hades in there?" Corey asked. He walked backwards in front of us. He had super-long legs, and his reverse walk kept him from striding too far ahead of the rest of our group as we crossed campus from Greek Row to our dorms.

"I don't know, but if I would have known you'd take that mask off, I'd have brought you out here sooner," I said, wrinkling my nose at him.

"Seriously, dude, it's creepy as shit," Maria agreed.

"It's a *clown* mask," Corey protested.

"Exactly," Whitney said.

"Creepy, pervy, stalker clown," Maria clarified.

"The kind that likes to lure little kids into white vans," I added with an exaggerated shudder.

"Or pretty girls," Corey said with a maniacal laugh as he jiggled the flaccid rubber mask in front of us. The thing was even creepier when it was empty.

Whitney squealed again. "Keep it away from us!"

"Don't worry. I'll keep you girls safe," Mike said as he maneuvered himself between Josie and me and slung his arms over our shoulders.

"You're the damn reaper," Corey said, referring to Mike's costume that consisted of a black robe, a mask, and a large scythe, which he must have left at the frat house, because he didn't have it now.

"Still less creepy than a clown," I said, and the other girls agreed.

Our conversation moved on to the best costumes we remembered from childhood as we crossed the grassy quad, punctuated by laughter at the stupidest things. Whitney and I nearly fell over from a fit of giggles but we couldn't remember why we'd even started laughing. The alcohol was still warm in my belly, probably the only reason my teeth weren't chattering. At least it hadn't snowed this year like it had last—here in the mountains, you never knew if Halloween would be part of an Indian summer or bring in a blizzard. Tonight was in between, with the perfect amount of chill for a fall evening.

Thin, gauzy clouds passed over the full moon, and we all glanced upward, then launched into a new tangent about whether a full moon on Halloween was classic or cliché. And that led to a drunken philosophical discussion—the kind college students are known for—about what makes something classic or cliché.

We reached Whitney and Maria's dorm building first, and the guy's building was right across from it.

"Are you sure you'll be okay?" Maria asked me as they all paused at the junction of sidewalks that everyone called the Crossroads because eight paths from various dorms and the rest of campus crossed here.

"I'll be *fine*," I said a little too enthusiastically. I poked my hand out of my jacket sleeve and pointed at my building about fifty yards away. "I'm right over there, you know. You can see my window from here."

Said window was lit up by my lame-o roommate who had probably spent the night studying. I kept trying to convince her that she was missing out on the best times of her life, and she kept trying to convince me that the next two semesters would be gone in a heartbeat, and I'd be jobless because of my GPA. Not that it sucked as badly as she made it sound—it just wasn't perfect like hers. We were complete opposites. In fact, I was surprised the light was even still on, because I was the night owl in our room, while she was the early bird always after that worm.

Thankfully, I had Maria and Whitney, my besties at college, who were always looking for fun. Mike and Corey were friends from freshman year, too. They'd been pledges then, pressured to bring more girls to the parties, and we'd been their first invites. Our group had been together ever since. Frat parties may not have been my top choice for spending the evening, but they were better than sitting in the dorm studying. Especially on Halloween, one of the greatest holidays of all time.

"Okay," Maria said, throwing her arms around me. "Be safe."

"The worst thing that can happen to me is I trip on these heels," I said, wobbling even as we stood there. "Go on. I'll see you in class tomorrow."

Whitney laughed. "Or not. It might be a sleep-in day."

She gave me a hug, too, and then she and Maria turned for their building.

"I wouldn't miss the chance to see you tomorrow," Mike said as he turned toward me, his blue eyes searching my face, as if for some kind of sign that I felt the same.

I sighed. Poor Mike. He was deeply entrenched in the friend zone with me, and that would never change. He just wasn't my type at all, but he didn't seem to realize that. Even as he leaned forward to kiss me, and I spun away. His lips skimmed my temple.

"I need my bed," I said with longing. "Good night, boys."

"'Night," Mike mumbled before striding away, his voice full of rejection. My chest tightened, but what could I do? I'd done my best to not lead him on, but the boy was persistent.

"See ya tomorrow," Corey said, then he turned and followed his roomie.

Without anyone to lean on, I knew there was no way I'd make it to my dorm in one piece. I slid off my heels before heading for the four-story building I called home these days. After leaving the well-lit area of the Crossroads, my walk home suddenly seemed unusually dark. I looked up. Well, no wonder. One of the path lights was out. *No biggie,* I told myself. Plenty of lights were lit ahead, and I made this walk at least twice a day, including at night. Laughter carried from somewhere not too far off, so I wasn't completely alone. Still, when there was a snapping sound behind me, I jumped and let out a little squeak. I glanced over my shoulder, but nobody was there. My heart picked up speed, and so did my feet.

As I passed some bushes and then a bench with a trashcan next to it, there was another sound. My breath caught as I looked around wide-eyed. Nobody. *Stop it. You're just freaking yourself out.* I forced a breath as I continued on my way.

And then someone jumped out at me. A snow-white face and blood red lips drawn into an insane-looking smile. Big eyes that were black and empty.

"Got ya!"

"Ahhh!" I screamed and jumped back several feet. My hand slammed over my chest and my racing heart as I took in the fake green hair, round red nose, and the familiar long, thin body. "COREY! You asshole!"

I punched him in the shoulder, and he doubled over in laughter.

"Sorry, but that was epic," he said when he'd finally stopped chortling. "You should have seen your face!"

I scowled at him, and he made his face as straight as he could manage.

"I decided you shouldn't walk on campus at night alone. Especially a night full of drunks and evil spirits."

I resumed my walk. "And you thought scaring the shit out of me with that damn mask would what? Help in some way?"

He strode next to me, doing his best to keep his strides in pace with my much shorter ones. "If it scared you, maybe it scared the evil spirits away."

I thought I heard something behind us, like a snicker, but when I looked over my shoulder again, all I saw was sidewalk, grass, and bushes leading back to the Crossroads. No people anywhere.

"I'll be fine, Corey," I said. "There's nobody around, and I'm halfway there."

I turned to face forward again and cut my eyes sideways when Corey didn't answer. He wasn't next to me. I turned in a circle, but no Corey. Nobody at all.

"What are you doing now?" I asked with annoyance as I headed toward my dorm. "If you scare me again, dickhead, my punch will land a lot lower than your shoulder."

Silence greeted me.

"Corey, come on," I said. "Where did you go?"

I looked around again even as I continued walking. He'd completely disappeared. Did he decide he wasn't so worried after all? Or did something happen to him? The worst of my imagination ran off with me, creating all kinds of terrible scenes in my mind.

"Corey?" My voice took on a pleading tone as I pulled my jacket tighter around me. "Dude, please. I'm done with this."

I picked up my pace. Then I heard footsteps behind me. I spun around, trying to startle him before he got me again.

I lifted my arms in the air and shouted, "*Boo!*"

But no Corey behind me.

There was someone, though.

"Oh, god, I want to die now," I muttered under my breath.

Him. The object of my daydreams during my history lecture. The one I'd been hoping to see at the frat house, and maybe catch his eye. Tall. Dark. And way beyond handsome into I-want-to-lick-your-face effin' *hot*. He stood right in front of me, dressed in a tuxedo with his hair slicked back, his face painted white, and his lips bright red. He was probably going for the Dracula look, and my mind quickly reeled through all the places I wished he would bite me, starting with my inner thigh.

And I'd just yelled "boo" at him.

"Um . . . sorry . . . I, uh . . . " I stammered, forgetting everything about the last five minutes as he gazed at me as though he wanted to taste me as badly as I wanted to taste him.

"I've been looking for you all night," he said, his voice low and sexier than I'd ever imagined. No, I hadn't actually talked to him in person before. Even though he was a frat brother to Mike and Corey, he was rarely around the house, at least when we were.

"Me?" I managed to squeak.

He took a step forward and brushed his fingertips up my arm. Even through my jacket, my skin tingled. My knees began to feel like jelly.

"You," he confirmed. "I've been watching you for a long time. Will you come for a walk with me?"

He offered his arm like a gentleman. I glanced at my dorm, but my empty bed suddenly seemed less attractive than it had a few minutes ago. My eyes darted around, but Corey must have made himself scarce and gone back to his room when he saw My Guy coming. He knew there would be nothing between Mike and me and also knew this was My Guy—after all, Corey sat next to me in history lecture and put up with my sighs every week.

"Um, I guess." I looped a slightly trembling arm through his, barely able to believe this was really happening. "Where do you want to go?"

"Not far—just over here," he said reassuringly as we walked back toward the Crossroads. His hand clamped over mine where I gripped his forearm. A calm, warm feeling swept through me, as though my buzz had returned, but even better.

Until he steered me off the sidewalk and toward a dark copse of trees that eventually led to the forest up the side of the mountain.

I tried to pull free and turn back for the sidewalk, but his grip tightened, his arm feeling like an iron bar as he pinned me against him.

"Hey! What are you doing?" I demanded.

"I'd hoped you'd make this easy," he muttered before sweeping me off my feet and into his arms.

The air swooshed by me at impossible speeds as he held me closely to his hard-as-steel chest. I inhaled deeply, his brown sugar-like scent coating my throat and tongue. By the time he stopped and set me down, we were far up the mountainside, and I could see the lights of campus over his shoulder, below us. The pitch black of night surrounded us. What'd happened to the full moon?

"What are we doing? Why'd you bring me here? Did you seriously just run all that way that *fast*?" The questions came pouring out of my mouth, but My Guy only sauntered closer to me without a word.

I backed up with each of his steps until my spine pressed against the rough bark of a tree.

"What do you want?" I breathed.

"You," he said simply. His hands gripped the lapels of my jacket, and he pulled it open. My belly warmed like it does when I take a shot of tequila as his gaze swept up and down my scantily clad body. Why had I chosen to dress like a slutty witch? I knew I should be freaking out a lot more than I was, but my panic switch seemed to be malfunctioning.

At least, until his eyes came up to my face. They glowed. Bright red. Like a fucking demon.

"What the hell?" I shrieked.

I shoved my hands out at him and prepared to run, but I might as well have pushed at a brick wall. He grinned, and fangs were revealed. Fangs! *They're not real. This isn't real. It's Halloween. Just a costume.* My logical mind tried to convince me, but everything else about me denied what made sense. Fear replaced the calming, almost dreamy effect he'd had on me moments ago. My heart raced at breakneck speeds. My body wanted to follow in a flight response, but I couldn't get past him.

"I just want a taste," he said as he moved in closer. I tried to push against him, but holy shit was he strong. "A long taste."

His tongue slid over his lips before he dove for my throat. I was being attacked by a mother-fucking vampire! This couldn't be happening.

He pulled back at the last moment, and when he looked at me, his eyes had returned to their dark brown. Had I imagined the glowing? They were even warm now as he cocked his head.

"I don't really want to simply eat you," he said as a long finger stroked over my cheek. "I'd prefer to turn you. You could be strong and invincible, like me. Have super speed and senses, and live forever. You could be mine for the rest of eternity. Would you like that?"

I stared at him with wide eyes. Was he for real? He'd make me a vampire?

"You have about three minutes to make up your mind," he said as he leaned in close again, "before I drain you."

My mouth fell open for a scream, but no sound came out.

The moment his fangs pierced my skin, something rammed into him. Something insanely large and furry and growling like a monster. My Guy, who was no longer *My Guy*, was knocked several feet away, but he landed on his feet. His eyes, red and glowing again, narrowed at the beast. An actual beast that stood taller than me, but looked like a wolf. They circled each other in a standoff, both of them growling, back and forth, as if having a conversation. The thought crossed my mind that I might be able to escape while they were distracted, but then the animal began to shrink before my eyes, and a strange fascination kept me planted firmly in place.

Within seconds, a naked man stood where the wolf had just been.

I was losing my mind! First a vampire, and now a werewolf. This couldn't be happening. I must have made it back to my dorm and fell asleep, because this could only be a nightmare.

"I told you she was mine!" the wolf-dude yelled at the vampire. He seemed familiar. Did I have class with him, too?

"I got her first, though, didn't I?" the vampire sneered.

"You were going to eat her! She's supposed to be my mate!"

"Not if I make her mine!"

They snarled at each other again, the sounds more feral than human. Without daring to move my body, my eyes slid side-to-side as I tried again to assess my ability to run. But at that moment, they both turned on me, their eyes full of lust and hunger. Something stirred within me, but I couldn't decide if it was the fight-or-flight response . . . or a mutual feeling of desire and need.

"We either have to kill you or turn you," the vampire said to me. "We know you have a dark side—yeah, we've been watching you—and we think you'd be a good addition. But if you don't agree, well . . . "

"We have orders," the naked man finished. Good lord did he have a smokin' hot body. My eyes couldn't help but roam even as they were hanging my future—or lack of one—over my head. "Straight from our bosses, Lucas and the Daemoni Ancients. Nobody gets out human or alive. And I'd really like to make you *mine*."

A shiver ran up my spine at his tone and meaning.

Daemoni. The word bounced around my head. Why did it sound familiar? Where had I heard it before? The word Amadis popped into my mind with the same vague sense of familiarity. Strange words, somewhat memorable. I was sure one meant demons, so the other must be good. Were there good people around, too? Amadis who could help me? I thought about screaming, but I didn't. I wasn't sure I wanted to be helped.

"So you decide, love," the vamp said, surprising me with both the offer and the sweet but sexy quality to his voice. "Do you want to have inhuman strength, speed, and abilities, as well as immortality like me? Do you want to be mine?"

"Or also have inhuman abilities, but a beating heart and the ability to have family and children, like me?" hot naked man asked. "And get to shift into a fucking wolf. You can't beat that."

He gave me a grin that could melt panties.

I stared at them, speechless. How could they expect me to make such a decision? The abilities would be pretty cool, and maybe immortality, too. But I didn't want to be a monster! Did I? Did I have any choice? At least as a wolf I could have the family I always wanted. But did I really want pups for kids? Oh, my god, why was I even thinking about this? They couldn't be real. This could *not* be happening!

"Or, of course, you have another choice," vamp-guy added, and the threat of his tone with his next words made my knees knock together. "We kill you."

They watched me, both with red eyes now, their hunger and lust growing with each beat of my heart. They moved in closer, expectantly, crowding me. I could either choose to be like them, or choose to die.

What kind of choices were those? What was I going to do?

"Hurry," wolf-man growled. "We don't have all night."

My throat tightened with each hammer of my heart as I continued to stare at them. They took a step closer to me. I tried to swallow as my gaze bounced between them.

"I, uh, I choose . . . "

What do you choose?

If you choose to become a vampire, go to Chapter 2 (page 22).

If you choose to become a werewolf, go to Chapter 3 (page 24).

If you choose to stay human and fight, go to Chapter 4 (page 26).

If you choose to drop into a ball and pray for the Amadis to rescue you, go to Chapter 5 (page 28).

Chapter 2

"I want to be a vampire," I said, and as soon as the words came out of my mouth, I knew they were true.

Superhuman speed and strength? Being at the top of the food chain? Being young forever with all of eternity stretching before me? Why would I choose anything else?

My Guy's lips turned up in a luscious smile, and if I hadn't been sure before, I was now with the promise that grin held. "Excellent choice, darling."

The next thing I knew, he had me in his arms again, and he was sprinting farther up the mountain. Over the top and down the other side, we stopped at a large log cabin overlooking a lake.

"Welcome to my home," he said as he carried me inside.

He lay me down on a sofa that faced a huge window with a stunning view as the sky began to lighten with dawn.

"I apologize for the rush, but I am out of time." He knelt beside me and pushed my hair away from my neck. "I have to drain most of your blood, and then replace some of it with mine. I'll do my best not to drain you completely."

He dove for my neck then, and his fangs slid into my skin. As he began sucking, a feeling of bliss swept over me. I lay limp in his arms until my world went completely dark.

Three Days Later

"Hey, you, it's about time you woke up." Maria's voice filtered into my foggy brain.

"Yeah. You've been like a corpse, in bed for *days*." Whitney now.

I tried to pull myself into consciousness. My eyes peeled themselves open, and I blinked against the white light until my vision focused. Not white light, only simple daylight streaming through the window. But damn, it was *bright*.

"What happened to you?" Maria asked.

I looked at my friends, who sat on the edge of my bed in my dorm room. I squinted for a moment as I thought about exactly what happened, until something caught my eye. And my nose, making my mouth water and my throat burn.

"Thirsty," I croaked as my gaze focused in on exactly what I needed.

Maria's vein thumped in her neck. She tasted as good as she smelled.

Chapter 3

"I want to be a werewolf," I replied.

The ability to live forever had never attracted me. Who would want to do that? Sure it could be fun for a while, but eventually the excitement would wear off, leaving you in a dull, monotonous state of existence for eternity. Nope, not my cup of tea. I wanted to *live*, not simply exist.

And to be able to change into a wolf? To have all the superhuman abilities they have? And to still be able to have a family? That's what I was talking about!

Naked guy bowed his chest, showing me who was alpha, as he nodded with confidence. He'd known my choice. Something inside me had been calling to him as his mate, drawing him to me. I knew that now that I'd made the decision. I felt our connection all the way to my bones.

The vampire narrowed his red eyes, let out one last snarl, and then disappeared.

"So now what?" I asked, the shake in my voice completely gone. I'd made the right decision, and everything within me knew it.

"Now we see if you have what it takes," my alpha replied, and then he exploded, gross, gooey stuff falling all around me and into my hair. A wolf stood where he just had, a deep chestnut color to his fur. His upper lip lifted in a growl, and then he lunged at me. I threw my hands up in front of my face, and his fangs sank into my palm.

Only for a moment, though, long enough to draw blood, and then he was gone.

I spun in a circle, looking for him, but there was no movement, no trace that he'd even been near. "What the hell?"

I sank to my butt and waited for his return until long past dawn, but he never came. Exhausted and confused, I made my way down the mountain and back to campus. I had no idea what had happened tonight, but by the time I was snuggled into my bed, I decided I'd been drunker than I'd thought and had passed out while on a walk. I could only chalk up the events into a weird dream.

One Month Later

Snow fell in big, fat flakes as I hurried across campus for the warmth of my dorm. The clouds in the sky reflected the white blanket of snow on the ground, making it look and feel almost like noon rather than nearly midnight. The light brightened even more when the clouds skidded away from the full moon.

I was near my dorm when movement in the trees to the side of the path caught my eye. Were those eyes glowing in the darkness of the forest? The events of Halloween night rushed back to me as something within me tugged toward those woods. Toward the beast I knew was in there. As though in a trance, I veered off the path and headed for the trees.

I'd no more than passed the first tree when my lower leg snapped in half, ripping a scream out of me as I fell to the ground. My throat seized when my other leg broke like a twig. My whole body lurched and convulsed as agony wracked through me. Every bone in my body felt like it was breaking. My skin ripped apart where shards of bone poked through. Pressure built in my skull until my head felt as though it were about to explode.

Then I did just that.

I exploded. I burst out of my human skin, out of my human self. I landed on my feet—four of them now—and shook myself out. Bloody, pulpy stuff rained to the ground around me.

The deep chestnut fur of my mate caught my eye, but then a waft of something delicious tickled my nose. Meat. I needed meat. I needed food. And I didn't care what kind. I turned toward the tantalizing smell . . . back toward the way I'd come when I was human only moments ago . . . toward two girls and two guys my human self knew . . . and my animal self craved.

I sprinted for them. For my first meal.

Chapter 4

All of those years in the dojo and the fighting ring would pay off. I'd taken martial arts since I was a toddler and had defeated bigger guys who'd gone on to become professional MMA cage fighters. Surely I could take on these two whack jobs.

"You're both fucking crazy," I snapped before moving into action.

I swung my leg out in a roundhouse to the naked dude's danglies, and as he doubled over, I thrust my arm up, plowing the heel of my palm into his nose. He grunted as he fell to his knees. Not stupid enough to count him down, I swung my foot into his temple, knocking him to his side. He lay there, motionless.

I spun to face the other one—the one I'd been stupid enough to daydream about. He lunged for me at the same time, but I twisted out of his grasp at the last second, then shoved my fist into the side of his ribs. They should have cracked with the force. Instead, *my* knuckles cracked, and I gasped with pain. His side was like concrete.

He gave me a sardonic smile.

When I jumped for him, he disappeared. Only to appear behind me. He wrapped his arms around me, and I swung the upper-half of my body down, flipping him over my back. He broke his hold on me, but landed on his feet. He smirked again. I swung at his chin. He caught my hand. Squeezed. I cried out as all the bones in my hand broke.

"Too bad you're not as bright as I'd originally thought," he said. His hand blurred toward me and sank into my hair, grabbing a fistful and yanking my head back, exposing my throat. "I should have known, though. You *are* only human."

His mouth dove for my throat. A beastly growl sounded beside us right before more teeth dug into my leg and pulled. As they ripped me apart, all I could think was, "At least I still have my soul."

Chapter 5

Life as a monster or death? I couldn't choose either of those! I didn't want to be like them. I didn't want to die, either. I just wanted to be in my room, in my warm bed. Why was this happening to me?

"What will it be, young one?" the vampire asked as he took another step closer to me.

My whole body trembled. My breaths were shallow, barely pulling in enough air. My heart raced, sending a pulsing rush into my ears. I sucked in the deepest breath I could manage and let out a scream. Then the tree bark carved into my back as I sank to my butt, curled in a ball, and sobbed.

"Someone please help me!" I cried.

"Nobody's coming for *you*," the werewolf guy sneered, but he'd barely finished his sentence when two *pops* sounded in the air. The attackers both growled.

"Alexis and Tristan," one of them snarled.

I dared to peek between my fingers. Two new figures stood in the woods behind the vampire and werewolf—a girl and a guy. He was big, with light brown hair and a powerful build. She was his opposite, with reddish-brown hair and a petite body. Both were beautiful, *inhumanly* beautiful. And both scary as hell as they fought the supernatural creatures that had almost killed me. Like warrior angels battling these demons.

They were a sight to behold as they flipped and turned, kicked and punched, and then most amazingly, the girl shot electricity out of her palm. The other two stopped fighting and looked as though they were surrendering. I dared to uncurl myself and push my way to my feet. A breath of relief slid past my lips. I stared at the couple with rounded eyes until the girl gave me a slight nod. Then I took off in a run.

I sprinted down the mountain, toward the lights of the campus below. Tree branches tore at my jacket and bare legs, but I paid the scratches little attention. I'd almost died tonight, but I'd been given a second chance at life. I just needed to get to the safety of my dorm, and tomorrow morning I'd wake up with this horrible nightmare as nothing but a memory.

As the residential buildings came into sight, I wanted to shout with glee. But then something huge and hairy plowed into me, knocking me off my feet. I flew into a tree and fell to the ground with a gasp. The wolf stood over me, air puffing out of his black nose, and his eyes glowing an unnatural red. His lip curled upward, and he growled. Just once.

Then he lunged for my throat.

His fangs tore into my skin. He whipped my whole body around like a rag doll as he shook me like a dog shakes a toy. The grip of his muzzle loosened, and I flew several feet away. My back snapped when I slammed into a rock. My vision began to gray. He growled again before latching once more onto my neck.

As my vision slid into darkness, my life slipping away with it, the girl who'd been my heroine stood behind the wolf. Unable to speak or to move, I tried to plead to her with my eyes, begging for her to rescue me again. To save my life.

She only gave me a small smile as she lifted her shoulder in a shrug.

"Sorry," she said, "but this is a Halloween story. Did you really think it'd have a happy ending?"

Recipes

Recipes for you to try this Halloween—or whenever—submitted by me and members of my street team, Kristie's Warriors. I hope you enjoy them!

Keep the Monsters Away Spinach Artichoke Dip

Submitted by Tammi Swartz

The garlic makes it extra yummy and with it on your breath, you'll keep the monsters away on Halloween . . . and everyone else.

Ingredients:

    ¼ c butter

    Heaping tsp garlic

    1 10-oz frozen spinach, thawed and drained

    2 cans artichoke hearts, drained and chopped

    2 8-oz packages cream cheese

    1 ½ cups sour cream

    1 ½ cups mayonnaise

    1 cup grated parmesan cheese

1. Melt butter and garlic together in microwave.

2. Add all other ingredients.

3. Bake @ 350 degrees until golden brown

Tristan's Birthday Cake

Submitted by Kristie Cook & Wanita Cook

Alexis loves to cook, but she's not much of a baker, especially compared to Tristan and Blossom. If she didn't have Blossom's help, this recipe, using a box mix, would be right up her alley. And I know Tristan would love it because all the men in my house request this for their birthdays. I know the recipe by heart because they have me make it so much. I actually make it with a full 8 oz can of evaporated milk, two packages of caramels, and a full (small) bag of chocolate chips, because we're just decadent like that.

<u>Ingredients:</u>
    1 German chocolate cake mix
    ½ cup evaporated milk
    1 pgk. caramels
    ½ cup chocolate chips
    2 cups chopped nuts

1. Preheat oven to 350 degrees.

2. Prepare cake mix as directed. Pour half of batter in greased 9x13 pan (reserve the other half). Bake for 15 minutes at 350.

3. Meanwhile, combine milk and caramels in saucepan and heat to melt.

4. When half of cake is done, pour melted caramel over the cake. Sprinkle with half of the nuts and chocolate chips. Pour remaining cake batter over the top, then sprinkle the rest of the nuts and chocolate chips. Bake for 20 minutes.

Graveyard Cake

Submitted by Kristie Cook & Wanita Cook

The family calls this Kansas Dirt Cake, since they're from Kansas and the cake represents the dark, rich soil of Kansas. Because it does look like dirt, it's a perfect recipe to use for a graveyard theme at Halloween. Add some gummy worms, fake bones, and headstones for a fun party cake.

Ingredients:
   1 ¾ cups chocolate cookies, crushed
   1 stick of butter or margarine
   Large container of whipped cream
   2 pkgs of coconut pudding mix
   1 8-oz pkg of cream cheese, softened
   1 cup powdered sugar
   3 cups milk
   1 tsp. vanilla

1. Mix pudding mix, milk, and vanilla in a saucepan. Cook on medium heat until thick. Set aside to cool completely.

2. Mix cream cheese, butter, and powdered sugar. Beat until smooth. Stir in whipped cream. Set aside.

3. Cover the bottom of a 9x13 cake pan with all of the crushed cookies except 1 cup. Spread cream cheese mixture over the cookies. Pour pudding mix over cream cheese mixture. Sprinkle remainder of crushed cookies over the top. Refrigerate.

Spirit Blasting Leek and Potato Soup

Submitted by Katherine Murphy

A warm soup before you go out in the cold for trick-or-treating or other spooky festivities. The leeks will keep the evil spirits away.

Ingredients:
    4 large Leeks
    2 medium Potatoes
    1 medium onion, chopped small
    1 ½ pint chicken stock
    ½ pint milk
    2 oz butter
    2 Tbsp cream
    1/2 Tbsp chives
    Seasoning

1. Melt the butter in a pan and add the leeks, potatoes, and onions.

2. Stir well and sweat with lid on stirring occasionally.

3. Add the chicken stock and milk.

4. Put lid on and simmer for 20 minutes on a low heat.

5. Liquidize and season to taste.

6. Add chives and swirl on cream to serve.

Blossom's Last-Minute Stew

Submitted by Chrissi Jackson

There's nothing better than a rich, hearty stew to warm your soul and fill your stomach on a cold autumn night. The beauty of this recipe is that it's really just a starting point. You can customize it with whatever you have in your fridge and pantry. As long as there's love in the kitchen, the results will be delicious.

<u>Ingredients:</u>

3 Tbsp. olive oil (if you want to really kick up the flavor, use half bacon drippings and half olive oil)

2 cloves garlic

1 large onion (diced)

4 carrots (diced)

4 celery stalks (diced)

2 lbs. steak (cubed)

6 Tbsp. flour

½ tsp. black pepper

1 tsp. Sazón seasoning*

1 cup red wine

4 cups beef broth

4 medium red-skinned potatoes (diced)

Optional additional vegetables: green beans, corn, spinach, squash, mushrooms, sweet potatoes, kale, canned tomatoes. . .

1 Tbsp. Worcestershire sauce

1 Tbsp. Maggi liquid seasoning (or soy sauce if you can't find Maggi)

1 tsp. dried rosemary

Optional: 1 Tbsp. cornstarch, 1 Tbsp. water

1. Heat half of the oil in a Dutch oven over medium heat. Add garlic and cook for 30 seconds, stirring constantly so that it doesn't burn. Add onions, carrots, and celery and cook until veggies begin to soften (about 5 minutes). Remove veggies from pot and set aside. Add remaining oil to the pot and increase heat to medium-high.

2. Mix 6 Tbsp. flour, pepper, and Sazón seasoning in a large plastic bag. Add beef cubes and toss to coat. Carefully add meat to oil and cook until brown on all sides. Add wine to the pot and stir to deglaze. Add the broth, cooked veggies, potatoes (along with any other veggies of your choice), and seasonings to the pot. Reduce heat to medium-low and simmer for at least 30 minutes or until potatoes have cooked through. Add more broth if liquid evaporates too quickly.

3. Adjust seasonings to taste.

4. If you would like a thicker stew, combine 1 Tbsp. cornstarch and 1 Tbsp. cold water. Stir mixture into stew and bring to a boil.

*Sazón is a complete seasoning popular in many Latin countries. It is available in many grocery and online stores. It's really worth trying!

Charlotte's Perfect Carmel Corn

Submitted by Char Wilcoxson

This is the best caramel corn I have ever had, thanks to my Grama and her excellent baking from scratch skills! I got the idea for this recipe to be used by Clair since she made Tony popcorn in the cabin. This could be for any holiday and was something I wanted to share with everyone.

<u>Ingredients:</u>
    2 sticks real butter
    2 cups packed brown sugar
    ½ cup corn syrup
    1 tsp salt
    ½ tsp baking soda
    1 tsp vanilla
    (Oil for popping corn)

1. Melt butter in a saucepan. Stir in brown sugar, corn syrup and salt. Bring to a boil stirring constantly. Then boil without stirring for 5 minutes (make sure it does not burn). Remove from heat and stir in baking soda and vanilla (this will cause it to foam up, so have a spoon handy if needed).

2. Next, have half of your popcorn in a very large bowl with a lid, slowly pour half the mixture over the popcorn, making sure it is all coasted, then place lid on tightly and shake vigorously. When finished, pour it out onto a large cookie sheet and bake at 300 degrees for about 10 to 15 minutes. Halfway through, use a spatula to mix it up and turn it over.

3. When done, spread it out onto foil and let cool. Repeat with remaining popcorn and carmel sauce. To store, place in plastic bowl with a lid if it last that long!

Vanessa's Blood Jam (Low Iron)

Submitted by Kelly Victorine

This is for Vanessa. It's a low-sugar jam recipe that actually tastes good. My husband and I spent multiple years perfecting the recipe so it is a little more tart and not overly sugared. It is also a little runny like blood! It sets up more if you include more pectin, but I like my jam in between runny and solid . . . so here you go.

Ingredients:

6 ½ cups Strawberries (liquefied or smashed depending on your desired consistency)

½ cup Lemon Juice

2 pkgs. Pectin

5 cup Sugar

1. Liquefy strawberries (leave two cups out to crush in hands).

2. Add lemon juice and berries into a large kettle pot.

3. Add pectin and mix thoroughly.

4. Let sit for 30 minutes, stirring every 5 minutes to dissolve pectin.

5. Heat mixture to boiling over high heat, stirring constantly for 10-15 minutes.

6. Crush remaining strawberries in hands and add to mixture.

7. Let cool slightly, then pour into jam jars.

8. Let jars and jam completely cool on counter.

9. Add lid and move to freezer, allowing jars to freeze overnight.

10. Enjoy Jam on toast, crackers, or crumpets after removing from freezer and thawing.

Thanksgiving Stories & Recipes

Amity

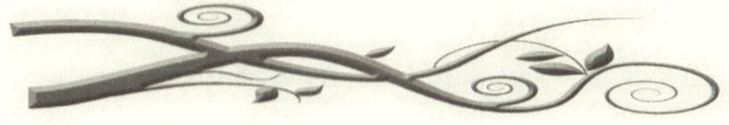

This first short story, *Amity*, introduces new characters in the Soul Savers world, giving you a peak into the Daemoni way of life. It does not fit in any particular place in the main Soul Savers Series chronology, although it would definitely be before the events that conclude *Wrath* (Book 5). I hope you enjoy these characters as much as I enjoyed writing this!

Chapter 1

Oranges, reds, and yellows painted the trees lining the path of the park as Mindy crossed it on her way to work. One tree blazed like a bright fire against a backdrop of evergreens. Another was nearly naked already, its bare, spindly branches reaching for the overcast sky. Although the cold air didn't bother her, Mindy snuggled her hands into her coat pockets, trying to look Norman, while flipping the blond strands away from her eyes and cheeks even as the wind insisted on slapping them back against her skin. She sniffed the air, tasting the crispness of fall along with the threads of humanity that floated in the cool breeze. Her mouth watered. But, strangely, not for her usual favorite meal of human blood.

No. Right now, she craved human food. More specifically, a Thanksgiving feast.

She hadn't craved human food for months. Not since the early weeks of being turned nearly a year ago. Sure, she could eat Norman food and drink Norman drinks, but except for pretty much anything alcoholic, she never strongly desired it. But Thanksgiving had always been her favorite holiday, and for the last couple of days, she couldn't stop thinking about a table loaded with a golden turkey, fluffy mashed potatoes and creamy gravy, buttery green beans, and her mother's famous stuffing that was never soggy or mushy, but perfectly browned like her turkey. She dreamt about Granny's pumpkin pie and Nana's apple cobbler, too.

Or, maybe, it was really Mom, Granny, and Nana, as well as her sisters, that she truly missed so much.

Not going there, Mindy told herself as she shouldered her way through the door of the bar where she'd serve drinks to humans for the next several hours while deciding which one she'd take for dinner after closing. Thoughts of family were unacceptable. Forbidden, even. But oh, so difficult to avoid this week. Which was why she focused on the food.

The night remained slow, most Normans doing the "family thing" this night before the holiday. The ones who weren't, though, were her best customers—they didn't have family to be with tonight or any other night. They'd left their families and never bothered to start ones of their own because they'd much rather spend their time in a dark, dingy bar run by creatures they didn't believe existed, no matter how many times said creatures drank from their veins. They were alcoholics, loving the bottle more than any soul, which was why they were Mindy's best customers. Not only did they drink a lot and tip well, but drunk and readily available, they provided easy pickings for her own dinner and were too far gone to remember it the next morning. Or at least, to believe it when they were sober.

Jewels, a fellow bartender and Mindy's roommate, handed Mindy a card toward the end of the night.

"We're invited to a Vampire Thanksgiving Feast!" Jewels danced behind the bar with excitement, her vampire gifts keeping her perfectly balanced on her six-inch stilettos when any Norman would have broken an ankle. Her long, brown hair spread like a fan as she spun, and when she stopped, a twinkle shone in her brown eyes. "Time to show our thanks to the Daemoni gods for our immortality."

Mindy lifted a brow at Jewels after reading the invitation. "It doesn't say that."

Jewels laughed. "Of course not, silly. But isn't that what Thanksgiving is all about—giving thanks? And what more do we have to be thankful for than being vampires?"

"You're British. You don't even celebrate Thanksgiving," Mindy pointed out.

"But I'm here right now. And a vampire *feast*? I can only imagine how nice that will be!"

Mindy had learned by now that "nice" had a deeper meaning to the English than to Americans. "Nice" to Jewels meant very good, maybe even spectacular, especially when she said it with such enthusiasm. Mindy wasn't sure about a vampire feast being spectacular. Or even nice. She still fought traces of humanity that lingered in her soul, and a smorgasbord of humans didn't sound so "nice."

"Oh, dear. Why don't you just go and be an Amadis bitch?" Jewels said at the look in Mindy's blue eyes. The dark-haired vampire shook her head. "Don't worry, I won't let you stoop to that. But really, Minz, you need to step it up. You know you feel it—the blood thirst. The craving for human blood. Stop fighting it so much."

Mindy chuckled as she eyed one of her regulars, and her tongue swept across the bottom of her teeth. Her fangs were retracted at the moment, but she could still feel the little points of her canines. "You know I don't fight it."

It was impossible to fight, even when she wanted to.

"Then you'll come with me to the feast tomorrow?" Jewels demanded. Mindy's eyes travelled back to her roomie's face, and she frowned. "That looks like a 'no'."

"I kind of . . . I kind of want a traditional dinner."

Jewels' nose wrinkled. "Like *human* food?"

She shuddered.

"It may be the last time I crave it, so why not?"

"And where are you going to do that?" Jewels' eyes narrowed. "You're not thinking about going home, are you?"

Mindy rolled her eyes, although the desire to see her family one more time remained as a pit in her stomach. "Of course not. That would be stupid."

"And forbidden."

Yup. And forbidden. A new idea struck Mindy. "I could make my own little Thanksgiving feast at the apartment." Her excitement grew at the idea. "You could join me, too, and we can eat like human pigs."

"Yuek. No, thank you. I'll be going to the vampire feast. And you should really go with me. It's much healthier, you know."

Mindy laughed. "Healthy and Thanksgiving feast don't even belong in the same sentence. You really should join me and learn what an American Thanksgiving is all about."

"Giving thanks and gluttony. I already know. And that's what I plan to do—with all of our new vampire mates." Jewels sauntered down to the other end of the bar, indicating the conversation was over.

Not quite wanting to throw it away, Mindy shoved the invitation into the back pocket of her jeans. As she served the few customers the rest of the night and even as she drank from one after, she made a mental grocery list. The craving for a traditional Thanksgiving became so strong, her mouth watering so much, she nearly drained her customer dry. She was a baby vamp herself, too young to be siring a newborn, but if she hadn't stopped in time, her only other choice would have been to leave him to die. So she was thankful she'd come to her senses when she did.

No, she wasn't full Daemoni yet. And that could likely get her killed. But for now, she wanted to enjoy these last bits of her humanity. She was thankful she hadn't lost her soul . . . yet.

"Much to be thankful about," she happily muttered to herself as she entered the twenty-four-hour grocery store near her apartment, but then she clamped her mouth shut and looked around. Too many Daemoni vamps around to be talking like that. But she could think it. *A real Thanksgiving dinner is especially something to be grateful for.*

Chapter 2

"What the hell are you doing?" Jewels demanded when she came out of her bedroom the next morning wearing nothing more than an extra large t-shirt and maybe panties underneath, but the shirt was too long to know for sure. She didn't really need to sleep—neither of them did—but sometimes a vampire needed some alone time in the privacy of her own room. Jewels' dinner-date still slept soundly in her bed. "And what the hell are you wearing?"

Mindy sat on the couch with her knees pulled to her chest, wearing her old pajamas left over from a life she no longer had—pink fuzzy ones with yellow elephants on them. Her eyes didn't leave the television screen where a four-story-tall Elmo floated by. "Watching the Macy's parade in my jammies. Thanksgiving Day tradition."

Jewels glanced at the TV, then glared at her roommate. "Are you daft? We have a feast to get ready for!"

"I told you. I'm making my own feast, and the turkey's already in the oven. But even if I was going with you, it doesn't start for twelve hours."

Jewels huffed. "Yes, well, it's the event of the year. At least, since I've been here, which has almost been a year. It's going to be glorious, and I want to look my best."

Mindy looked at her roommate and pretended to gag. "Are you actually going to wear a *dress*? Gads!"

"Hmph. I might." She spun on her heel and returned to her bedroom.

Daylight was only a nuisance to them, although direct sun could be a little more problematic, but less so for Jewels, who was a couple of years older, in vampire age, than Mindy. Jewels showed no repercussions as she had another go with her dinner before kicking him out of her bed so she could get ready for the night's gala. After the parade was over, Mindy moved a little slower than she did at night—but still faster than any Norman. By noon, she was dressed in dark blue jeans and a festive brown and red sweater, her turkey was sitting on the counter resting, and she'd finished whipping the potatoes, buttering the green beans, and now stirred the lumps out of the gravy. Her stuffing hadn't turned out nearly as good as her mother's, and she wasn't sure she even wanted to eat it.

"I have to admit, it smells nice," Jewels said. She still wore only a silk robe and walked on her heels, cotton woven between her freshly painted toes. She took a spoon out of the drawer and scooped out a bite of potatoes. She wrinkled her nose as she swallowed it. "Ugh. How can you eat this?"

Mindy took her own bite with petulance, sure Jewels was just being difficult. Teasing her again for wanting human food. But she frowned as she moved the creamy potatoes around her mouth with her tongue.

"Something's not right," she admitted. "It's missing something."

"Norman," Jewels called to the guy who had left her bed and found his way to the couch to watch football. Why he was still there, Mindy didn't know, especially when Jewels wouldn't need him tonight—not with the feast the girl was so excited for.

"I'm sure he has a name," Mindy hissed at her roommate.

"That *is* his name," Jewels said, and she giggled. "He's a Norman named Norman. And he's *delicious*, isn't he? I think I want to keep him."

The guy—a rough and rugged type with tousled brown hair and a scar on his cheek—looked up at Jewels with complete adoration in his eyes. Mindy shook her head with amusement. How did Jewels do it? Her roommate always managed to get what—and whom—she wanted.

"Come here, baby," Jewels crooned. "We need your help."

Norman the Norman crossed the living room in three long strides and joined the vampires in the kitchen. Jewels fed him a spoonful of potatoes.

"What does it need?" Mindy asked.

"Salt?" Norman asked, unsure of his answer.

"Oh! Of course." And Jewels lifted Norman's arm to her mouth and with what looked like an intimate kiss, slashed her fangs across his wrist.

"Jewels!" Mindy screeched as the other vampire held Norman's wrist over the bowl of potatoes and stained the white spuds red. "Salt. Not blood. You've ruined—"

"Oh, Minz, you *have* to taste these now." Jewels' eyes sparkled with delight as she licked the spoon while taking another from the drawer, filling it with potatoes and shoving it into Mindy's mouth.

Mindy's eyes sprang open. "Oh, my god. Those are the best potatoes ever!"

Mindy glanced over all of the bowls and platters spread out on the counter, and she knew exactly what all of her dishes lacked. Blood. Human blood was the missing ingredient that would make this the best Thanksgiving feast ever.

"Mind if I grab a plate before you do that?" Norman asked as Mindy grasped his arm in a tight grip and began making him bleed all over her Thanksgiving feast.

"Ugh. Hurry," Mindy barked, her mouth watering even more at the spread of food before them. She couldn't wait to dive into it, hoping she'd have the self-control to be able to savor all the goodness. The way her heart sped at the thought of such gluttony, she wasn't sure. At least there was a lot of food here, enough to keep her happy for a while. Just grabbing a serving spoon took Norman too long, so Mindy moved in a blur as she dumped spoonfuls of this and that until food heaped in a mountain on his plate. She had it filled in less than three seconds. Then she grabbed his arm once again, slashed it open, and made him rain blood over her feast.

After several minutes, before she'd even made it to the platter of carved turkey, Norman's body began to slump. Mindy's brain suddenly clicked back on. Or maybe it was her humanity. She jumped away from the guy and gasped.

"What have I done?" she cried aloud. She shoved Norman's plate at him and pushed him out of the kitchen. He stumbled for the couch, while she stared at her so-called traditional Thanksgiving feast. Tears filled her eyes.

"What's wrong?" Jewels said, confusion lacing her voice. "Isn't this what you wanted?"

"No!" Mindy nearly shouted while her eyes never left the crimson-stained food. "I wanted a real Thanksgiving. Not one soaked in blood!"

Jewels laughed. "Ah, Minz. You're a vampire now, remember? Maybe this needs to be your compromise."

Mindy shook her head, then stomped to her bedroom. She threw herself on the bed. What was wrong with her? Jewels was right. A perfect compromise of a feast waited for her out in the kitchen. But that's not what she really wanted. Not what she craved—not her heart or her soul. And she could no longer deny it.

What she really wanted—what her soul desired more than anything—was to be with her family on this favorite of all holidays. This little apartment shared with another vampire and a guy she didn't know but had nearly drained to death was not where she wanted to be. Where she *needed* to be. She wanted to be at her Nana's with everyone else, enjoying the company just as much as the food.

"I miss my family," she cried to herself. "If only . . . "

She didn't even finish her sentence as a new thought occurred to her. *I still have a little bit of my humanity. Surely it will be okay.*

Chapter 3

Mindy took her time as she chose a new outfit and dressed for the second time that day. Nana always served Thanksgiving dinner later than most people, much closer to a normal dinner time. And she expected everyone to look nice when they came to the table. She didn't require dresses or suits or even sweater vests, thank God. But sweatpants, jeans, and t-shirts were not allowed. Mindy used to grumble at Nana's dress code, but not now. Although she rarely wore skirts or dresses, she was happy to be pulling on an ankle-length, dark brown pencil skirt, the only skirt she owned besides her "vampy" ones that barely covered her ass. And those would be a definite no-no at Nana's table—or anywhere in or near her house.

"That's what you're wearing?" Jewels asked when Mindy came out of her bedroom in her skirt, a cream-colored sweater, a scarf wound around her neck, and peasant boots. Jewels sounded appalled, although she still only wore a robe even as the church down the sheet chimed three o'clock in the afternoon.

Mindy looked down at herself and grinned. "It's perfect."

"Don't you know by now the appropriate dress code for these kinds of things?"

Mindy cocked her head, confused for a moment, but realization dawned on her. Jewels thought she'd been dressing for the vampire feast.

"I'm still not going to the feast with you," Mindy clarified.

Jewels' brows pushed together as her eyes skimmed over Mindy's form. "Then where are you going?"

Oh, shit. Mindy couldn't exactly tell her. Jewels would do everything in her power to stop her, and if that didn't work, she might even go to the head of the local nest. The Daemoni could not know Mindy's new plans for the day.

"Um, well," Mindy stammered as her mind raced. "I'm, uh, I'm just going to go for a walk around the city, take in the holiday a different way, and, I guess, find some poor Norman who needs some company tonight so he doesn't kill himself."

Jewels' gaze flitted over to the couch, where her Norman lay snoring, his hand tucked into the waistband of his jeans. At least he'd been able to enjoy Mindy's Thanksgiving dinner before she'd ruined it all.

"Just stay away from *my* Norman," Jewels said, and she turned back for her bedroom. She looked back over her shoulder as Mindy made her way to the front door. "You still have the invitation, though, right? You can always change your mind."

Mindy nodded, although she didn't have the invitation with her. She wouldn't be going to the feast. She still hung onto the need to make this day as normal and as traditional as possible.

Except how she traveled.

Nana—and the rest of her family—lived outside of the city, and Mindy no longer had a car. She could take the train and the bus, but she figured they ran on a holiday schedule, which meant she'd never make it to Nana's in time. She didn't have a choice. Once she reached the edge of the city, she slipped into the woods, hiked her skirt above her knees, and ran at vampire speed. She laughed to herself as she jumped the twenty-five feet to cross a stream. *This gives new meaning to over the river and through the woods.*

As she came closer to Nana's, however, anxiety began to replace the hope she'd been feeling since making her decision. She hadn't seen her family in nearly a year, since last New Year's Eve. She'd left on a bad note, fighting with them about wanting to go into the city for the New Year's celebration. They didn't think it safe . . . and they were right. However, they warned her about being mugged or drugged and raped. Not about being attacked by a vampire and turned. Of course, they wouldn't know anything about such fantastical things that shouldn't exist. But here she was. That was exactly what had happened to her, and she hadn't been able to come home since. She couldn't even call them. Her sire had said they needed to believe she was dead. She hoped they simply believed she'd run away—and that they'd accept her again, at least for one night. But what if they didn't?

Still keeping to the woods, she passed the small town where she'd grown up, and slowed as she approached Nana's farm a few miles outside of town. A line of cars filled the long driveway. Although still several hundred yards away, Mindy could already hear the laughter and chatter coming from inside the house. Everyone was there—Mindy's mom and uncles and their families, her sisters and their boyfriends, a couple of babies. Her two older sisters, already married before Mindy left, had been talking about babies. Had they already had them?

Sorrow filled Mindy at this thought. She could be an aunt and hadn't even known. And after tonight, she'd never see any of her nieces or nephews again. She'd never watch them grow up, go to their sports games and birthday parties, be a bad influence on them when they reached their teenage years. She'd be the aunt nobody ever talked about. The black sheep every family had. The one they'd pretend didn't even exist. Because she really shouldn't exist.

They needed to believe she was gone for their own safety, Mindy knew. *Just this last time and never again.* Although Mindy was glad she still held on to a tiny bit of her humanity, she'd never bring herself to go to the Amadis. She didn't believe for one minute what they promised and couldn't imagine the horrors they'd put her through, if they even allowed her to live. No, she'd always be Daemoni, even if it meant losing all of her humanity. So she only had this last chance to say a real good-bye to her family.

She snuck over to the house, still full of trepidation and near cowardice. The desire to leave almost overcame the need to see them.

She peaked into the dining room window. Dusk had darkened the sky outside, but the interior of the house glowed a bright yellow. As expected, the long table was piled with china full of delectable food and beautiful centerpieces handmade by Nana herself using evergreen branches, pinecones, and berries gathered in the very woods from which Mindy had just emerged. Flames danced on top of candles, their glittering light reflecting in the gold trim of the plates and silverware already set out. Mindy's eyes scanned the settings and filled with tears when she saw her own name.

Nana had set a place for her.

She would be welcomed. They may be angry and hurt that she'd disappeared without a trace, but tonight they would welcome her in. That's how her family was. The questions, the demands, and all of the drama would be saved for tomorrow. And for her, that would never come. *I can really have this night with them.*

Mindy drew in a deep breath, taking in the late November air that was laced with the smells of a lifetime of memories—the scents of pine, fallen leaves, not-quite-winter-but-almost air, colognes and perfumes, Nana's favorite cleaning detergent, and so many different foods. Memories of leaf fights with her sisters and cousins, drinking hot cocoa by a bonfire, playing hide-and-seek in the woods and dress-up in Nana's attic, hugs from various relatives she saw only once or twice a year, laughter and good cheer, and, of course, those mouth-watering dishes. Her soul warmed. This was exactly what she needed.

She slowly climbed the three steps to Nana's front porch as though they were five stories high and at the top was a temple of doom rather than the family she so longed to see. Her hand felt as though it pushed through molasses as she raised it to the doorknocker. The air in her lungs thickened and became trapped when the door flew open before she could even knock. This was her chance. She could do this. She would not kill them. She wouldn't even smell them. She'd just enjoy the time she had and disappear once again. *I can do this.*

"Mindy!" Regina, her youngest sister, screeched. "Is it really you?"

And the next thing Mindy knew, she was yanked inside and surrounded by family. Arms enveloped her in hugs. Hands ran over her short, blond hair. An uncle—or maybe that was her cousin who'd grown up so much already—took her coat from her. The crowd moved as a blob into the dining room. Mindy could barely see over their heads to where Nana stood in the doorway to the kitchen. The crowd parted.

She and Nana stared at each other. Mother came up behind Nana, her jaw dropping. People whispered and giggled and someone finally gave Mindy a gentle push.

"Nana," she whispered. "Mother?"

Both women stepped into the room and held their arms wide open. Mindy rushed into them. Tears streamed down her cheeks as she once again embraced—and was embraced by—the people she loved most in the world.

"Carl, get the turkey," Nana ordered one of her sons without letting go of her long-lost granddaughter. "Where's George? He should carve it."

"Probably shooting up in the bathroom," someone muttered under their breath. Mindy didn't know who, and nobody else in the room heard it. She looked around for George, her eldest aunt's latest husband, but he was nowhere to be seen.

Nana finally let go of Mindy, and everyone moved to their set places marked by place cards. Finally, George staggered into the room, his eyes bloodshot, and he certainly wasn't dressed to Nana's code. Rather, his button-down shirt was completely unbuttoned and untucked, a stained undershirt strained tightly against his chest, and his belt buckle hung open.

"George," Nana quietly admonished.

Ignoring her, George grabbed the carving knife and eyed the beautiful turkey with its perfectly brown and crispy skin, juices dripping down its sides.

"Shut up, you old hag," George drawled, and everyone gasped. Mindy's spine went ramrod straight as anger filled her. George waved the knife in the air, vaguely pointing it at Nana. Then he palmed the turkey with his other bare hand and slammed the knife down. The tip of a finger rolled over the turkey's breast and onto the plate. Blood spurted out of the end of George's finger. "Now look what you made me do, stupid bitch."

And without further thought—her brain completely clicked off again—Mindy soared across the table and landed on George. Rather than taking his hand in her mouth, though, she tore through his throat. She barely registered the screams in the distance, the hands on her shoulders trying to pull her off. Her focus remained on teaching this disrespectful asshole a lesson.

"Mindy, stop!" Nana bellowed, and she definitely heard that.

Mindy's head snapped up, blood staining her lips and dripping from the corners of her mouth and the tips of her fangs that had fully let out. Her eyes glowed a bright red. And as her gaze skimmed along the shocked faces of her family, all she could see was the pulses in their throats.

"Oh, my god," she choked, and she blurred away.

Chapter 4

Mindy berated herself with all kinds of profanities as she bolted for the city, her form nothing but a blur in the dark woods. Animals ran away, scurrying for cover as she approached and then whooshed by. How could she have done such a thing? Had she killed him? She didn't know. She hadn't stayed long enough to find out. How stupid of her! George was the jackass douche-canoe, but she'd been the one to ruin everything.

She ruined Nana's meal. Ruined everyone's Thanksgiving. And she'd ruined her last chance to be a part of her family. To be somewhat normal. To enjoy the feast and the company she desired so much.

"I'm a monster!" she cried as she burst into her apartment. She hadn't thought about anyone still being there, although some part of her brain knew it was too early for Jewels to have left yet. So she was surprised when Jewels came running out of her room, wearing only a bra and panties—if you called that little scrap panties.

"You're a vampire," Jewels corrected, taking Mindy under one arm. She wiped her fingers over Mindy's lips, but the blood had dried on her run home, and guided Mindy to the couch. She pulled the other vamp down, practically into her lap, and cooed softly into her ear. "It's okay, Minz. This is what you are. You can't help it."

"It's not okay," Mindy cried. "And I *can* help it. I help it all the time when I'm out in the world around the Normans. Why did I have to do this? Why this time? Why today?"

"Hush, hush, now," Jewels crooned. "Tell me what happened. It can't be as bad as you think."

"It's worse!" Through her sobs and hitched breaths, Mindy told her friend the horror of what she'd done.

"Oh, Minz," Jewels said with a dark chuckle, "you really should have known better. There's a reason we aren't allowed to see our family."

"I thought I could control it. I thought I still had enough humanity left."

"Silly girl. Silly little baby vamp. Your humanity is worthless. You need to let it go." She stroked a hand over Mindy's hair as the other vampire lay her head against her chest. "But our humanity has nothing to do with why we can't see family. Well, little to do with it. Families bring out *all* of our emotions to the extreme—annoyance, companionship, disgust, joy, hope, disappointment, hatred, and love. Gatherings heighten those feelings. That's why we get all excited about the idea of bringing our families into one room for a party, although we know how dysfunctional they are and someone's likely to leave in tears or in a riot van. We're excited for the emotional buzz, even as humans. But as vampires, their emotions only fuel us, like blood does, but in a very different way—their feelings build our need. Our need for *blood*. If you went there thinking you'd get away with being Norman, you set yourself up for utter failure."

Mindy sniffled against her roomie's chest, then realized said chest was nearly naked, as was the rest of Jewels' body. Mindy pulled away.

"Nobody explained it like that," Mindy admitted.

"Your sire should have, but we know he's an arse of a parent. That's why you have me. If you'd told me your plans . . ."

"I knew you'd try to stop me."

"For good reason, wouldn't you say?"

Mindy nodded. "What am I going to do?"

Jewels blew out a firm breath. "You're going to wash your face, change into something vampy, and—"

"I mean about my family. What I did! I—"

"You did nothing. You're going to do nothing. They're never going to accept what really happened, and nobody else will believe them if they try to explain. They'll figure it out. The only thing you're going to do is never go back." She paused, then added with a nonchalant shrug, "Unless you want them all to die, of course. That's up to you."

The thought of never seeing her family again pained Mindy as freshly as it had the first time she was told, but she now understood better. She didn't want them all to die. She wasn't that type of vampire. Not yet, and she hoped she never would be. She hadn't chosen this way of life, and she hoped that by hanging on to at least a thread of her humanity, she could hang on to her soul. Jewels seemed to be walking the line just fine. Mindy decided she could do the same.

"So, as I was saying, go wash your face, put on something more vamp-like, and come with me to the vampire feast," Jewels said.

Mindy stood, but didn't plan to follow her roomie's orders. "I think I'll just zone out in bed and wait for this day to be over. I only wanted one last traditional Thanksgiving, and I ruined it all."

"So try a vampire Thanksgiving."

Mindy shook her head and headed for her bedroom. "I can't handle any more of that."

The thought of any more blood, of people hurting for her, disgusted her. She'd had enough of it for one day. She didn't want to be any part of a vampire feast, whatever it entailed.

"Come on, Minz. Please don't make me go alone," Jewels begged. "And you really don't want to miss this lovely time, now do you? All of our mates will be there. You don't even have to drink or have anything to do with the actual feast. But you shouldn't be alone on this day of all days. Come be with your new family."

Mindy sat on her bed and dropped her head into her hands. Her new family. Well, maybe it *was* time to accept that. She certainly could never go back to her original family. She had a new life now. New holidays to celebrate, or, at least, new ways to celebrate the Norman ones. And Jewels was right—she didn't have to drink. She certainly had no thirst now, already having her fill for the day. She slid the invitation from her dresser and stared at it for a long moment, then tapped the corner against her hand as she thought, trying to talk herself into going.

Thirty minutes later, she joined her roomie at the door, vamped out in a sleek black dress that clung to her body, ending at the top of her thighs, and heels almost as high as her roommate's. Jewels wore a blood-red, skintight dress that hugged her curves perfectly and dangerous stilettos that could easily be used as a weapon. The white skin of their bare shoulders shone in the moonlight, and Normans looked at them with expressions mixed with lust and disbelief that they weren't freezing in the night's dropping temperatures. They glared back with glowing red eyes, and the Normans cowered away, forgetting they'd even seen the strange but inhumanly beautiful women.

"Here we are," Jewels said as they approached a gothic mansion on the outskirts of the city. Limos and luxury sports cars lined the curved driveway. A doorman checked their invitations before allowing them to saunter through the two-story-high doors and into the elegant foyer with a chandelier dripping in gold leaf and crystal.

They were swept through the grand foyer and into a great hall where an orchestra played and vampires danced and mingled. Jewels took Mindy's hand and led them around until they found their friends. They chatted, and Mindy even danced with a friend from work, grateful Nana had taught her how to waltz. She immediately pushed the thought of Nana out of her mind and forced herself to focus on the here and now. That had been the final decision maker to even come—knowing she needed a distraction from the day's events.

And what a distraction this had turned out to be. Not at all what she'd imagined, which had been a dark basement with Normans being taken by the vamps in whatever way they desired, passing the humans along to each other, both mouths and legs open wide. She'd expected a bloody orgy, in other words. The Daemoni were known for such things even when it wasn't a holiday.

She certainly hadn't expected a glamorous mansion, ballroom dancing, and champagne. But, she concluded, vampires were gluttonous in all ways, so she really shouldn't have been surprised that some—most from her city, it seemed—reveled in the luxuries only money could provide.

A dinging sound rang through the room. The orchestra fell silent and all conversation ceased.

"Dinner will be served momentarily," a bodiless voice carried through the grand hall. "We ask that you make your way to the banquet room."

As a whole, the crowd moved for the double doors in the side of the hall, to where, apparently, dinner would be served. Mindy paused, hesitating. She'd assumed too soon that this would be a night of elegance and propriety. This was the part she didn't want to participate in.

"Come on," Jewels whispered as she hooked her arm into Mindy's. "You don't have to drink. Or eat. Or whatever. But don't stay here by yourself. It will look . . . uncouth."

Uncouth. Mindy tried not to laugh at the word and strode alongside Jewels. Shock once again hit the vampire when they entered the banquet room. Several round tables were scattered about, each of them covered in a spread of traditional Thanksgiving food—dozens of turkeys, bowls of stuffing and mashed potatoes, boats of gravy, platters of vegetables, and dinner rolls.

The vampires chose their seats, but none of them sat down, so Mindy stood behind hers like everyone else did. She looked around the room with curiosity as the vamps all took their places and the room settled into a disturbing quiet. Then Normans filed through one door and into the room. Mindy began to gnaw on her lip as the humans made their way to the tables and took the seats. A very handsome young man about Mindy's age, with a head-full of dark hair and the sexiest lips she'd ever seen, sat in the chair before her. As if her mouth could fall open even more, it did when Jewels' Norman sat in the chair in front of her.

"Let the feast begin!" called out the same voice.

The humans dug in. And so did the vampires. The Normans feasted on turkey and the trimmings and the vampires feasted on the Normans. Mindy only watched, not able to bring herself to partake.

"Oh, Mindy, the turkey is delicious," Jewels said when she came up from Norman's throat for a breath. "Try it."

Mindy's brows pushed together.

"Yes, try it," said the man sitting in front of her. He tilted his head, exposing his neck to her. His vein pulsed invitingly. His tongue slid over his lips as his hand reached up to her face. He pulled her down to him. "*Please* try it. I've been waiting for your lips on my throat. I guarantee you'll like it."

As his scent, mixed with the fragrance of the food, filled Mindy's nose, her mouth salivated. He pulled her closer until their lips touched. Kissed her until her knees nearly buckled. Opened his mouth so she could taste the turkey on his tongue. But that's not what he meant. He suddenly twisted, his hand clamped against her head, and practically forced her to drink from him. And when his blood filled her mouth, it was the most delectable flavor she'd ever tasted. Sexy man mixed with a holiday feast.

They all ate beyond their fill. Drank until they were daft. Kissed and sucked and stroked until they climaxed. It really was a bloody orgy. And Mindy loved every minute of it. She ate and played with her new guy, and he ate and played with her, both of them enjoying each other's bodies until the new day dawned and Thanksgiving was over.

And then they went back to her apartment for dessert.

Every tradition has a start somewhere, Mindy thought as she lay in her new guy's arms (she really needed to find out his name), and she'd now started a new Thanksgiving tradition for herself: The Vampire Thanksgiving Feast. A feast like no other.

Belonging

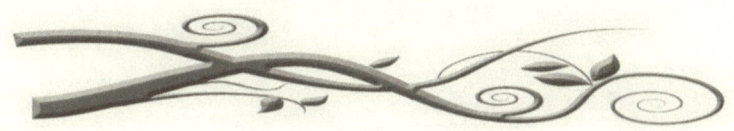

This next short story, *Belonging*, introduces a couple of new characters in the Soul Savers world, as well as including some secondary characters you've already met. Again, it does not fit in any particular place in the main Soul Savers Series chronology, although it would definitely be before the events that conclude *Wrath* (Book 5). This couple has found a special place in my heart. I hope you love them as much as I do!

Chapter 1

The wolf sprinted through the woods, the sounds of heavy footfalls not far behind and the echo of the gunshot still ringing in her ears. Her powerful legs carried her faster in a rhythmic pace, the air sucking in and out of her nose, a growl at the base of her throat. She sprang over a fallen tree and scurried under another, before pushing her legs harder. Her ears twitched backwards as she listened for her pursuers, but she seemed to be putting a nice distance between them. Not a safe distance yet, but hopefully soon.

She imagined what she looked like—all beast with midnight black fur and the distinct white marking on her chest—as she ran through the forest. The awe-inspiring image of her pack mates when they ran came to mind, and she hoped she looked just as majestic. She certainly felt as though she was beautiful and powerful, a gorgeous creature outrunning the enemy. She felt that way for now anyway.

But the soul within her didn't truly believe she was a gorgeous creature, not when she knew the kind of blood that ran through her veins, the grotesque hunger that made her wolf's stomach growl. Not when she knew that the so-called enemy were merely normal humans—Normans—who simply protected themselves. Just as she would have done not too many years ago. After all, she may have been a lone wolf this time, but a pack, either her old one or another, had left their mark on the Normans' village. And how were they to know she had nothing to do with those killings?

The wolf quirked her ears again to listen, but heard nothing. Not the signs of Normans, anyway. Only a stream rushing nearby, the wind in the few leaves that remained overhead, and the sounds of scurrying animals on the forest floor. She'd outrun them! She slowed to a trot then an amble as she sniffed the air. She followed her nose and ears to the squirrel under a pile of leaves. One quick strike and the rodent was hers. Not exactly her preferred dinner, but likely the only meal she would have until tomorrow. She tried not to think about what she was doing as her teeth picked the meat from the squirrel's bones. *It's better than a human*, she reminded herself. The thought sent a shiver down her spine, and she shook it out.

While hunting for a place to curl up for the night, she came to the edge of the forest, and a spectacular sunset lit up the sky over the low Appalachian mountains. The wolf sat on her hind haunches and gazed at the glowing pink and yellow sky. A thin stream of white smoke caught her eye, and her gaze followed it down to a chimney on a small house at the base of the mountain. She sniffed the air and inhaled the wonderful scent of burning leaves and wood—a scent of memories, of happiness, of coziness and warmth. The scent of a lifetime long gone. The wolf looked back toward the sky and, unable to help herself, let out a long howl.

She turned back for the woods, skirting its edges as she returned to her hunt for a safe place to sleep. Her eyes kept darting back to the little house, and her heart ached to go nearer. But that would be stupid. Unsafe. Normans were there, and she'd spent half the day running away from them. Why on Earth did she so badly want to run for them? She knew that answer deep in her heart, but she ignored it.

Just as she eyed what appeared to be a hollow log big enough for her to curl up inside, a snapping sound tore through the quiet and pain clawed at her back paw. The wolf yelped and turned. A steel trap! She remembered her brothers setting such contraptions many years ago. And now one had her. The thing's teeth dug into her flesh, and she couldn't help the whimper. The animal lay down on her side, stared at the sky, and whined. But she'd only allow such self-pity for a minute. Then she'd suck it up, knowing the one thing she had to do to free herself from the trap. With a sigh—the air was cold and she'd soon be freezing—the beautiful black beast closed her eyes and forced the change.

"What the hell?" a low voice demanded. A Norman jogged into the woods, coming to a full stop when he saw Rissa lying on the ground, completely naked, the trap enclosing her ankle. "I thought . . . good thing I heard that wolf and came running. He could be anywhere. How the hell did you get caught in this?"

Rissa ignored the man, not able to even bring her eyes up to his face. She tried to curl into a ball, hiding what she could of her girl bits, but the trap dragged at her ankle, the steel teeth still gnawing at her skin. She bit back another cry. The man knelt down beside her. Rissa tried to spring away and let out a gasp with the pain.

"Relax, sweetheart," the man said. "Let me help you before you make it worse."

She peered at him, but couldn't see his face. He kept it turned to the side, toward her feet, averted from her nakedness. All she could see was dark hair curling over the edges of a gray beanie, dark scruff on his jaw, and a tall body clad in an orange winter vest, a black hoodie underneath, and jeans. His large hands grasped at the metal jaws of the trap, and the golden words *Georgia Tech* that decorated his hoodie's sleeves rippled as the fabric strained against his bulging muscles. As soon as her ankle was released, Rissa quickly pulled her leg away. She curled into a ball, trying to hide her most private parts. Her body shivered from both cold and fear. This man would have questions. All kinds of questions. She needed to get away and fast.

Gentle fingers skimmed over her foot, and she looked down with terrified eyes. The man—who was about her age, barely more than a boy—wiped away the blood trickling down her ankle. She jumped back at his touch. Pain shot through her leg.

"I'm so sorry," he said. "I thought I'd cleaned up all the traps, but it's not like there are usually people traipsing around these woods. What were you doing out here, sweetheart? And if you don't mind me asking, where the hell are your clothes?"

And there were the questions. They were only the beginning, she was sure. His eyes skimmed over her shins and her arms—the only parts he could really see, thankfully the light was dimming as the sun fell further behind the mountain—and to her face. Something flickered in his dark eyes, but Rissa nearly missed it, too busy staring at his mesmerizing face. Especially his lips—full, kissable lips. She wondered what they tasted like. She licked her own lips and moved her gaze to his eyes, a dark brown like her own. The initial glint brightened into a twinkle as he watched her stare at him and he returned the favor.

I have to get out of here. As though the reminder were a prod in the ass, Rissa sprang to her feet to run. But more pain jolted through her leg, all the way to her hip. Her ankle immediately gave out, and she fell to her hands and knees, giving the stranger quite an eyeful. With a frustrated cry, she collapsed to her side again and returned to her ball shape. Every profane word she knew flew through her mind.

"Looks like it's broken," the stranger said.

"It's fine," Rissa said through clenched teeth, her human voice rough. "I'll be fine. Just leave me alone. Please."

The guy chuckled, the sound laced with disbelief. "You're a young woman alone in the woods, severely injured, and naked at that. No way can I just leave you here."

"I said I'll be fine," Rissa snapped. "Just go!"

The man rose to his feet, took one stride over to her, and knelt beside her again. Too quick for her to react, he scooped his arms underneath her and lifted her as he stood.

"Not a chance, sweetheart," he said.

Rissa struggled but only for a short moment, because the movement only increased the pain in her foot. She considered changing back to her wolf form, but he held her so closely against his chest, she wasn't sure she could. On the other hand, the transformation would surely surprise him, giving her an opportunity to escape. Yet, something kept her from doing so, kept her in his arms as he headed for the house with the smoke rising from the chimney.

"The holiday season's coming, you know," he said as he walked up the front steps. " I won't exactly be making brownie points with Santa if I leave you out there, unable to walk, and no place to go for miles. Let's get you inside and warmed up, then I'll take you wherever you want to go."

Rissa held back a snort. *The holidays*. Was it that late in the year already? She didn't really care. She didn't have a home. No family to go back to. The holidays were a part of her old life. Now she had nothing to be grateful for, no comfort or joy in her life.

As the stranger carried her inside his home, laid her on the couch, and covered her with a heavy blanket, she looked up into his kind eyes, and for the first time since she'd been bitten six years ago, she wondered if there was something left in her to live for. To be thankful for.

Chapter 2

"What's your name?" the guy asked as he stood over her.

Rissa's nose twitched—something here smelled strange, but she couldn't pinpoint the faint odor—but she kept her mouth shut. He didn't need to know her name. He didn't need to know anything about her. She needed to get the hell out of here before this went any further.

He continued staring at her expectantly, and when she didn't answer, his dark eyes twinkled. "Well, then. I guess I'll start. I'm Gray."

Rissa's brows pushed together. Gray? What kind of name was that? Was it even a name? The stranger must have seen the curiosity killing her because he grinned widely. Dimples punctuated his smile, and Rissa's thighs quivered in response.

"That's what everyone calls me, for many reasons. Maybe I'll tell you one if you tell me your name."

Her eyes cut away from him and his fabulous smile, and she scowled at the blanket. After another long moment pregnant with expectation, Gray must have given up on her. He rose to his feet and strode away, and Rissa watched him through her lashes. He had wide shoulders, a narrow waist, and a confident stride that screamed, "Hot sex here." Rissa swallowed, her throat suddenly dry. Once Gray's perfect ass disappeared through a doorway, she came to her senses and seized the opportunity.

She bolted to her feet and quickly gathered the blanket around her. Once she was outside in the dark night and far enough away, she wouldn't need it. She could change and stay warm in her own fur coat. But for now, she'd already given Gray enough to look at; he didn't need to see any more. She tested her weight on the injured ankle. It had already begun to heal—a nice, wolfy benefit— but remained pretty sore. She'd toughed out much worse, though.

Gritting her teeth, she rushed for the back door in the kitchen, the one Gray had carried her through only minutes before.

He already stood in front of it, something in his hands, a smile on his face, and a challenge in his eyes. "I told you, I can't let you go back out there alone, especially in the dark. There's nowhere for you to go, and it's too dangerous."

"I—I can take care of myself," Rissa said.

Gray's gaze skimmed over her, and though the blanket covered everything but her head and feet, the look in his eyes remained appreciative. Yep, he'd seen too much earlier. He didn't have to see her now to know what she kept covered.

"I'm sure you can, sweetheart," he said. "Until you step into another trap, anyway."

Rissa's nostrils flared. "Did you set those?"

She'd grown up with brothers who loved to hunt and trap, and every season she'd begged them not to do it. Sometimes she'd even follow them into the woods behind their house and spring the traps herself so no animal would get caught up in one. And when they did, she'd set them free every chance she had. Now that she'd become one of those animals who could be caught, she hated the things even more.

Gray chuckled darkly. "Not a chance. Some assholes around here come on our property and set them like they own the place. Whenever I get up here, cleaning them up is one of the first things I do."

"Why?" Rissa blurted, forgetting that she was trying to get away from this guy, not hold a long, drawn-out conversation.

"Damn things are a nuisance. Dangerous to humans and animals alike."

Score one for Gray. Rissa shook her head, both to that thought and to Gray's answer. "No, I mean, why do they come on your property if they know you don't want the traps there? Isn't that trespassing or something?"

"Yeah," he said, his voice suddenly gruff. "Trespassing. But they don't give a shit. They'll do anything to capture the wolves." Something dark and dangerous flickered in his eyes, but then he shrugged and held out wads of fabric toward her. "I don't even want to know what happened to your clothes, but you can wear these until I get you home. Mind if we eat first, though? I was just about to start dinner when I heard the wolf howl and then found you."

Rissa's eyes flickered to the window in the back door. Night had settled in completely, and the dark outside made the window more of a mirror. She nearly jumped at her own image reflecting back at her—dark eyes that looked too big for her face, hollowed cheeks, and a rat's nest of curly hair. Her mouth already watered at the thought of real food, and by the looks of her, she really needed it.

"You look like you could use a good meal," Gray said, echoing her thoughts. He thrust the clothes at her again, and she had no choice but to take them. As soon as she did, he nodded toward a door off the kitchen. "Bathroom's over there. Help yourself to whatever you need."

Rissa simply stared at him. *Why is he being so nice? If he only knew . . .*

"Go on," he said as he turned for the refrigerator. "Get cleaned up while I make dinner. Then I promise I'll take you wherever you want to go, as long as it's not in those woods."

Rissa looked down at the clothes in her hands, then sighed to herself as she took the three steps from the small kitchen to the even smaller bathroom. Gray obviously wasn't giving up, so instead of trying to run, she'd just have to play it cool. Hopefully he'd be good on his word and take her wherever she wanted to go after dinner. Problem was she didn't know where that was. She didn't belong anywhere except in those woods.

Let's just get this over with. She closed the bathroom door and dropped the blanket, ready to throw on the clothes and hurry through dinner so she could get out of there. But when she saw her reflection again, in a full-length mirror on the back of the door, she gasped out loud at the ugly sight. Her olive skin stretched tightly over her bones, barely enough muscle between them to show any kind of definition. And she probably only had that much because of the wolf inside her. Her collar bone angled sharply from her chest, her once full breasts had become almost non-existent, and her soft hips had disappeared, leaving more angular bones jutting against her skin. And dirt smudges graffitied her body from face to feet. How embarrassing!

She couldn't believe Gray hadn't been appalled by the way she looked and probably smelled after spending weeks in the woods. And he wanted to eat dinner with her? *Not like this. No way in hell.* Rissa stepped into the small shower stall, pulled the plastic curtain shut, and blasted herself with hot water and soap that smelled like man. The metal rings scraped against the rusting rod when she opened the curtain again and found a fresh towel folded neatly and sitting on the closed toilet seat. She held it to her face and inhaled the scent of fabric softener. Oh how she missed the little things like clean skin and the smell of freshly laundered towels.

She didn't miss having to brush out her unruly hair. After pulling on the red sweat pants that she had to roll up at the legs and tighten all the way with the drawstring and a black t-shirt so large, the pants were practically unnecessary, she snooped around the bathroom for a hairbrush. She only found a plastic comb that would never make it through her thick hair in one piece. Not knowing what else to do at the moment, she wrapped the towel around her head and stepped out of the bathroom, steam following her out.

Gray glanced over at her, and his mouth fell open. His hands shook so badly, she thought he was going to drop the bowl he held, filled with something steaming and delicious smelling. After a long moment, he finally blinked and his adam's apple bobbed as he swallowed. A sexy glint sparked in his eyes.

"You, uh, feel better?" he asked as he set the bowl on the counter.

"Much. Thank you," Rissa said, offering a small smile for the first time. Gray's eyes went wide again, but he quickly recovered.

"My sister probably has a brush in the upstairs bathroom," he said, nodding at the stairs by the front door in the living room.

Rissa blinked, and a new wave of anxiety rolled over her. "Your sister? Is this her house?"

He turned back toward the stove and picked up a second bowl. "It's ours. Just a cabin our parents left us both. Neither of us lives here, and she hardly ever makes it up anymore, but she keeps pretty much everything she needs here. Just in case . . . "

His voice trailed off.

"Just in case what?"

He paused, then cleared his throat and gave a nonchalant shrug. "In case she forgets something when she packs. You know how you girls are—can't live without your hair stuff and makeup and everything." He turned around, the second bowl filled with some kind of stew. "Of course, you might be a little different?"

Rissa heard this as a question, one she wasn't about to answer. "I'll, uh, see if I can find a brush. It might take me a while, though. My hair's a pain in the ass like that."

Gray eyed the towel-turban around her hair with curiosity. "This stew needs to cool for a bit anyway, and the bread's still in the oven warming."

Rissa gave him a small nod then headed for the stairs. The stew would be ice-cold and the bread burnt to a char if he waited on her, so she tried to hurry. Although the upstairs bathroom was a little bigger and even had a tub and a linen closet, she found the brush easily enough, but pulling it through her wet hair wasn't so simple. She took the systematic approach that she'd learned years ago, and ten minutes later, she'd tamed the biggest knots. As she reached back to start the next round, a hand caught her wrist, and a jolt of something exciting and promising nearly brought her to her knees.

Her eyes caught Gray's in the mirror, and his smoldered as he took the brush from her.

"You were, uh, taking so long," he said, his voice husky. "Thought you could use some help."

Rissa's brain had turned to something soft and senseless, and she couldn't bring herself to protest as he gently pulled the brush through her hair from crown to nape, easing his way through the smaller tangles. They both remained silent as Gray continued brushing, and by the time he finished, her whole scalp tingled, and her nipples were hard. He reached around her, his arm pressing against hers as he placed the brush on the side of the sink. His head bent near hers, his mouth close to the skin of her throat, their eyes locked in the mirror once again. Rissa's were wide, and her pulse thundered with anticipation.

Then her stomach growled with the ferocity of a lion.

Gray straightened up, and a small smile danced on his lips. "Dinner's ready."

Chapter 3

Rissa had always spelled her name a-w-k-w-a-r-d, but it'd been a long time since she'd felt as awkward as she did while eating dinner with Gray. A table could never fit in the tiny kitchen, so they sat in the living room, Gray on a weathered leather recliner and Rissa on the couch. The beef stew was delicious with a gravy that hinted of red wine, the bread warm and buttery, and the silence as heavy as the blanket she'd been wearing earlier. Rissa shamelessly devoured two bowls of stew and half of the baguette, and between the two of them, they finished the bottle of wine Gray had opened for the gravy.

"You seriously cooked that yourself?" Rissa asked with disbelief as her tongue ran over her spoon. Realizing her lack of class, she quickly dropped the utensil in the bowl and placed the dish on the glass coffee table.

Gray smiled, and the sweatpants she wore nearly dropped as fast as the spoon had. "One of my many specialties. I'm guessing that you liked it?"

"I have to say I'm impressed," Rissa admitted as she leaned back on the couch. Her belly hadn't felt so full in weeks, nor her psyche so content. She stared at the flames dancing in the hearth until her eyes drifted closed, the smell of burning wood filling her nose and the pops and crackles of the fire singing her a lullaby.

When she opened them again, daylight flooded the room, she was in a strange bed, and the sounds of cooking came from a distance. Downstairs, she realized when her senses came back to her. She was in the bedroom upstairs, next to the bathroom where she'd found the brush. She felt as though she'd just eaten, but the smell of bacon had her mouth watering again.

"You sleep like the dead," Gray said when he sensed her presence in the kitchen. Her mouth fell open, and she couldn't move her eyes away as he worked at the stove. He wore pajama bottoms and nothing else, and she'd never seen anything sexier than a half-naked man cooking. "You didn't even wake up when I carried you upstairs."

He glanced at her and grinned when he saw her eyes widen. "Don't worry. I slept on the couch." His gaze swept over her, and his tongue darted over his lips. "Not that it wasn't tempting, trust me, but like I said, you sleep like the dead. And I'm not into necrophilia."

Heat rose into Rissa's cheeks, and she finally tore her eyes away, looking down as she twisted her hands together. "I'm, uh, so sorry. I didn't mean to—"

Gray stepped toward her, and her eyes moved on their own accord, skimming over his six-pack abs and hard chest before coming to his face. He gave her a cocky smile loaded with dimples. Shit, she was so transparent.

"No worries, sweetheart," he said, his voice low. "You were obviously exhausted and needed the rest." She could only nod in response. He lifted a plate in front of her. "I hope you're hungry again."

Rissa gladly took the plate of bacon and pancakes and turned for the living room before she could make a bigger idiot of herself. Unlike last night's awkward silence, Gray filled the space with conversation. First he tried probing information out of Rissa, but when she refused to answer a single question, he decided to share more about himself. She didn't know why he felt the need to spill so much, but she listened as he told her about his senior year in college, his part-time gig at a shop that built custom motorcycles, and how he came to the cabin on the occasional weekends he had off from work.

"I try to get here at least once a month," he said, "but it's not always possible. My sister used to come every full moo—month, too, but she stopped when . . . well, after our parents died."

Rissa's breath caught. "I'm so sorry," she muttered, unsure what else to say.

"Thanks." Gray gave her a small smile. "It was several years ago, and then my sis had to take over the family business. It keeps her plenty busy, although she could bring her work here if she really wanted to. I think it just reminds her too much of Mom and Dad." He let out a soft chuckle and shook his head. "I have no idea why I'm telling you all of this."

Rissa didn't know either, and an uncomfortable silence passed between them. She bounded to her feet.

"I'll help you clean up," she said a little too enthusiastically.

After they finished cleaning the dishes and the kitchen, Gray disappeared for a few moments before returning with a small duffle bag with a Georgia Tech logo on it.

"I need to head back to Atlanta and get ready for classes this week," he said and added something about a meeting that made Rissa's ears perk.

"A what meeting?" she asked, though it sounded more like a demand.

Gray's brows pinched together for a brief moment. "A chapter meeting. For my fraternity. We have one every Sunday."

Rissa eyed him. She could have sworn she'd heard 'pack meeting', but maybe that's what she'd expected, used to hearing 'pack' and 'meeting' together. Although, it'd been over a year since she'd been to one.

"But first," Gray said, "I promised to take you wherever you want to go."

As they climbed into his extended cab pickup truck, Rissa berated herself for feeling so sullen at the prospect of leaving. She'd enjoyed the comforts of home a little too much and enjoyed the company of Gray *way* too much. She should have left last night. She had the animalistic power to escape, no matter how strongly he'd held her, but she'd given in. She'd let herself be soft, but now it was time to be tough again. Cut ties and move on. Except she didn't know where to go.

They drove the two miles to the closest town, and while Gray filled his tank with gas, Rissa used her inhumanly sharp eyes to gaze down the street where she saw the town square. She turned back to Gray who was hanging the gas pump up.

"I can walk from here," she said, throwing her thumb over her shoulder. "There's a bus station by the town square, which is just up the road."

"You're wearing flip-flops, and it's freezing," he said pointedly. Rissa looked down at her feet and wiggled her toes over the sandals that belonged to Gray's sister, who had left them by the back door months ago.

"I'll be fine," Rissa said.

"Please let me—" Gray's phone rang, interrupting him. He blew out a frustrated breath and answered it, and he immediately reacted to whatever he heard on the other end. His back straightened, and his eyes narrowed. He said a lot of 'uh-huh's' and 'okays' before hanging up and looking at Rissa with apology in his eyes. "I'm so sorry, but I really have to go now."

Rissa gave him a nod. "It's fine. Really. Don't worry about me."

He considered her for a moment until his phone beeped again. He glanced at the text message and groaned. Then he pulled something out of his back pocket.

"I know you have no money. You have no way of getting anywhere and here I have to abandon you. I wish I could do more but—" He grabbed her hand and pushed something into it before jumping into his truck and driving away. Before he drove five yards, though, he slowed as he rolled down his window. "I still don't even know your name."

What the hell, Rissa thought, *it's not like I'll ever see him again.*

"It's Rissa," she said, but he was already pulling away. She wasn't even sure that he heard her.

Once he was gone, she looked down at the paper in her hand. Gray's name and a phone number were printed on what looked like a business card, though it included no business name. She chuckled. As if she had any way of ever calling him. Behind the card were two folded twenty-dollar bills. She frowned at these, and anger immediately blossomed. She didn't need his charity! That's how he'd seen her this whole time—as a cause! She huffed and growled and stomped off down the road, as though to get away from him although he'd already left her. Then she considered what she'd do with the money.

She really did need it. She had the clothes Gray had basically given her, flip-flops on her feet, and nothing else. Forty bucks wouldn't get her far, but it could put a few meals in her belly. Or maybe a night at a motel. Nah. That wasn't a good trade. She only had enough for a seedy place rife with various body excrements. She'd rather sleep on the forest floor. But a few good, human meals . . . those were definitely worth it.

She already had a full belly from breakfast, so she tucked the money into her shirt pocket, then she headed out of town. Once she was far from anyone's prying eyes and hidden deep in the trees, she stripped out of her clothes and tied them into a bundle. Then she changed, picked up the bundle with her mouth, and ran. She didn't realize it at first and told herself she hadn't meant to head in that direction, but before long, she found herself at the edge of the woods by Gray's little cabin. Just like she had the evening before, she sank back on her haunches and stared.

No smoke rose from the chimney now. No light shone through the windows. The house was lifeless now, its occasional occupant gone for a while. Such a shame it sat empty, Rissa thought as she began searching for a place to sleep that night, carefully watching for more traps. She stopped in place and looked back at the house. She paced a few times, her gaze never leaving it. Did she dare?

She did.

Nobody will ever know. I'll just stay for a couple of days, then leave it the same way we did this morning. No harm, no foul. She continued talking herself into it even as she carried her bundle of clothes across the field and to the back door. After sniffing the air and looking around to ensure nobody could see her, she morphed into her human form and put on Gray's clothes, then picked her way through the flimsy door lock, her heart pounding the entire time.

As night settled in, she was still unsure of her decision, and several times, she almost bolted for the woods. But eventually she fell asleep. She headed for town the next morning and bought herself some groceries, then headed back, her conscience bothering her less. *After all*, she told herself once again, *it's not like it's hurting anyone. They won't even know.*

Days passed, and she felt more and more comfortable, although she still remained on alert. During the daylight, she'd walk through the woods, looking for traps and releasing them in case she had to run through there again. At night, she snuggled up on the couch under the blanket that smelled like Gray, the strange, faint scent making her nose tingle only at first. Then she grew used to it. In the wee hours of her third morning there, sounds in the woods woke her. She crawled over to the window and peeked out. Her heart picked up speed as she watched three figures move about the woods—male humans. Later that day, she found new traps set out.

When she came around the corner of the house after traipsing through the woods, she cursed herself for not paying closer attention. A familiar gray truck sat in the driveway, and its owner bounded the steps from the kitchen door.

Rissa turned on her heel and sprinted for the woods.

Chapter 4

"Rissa," Gray called after her, but she ignored him and ran for the woods. Within seconds, he stood in front of her, forcing her to stop.

Her breath caught as a mixture of emotions swirled inside her. Bewilderment because she'd been running as fast as she could in human form, which was faster than almost any Norman, and he'd not only caught up with her but had passed her. Anger at herself for being so stupid to get caught. Embarrassment because she'd had to sneak around and invade his house in the first place.

"You're the one who's been in the cabin?" Gray demanded, his voice filled with confusion and . . . was that relief she heard?

Rissa didn't answer. She looked over his shoulder, measuring the distance to the woods, where she could change and run away from here forever.

"Rissa," Gray said, trying to capture her attention. When she still didn't reply, he lunged forward and grasped her wrists in his large, warm hands. "I've been looking everywhere for you."

Before she could respond, he pulled her forward, into his arms.

"Thank God I found you again," he breathed as he hugged her against his hard chest. "I couldn't stop thinking about you. I came searching but no one had seen you anywhere . . . and I had no clue where you live. I came out here and found you—"

Rissa wiggled and squirmed her way out of his embrace. Once free, she stepped back two paces, and her head dropped.

"I'm sorry," she murmured. "I . . . I didn't have anywhere else to go."

Now Gray remained silent. Rissa looked up at him through her lashes, her hands wringing together in front of her. He cocked his head.

"Rissa, are you . . . are you homeless?"

She immediately dropped her gaze and stared at the brown grass which had gone dormant for the winter. How was she going to explain her life without giving everything away? There was no way. She needed to run. Now. Get as far away as possible and never return. Never see Gray again.

"My stepfather kicked me out of the house when I was 16," she blurted instead, and before she could think about what she was doing, she told him everything. Well, sort of. In Norman terms, anyway. "A couple found me in a city park, about to starve to death—if I didn't freeze overnight first. They took me in, like a foster kid, and they tried to make me like one of their own. But I never felt right there. They were . . . wrong. We had different values, I guess you could say. I tried to run away several times, but even after I was of legal age, they kept finding me and dragging me back. I'd become more like their slave, and they never let me forget that I was indebted to them. A few months ago, I finally got away for good. I've been running and hiding ever since. And then you helped me, and you were so nice, but then . . . then you were gone and that house, it was just sitting there empty and . . . "

"Rissa," Gray interrupted, his voice low and husky. Once more, his hands encased her wrists, and he pulled her into him in another hug. "Rissa, Rissa, Rissa. You're always welcome in my home."

Tears stung her eyes by now, and she pressed her face against his chest, refusing to let them fall. Her body trembled, though, betraying her emotions. He tightened his hold around her and pressed his cheek against the top of her head. She breathed his scent in, stronger than what had been left on the blanket, and once again, it tingled in her nose, but now almost pleasantly.

She couldn't believe she'd told him all that she had, but she felt a sense of relief at letting it all out. Of course, she couldn't tell him that the so-called family was really a werewolf pack, and that the values they differed on had to do with the sanctity of human lives and souls. He didn't need to know the true horrors of her past life, but there was still a release in being able to tell him what she did.

"I was so worried about leaving you like I did," he said. "I felt like a major douche bag, taking off like that. But something happened with the . . . the family business, and my sister needed help. If I would have known, well—" He chuckled softly. "Well, I would have let you stay at my place. And I certainly would have made sure you had more food."

"Why?" Rissa asked, her voice muffled against his chest. "Why are you so nice to me?"

Gray pulled back, just enough to look her in the eye. He raised his hand to her face, and she immediately missed his arm around her. At least, until his knuckles brushed lightly against her cheekbone and his thumb over her lip.

"Because there's just something about you," he said. "Something that makes me want to take care of you."

Rissa swallowed. "I don't need your charity."

His eyes squinted. "Um, yeah, you do. You've been helping yourself to it." He smiled at the flush that rose in her cheeks. "And I'm glad you do. I like it—taking care of you. Providing for you. I'm serious about not being able to stop thinking about you. I've been wondering what you've been doing, where you went, what I could have done to make sure you were okay. You don't even want to know the anger I felt when I thought about how I found you—naked and dirty—and the visions that ran through my head about how you got that way. I couldn't help but worry that you'd go back to that, whatever it was, and I didn't have any way to get a hold of you to know. I really set myself off, worried about you so much, until I couldn't stand it another moment. I skipped classes to come up here to look for you."

"You really shouldn't have."

"Yes, I should have."

"I was fine."

"I see that now. But I wasn't."

She looked up at him with big, brown eyes. "Are you now?"

He smiled, bringing out his dimples. Then he gripped her chin with his thumb and finger and leaned in toward her. Without even the slightest hesitation, his lips skimmed over hers, sending a jolt down to her navel. The light kiss became firmer and then urgent. Their mouths parted, and his tongue slid into hers, tasting like cinnamon gum. The kiss went on until they were both left breathless.

"Come on," Gray said, taking her hand and pulling her toward the house. "I'll make you dinner."

He skipped the next day of classes, too, and stayed with her through the weekend. Before he left, he made sure she had plenty of food for the week, and then he returned the following Friday. The weeks passed as the leaves fell, leaving the trees in the woods as naked as Rissa had been when Gray first found her. As naked as he left her in bed every Sunday afternoon. The days grew shorter, but seemed to drag on during the week, and the nights grew colder, but at least on the weekends they could snuggle under the blankets, sometimes outside on the porch swing as night fell, and other times inside by the fire. Thankfully, the full moon came during the middle of the week, and Rissa was able to run the woods those nights without Gray ever knowing.

"I tried to apply for a couple of jobs in town," she told him one Friday night over dinner. She'd been worried at first that her old pack would find her, but they hadn't come around since chasing after her over a month ago now. Maybe they'd finally given up. So she took the chance and walked to town, hoping to earn her own money so she could pay Gray back for all of his hospitality. "But, of course, they want I.D., and I don't have any."

"Hmm. . . " was his only response as he took another mouthful of the homemade spaghetti she'd fixed for him.

"I need to work, Gray," she said.

"You do. You take care of this place for me."

True. She'd been doing the cleaning and upkeep during the week so he didn't have to when he came on the weekends. But that was the least she could do. She needed to pay him rent and buy her own food. And if he wouldn't let her, she needed to save enough to be able to support herself elsewhere.

"I need a job," she said again.

He swallowed another bite and considered her for a long moment. "Tell you what. Come to Thanksgiving with me on Thursday."

Rissa's heart skipped a beat at the thought, but her brow furrowed. "You're changing the subject."

He wiped the napkin over his mouth. "No, I'm not. Come to Thanksgiving with me. Meet my sister. I've told her all about you, and she's dying to meet you."

"Gray! You did not!" Anger flushed through Rissa's cheeks.

He reached out and placed his hand over hers. "Relax. Not *everything*. The good things . . . which is almost everything. She really does want to meet you. And she might have a job for you."

"I don't think it's a good idea."

"It's a great idea! Or do you have plans for Thanksgiving?"

He knew she didn't. She didn't have a family or a home to go to for the holidays. A month ago, she'd truly had nothing to be grateful for. Now she had Gray, though, and a roof over her head, clothes on her back, and food in her belly. But she knew in her heart this could never last. She had a certain lifestyle that would never change—one that a human could never know about. It would be hard enough to say goodbye as it was, but meeting his sister . . . working for their family business . . . that was getting in way too deep.

"I can't, Gray," she said firmly, then she rose to her feet and carried their dishes into the kitchen, needing to put space between them. He followed her in, of course,

"Please, sweetheart. Don't make me go alone." He walked up behind her as she stood at the sink and wrapped his arms around her. "I kind of already told her you were coming."

Rissa groaned. "You didn't."

He pressed his lips against her neck. "I did. So please don't make me go stag another year. Don't make me look like a fool."

He pleaded with her all weekend and called every day from his apartment in the city. When he came Wednesday night, she finally acquiesced. She didn't exactly cherish the idea of spending the holiday with a group of strangers—their extended family would be there, too—but she hated even more the idea of missing a day she could have with Gray. And, admittedly, the idea of spending the holiday alone. Again.

As they pulled into the small town east of Atlanta, though, she immediately regretted her decision. She knew this place. It wasn't all that far from Savannah. When Gray pulled his truck into the parking lot of a bar, her hackles raised. A dozen people poured out of the bar's door, led by a woman with long, dark hair, wearing low-rise jeans and a tight-fitting button-down top. Rissa saw the obvious resemblance to Gray, and every instinct in her told her to run . . . or to prepare to fight. That odd trace in Gray's scent slammed into her like a wall of fire, so strong now that it seared her nose and lungs. The wolf inside her became alert. Grew within. Wanted out.

Amadis. Everywhere. She was surrounded.

"You set me up!" she snarled.

Chapter 5

Gray jumped out of the truck at the same time Rissa did while the others from the bar fell into formation in the parking lot behind the dark-haired woman, all of their eyes on Rissa. She scanned the area and found her point of escape—what looked like a forest about a hundred yards behind the bar. She just had to get past this Amadis pack, the bar and building behind it—

More Amadis wolves came from around the back of the building. Five men and three women, all dressed in denim, leather, and chains. No way could she outrun all of these wolves. Her head snapped toward Gray, her eyes wide and her nostrils flaring.

"*You*," she spat. "How could you?"

"No, you don't understand—"

"Oh, I understand all right. I see it all right in front of my eyes. I *feel* it." She paused and narrowed her eyes. "How did I not sense you?"

"Are we doing this or not, Henry?" the woman who had to be Gray's sister asked.

"Just . . . just give me a minute, Sundae," Gray said in response.

"*Henry?*" Rissa let out a dark chuckle, but then her voice rose as her body began to shake uncontrollably. "Was everything you told me a lie? Even your name? And you assholes accuse the Daemoni of being the deceivers!"

"Rissa," Gray said, "I . . . I wanted to help you."

"Help me?" Her voice rose another octave, and her form trembled even harder. She wouldn't be able to control the wolf inside her much longer. Her fingers ached from the growth of claws already protruding through her skin. "I don't need your help! I don't need your charity, and I certainly don't need your fucked-up idea of a Thanksgiving feast."

With no further warning, her human shape exploded. Were-goo rained to the gravelly parking lot with thick splats as Rissa shook her wolf-self out. Her hackles already stood high, her black fur from the back of her neck down her spine to her tail standing on end. She bent her head down low, twisted her ears back, and lifted her upper lip in a snarl, her now golden eyes sweeping over the group.

Several of the Amadis wolves, still in their human forms, began to tremble, but they didn't break rank or formation.

"Don't let them, Sundae!" Gray yelled at his sister as he threw her a look of warning.

Sundae raised her hand, and the others' shapes stilled. Gray's sister was apparently the leader of this pack. But wait. No, the others who'd come from the back of the building stood in formation behind another leader. A tall man with arms the size of Rissa's human legs and covered in tattoos, exposed as he only wore a black leather vest with his jeans. Apparently, even the Amadis wolf packs looked like biker gangs. And here she'd let herself be taken right into the hands of two such packs. What, were they going to fight over her? Or kill her and then split the goods? Either way, she wasn't going down without a fight.

Gray took another step toward her. She growled and snapped at him.

"Rissa, please," Gray said, holding a tentative hand out like a Norman does with a strange dog. "Listen to me. We don't want to hurt you. We want to help you."

She snarled again in response. Amadis don't help Daemoni. She'd been warned since the day she was bitten that they wanted to do nothing but kill her kind. They'd told her of attacks like this, reminding her to always stay with her pack. She'd thought them full of shit, though. Just trying to scare her. After all, she was a werewolf. She could defend herself. Yet, here she was, in the middle of these two packs who had quietly moved into a circle around her.

Effectively trapping her. Damn. She *hated* admitting that her old pack leader had been right all along.

"I'm not lying," Gray continued, standing in the center of the circle with her. "You have a good heart. You are a *good* soul. You don't have to be part of the Daemoni."

No, she didn't. If she could get through this, she could go back to her loner status. Be apart from all of them. She'd known all along that getting involved with Gray was a mistake. Now she just had to figure out how to escape this nightmare.

She paced a few times, a low growl rumbling in her throat as her gaze scanned over the others who watched them carefully. Gray stepped in front of her, his own shape quivering as he tried to maintain control over his wolf.

"You can still be good," he said. "You don't have to be a murderer. You don't have to hurt humans—I know you don't want to. I know you don't want to be one of *them*. You only have to let us convert you."

The word 'convert' sent a chill up her spine, and the Daemoni in her rose. She growled loudly this time and snapped at Gray again, her elongated teeth cracking against each other.

"Please, don't," Gray pled, but she didn't know to whom he spoke because four of the others had exploded into wolf form.

Another chill ran down Rissa's spine. She became agitated as adrenaline shot through her veins. She paced in a circle now, around Gray, taking him as her hostage. The other wolves growled back at her, their own heads down and their ears back. She snapped at them. They snapped back. But Sundae and the other pack leader apparently kept control of their wolves. Rissa had to admit they did a better job at doing so than her old pack leader had. The Daemoni wolves would have torn her into shreds by now. Or, at least, tried to. They possessed no control.

And the only way she'd escape right now was if she owned who—and what—she really was: a Daemoni werewolf.

Unleashing the self-control she'd barely been hanging on to, she lunged at one of the Amadis wolves. Her claws sliced into its neck at the same time pain pierced into her own shoulder: fangs from one of the others. She couldn't control the yelp.

"No!" Gray shouted, and the next thing she knew, a silvery-gray blur streaked to her side.

But Gray didn't attack her. He didn't defend his own pack members. He attacked *them*. And everyone else exploded into their wolf-selves, too.

Except Gray didn't really attack. He only snarled and snapped at them, pushing them back. A white wolf with a black streak down her back and a bigger one, black and gray, growled in return as they sauntered forward. The others once again dropped into formation behind their leaders. Everyone but Gray, who still stood by Rissa's side, his upper lip lifted, though he held the growl back.

Rissa could only stare in shock. This was nothing like how her old pack behaved. Not only would she be dead by now, but they'd be so hyped up, they'd be running off to find someone else to kill.

After several long moments passed, Gray's body began to shrink. He morphed into his human form—his beautifully naked form—and turned toward Rissa.

"We're not going to hurt you," he said, and she whined in response, referring to the bite in her shoulder. "We'll defend ourselves, but we don't want to harm you. We *do* want to help you. But it's up to you, sweetheart. Only you can make that decision. If you don't want to learn how you can have a much better life than you've had, we won't stop you from leaving."

She backed away, testing them before she made a run for it. She had to get out of here. No way could she ever trust any of them. Not even Gray, who'd been lying to her for weeks. Of course . . . she hadn't exactly been truthful with him. But he knew what she was, and, somehow, he'd been able to mask what he was. No, she couldn't trust him. No matter what her heart tried to tell her.

Nobody moved when she did. She took several more steps back, and still, they all remained frozen. Except Gray's face—his eyes. Sadness and disappointment flickered in them. Did he really care? *No. He's the enemy.* As she turned her body toward the forest without moving her gaze from him, she saw his face break. And her heart nearly broke with it.

Run, she told herself, and she sprang into action, hurdled the wolves, and sprinted for the treeline, pain screaming through her shoulder from the bite. She'd barely reached the edge of the forest before she had to stop for a rest. As soon as she did, grief and regret filled her being, and she morphed from wolf to human. She sat against a tree on a carpet of fallen leaves and sobbed, the image of Gray's crushed expression flooding her mind. When she stopped crying, conversation filtered to her sensitive ears as someone moved toward her.

"I'm sorry," Gray's familiar voice said, its tone heavy. "I knew she'd been running from them for a long time. I thought she was ready, that she'd want to."

"Well, you probably blew any trust she might have had in you by having that warlock mask your scent." The voice sounded like Sundae's, from the small bit Rissa had heard from the pack leader.

"I had to, or she'd never let me get close. You saw her. She thinks we're the enemy."

"We are, little brother. In her eyes, we are."

A long pause. "She's not my enemy, Sundae. Not any of ours. She was practically starving herself to death, and I'm sure it's because she can barely bring herself to eat a squirrel or rabbit. I just can't see her eating a human."

He paused again, giving time for Rissa to process their words. He'd been right about the eating a human part. That was the exact reason for leaving her old pack: they'd given her the ultimatum of devouring a Norman or being killed herself. She chose to run, even if that made her a coward, according to them. She didn't care what they thought. They didn't matter to her.

But, for some stupid reason, she did care what Gray thought. He did matter to her. She realized now that she'd allowed him to get under her skin much deeper than she'd known. He seemed to actually *see* her for who she really was.

Rissa squirmed to the side so she could see him now. Gray and Sundae walked along the back of the building that looked like a garage for motorcycles, from what Rissa could see. She remained hidden behind the tree trunk while watching them.

"I thought she was perfect for the Amadis," Gray continued, his voice becoming even more forlorn, and his next statement came out so low, Rissa almost missed it. "I thought she was perfect for me."

"Henry Grayson," Sundae said, her tone firm like a mother's as she turned and gripped his shoulders, "you need to go after her. From everything you've gushed about her over the last several weeks, she *is* perfect for you. And you're exactly what she needs. Go get her."

"But what if—"

"No what ifs! Go now," she barked. "And that's an order from your alpha."

Gray stared at his sister for a long moment, then his human shape was gone, replaced by the beautiful silvery-gray wolf. The magnificent beast took off for the forest, galloping straight toward Rissa. Her heart flew into double-time as she watched his majestic form run toward her. After her. To claim her. To make her his. And she suddenly realized that's what she wanted more than anything. She wanted to be Gray's mate. Even if that meant being Amadis.

Actually, she dared to admit, something deep down in her heart wanted that, too.

She stepped into the wolf's path, and he plowed into her, knocking her on her back. He immediately became human again, laying on top of her, both of them naked. He pushed himself onto his hands and locked his elbows, taking his weight off of her. He opened his mouth to say something, but Rissa wrapped her arms around his neck and pulled him back down until their lips crushed together.

After rolling around in the leaves together until their bodies were spent, they became wolves again and ran for the Amadis pack. A few younger pack members were outside, tossing a football between them. When they saw Gray returning with the raven wolf next to him, they ran inside. Sundae came out with a big grin and a pile of clothes in her arms.

The two packs gathered inside the bar, ready for a Thanksgiving feast. The entire bar and two pool tables were laid out with the biggest spread of food Rissa had ever seen. As they waited for Sundae and some of the others to bring out the last items, Gray took his new mate around to introduce her to the others, never letting go of her hand. She learned that his sister's pack had teamed up with a pack from Florida, the reason there were two packs in this small town. The Florida pack was led by the big man named Trevor. It appeared he and Sundae were mates, too.

After they filled their plates and sat down, Trevor led everyone in prayer. Rissa's body stiffened, but Gray wrapped an arm around her shoulder and pulled her close.

"Relax," he whispered into her ear. "You're right where you belong."

As Rissa looked around at these badass wolves who were also kind and caring, she knew Gray was right. She'd found a pack she could be a part of and had even found her mate. And for the first time in six years, she had something to be thankful for.

Gratitude

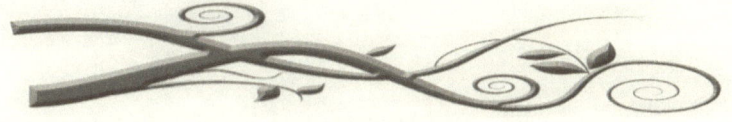

This last short story for the Thanksgiving part of the collection returns us to the lives of Alexis, Tristan, and the rest of the gang from the main series. Please note especially for this one that it does not fit in any particular place in the main Soul Savers Series. What happens in this short may never be a part of the events in the main storyline and the events of the main storyline are only vaguely relevant to the plot here. I've tried to write it so that if you have not read up to *Wrath* (Book 5) in the main series, you won't be completely spoiled here. However, your curiosity may be piqued. I hope it is! And for those who are completely caught up on the series, I hope you enjoy this extra little glimpse into the lives of the Knights and the Amadis.

Chapter 1

I stepped through the backdoor and into our shining white kitchen, finding it surreal to even be here on Sanibel Island, let alone back in our own home. My fingers trailed over the granite countertop of the island as Tristan and Dorian followed me inside. Sasha bounded in, passed all of us, and ran through the house, checking things out. Of course, I'd already done a mental sweep for mind signatures before we'd even come close, but the lykora wouldn't be too careful. She'd become more protective of my son than ever.

I headed into the living room and stood in front of the windows, staring out at the Gulf of Mexico as it spread out to the horizon. The November sun remained warm in this part of the world, and it shone brightly in the western sky, reflecting off the water. From the Amadis Island, I'd seen the same sun set over the Aegean Sea many times, but it felt different here.

"It's good to be back," Tristan murmured in my ear as he wrapped his arms around me from behind.

"I guess," I said. "It's *ours*, at least. No one else can tell us what to do here. But there's just so much going on. I feel like it's too much of a luxury to spend even one night here."

"It does feel like another world, doesn't it?"

"A little too peaceful. Too tranquil," I agreed. We'd seen so much war lately, so much fighting and blood and lives lost, that being here—*home*—while our people were still battling around the world felt wrong.

"Does that mean you don't want to watch the sunset with me?" His breath was hot against my ear, sending a shock of tingles to my core.

He took my hand and dragged me outside to the beach. He plopped onto the sand and pulled me down with him, positioning me between his legs and my back against his chest, just like old times.

I breathed deeply, trying to relax, wanting to feel the contentment this would have once brought me, but unable to.

"Sometimes we have to stop and appreciate this beautiful world so we can remember what we're fighting for," Tristan said, his voice low, nearly a whisper.

"I know you're right," I said with a sigh, "but it still feels wrong. I feel like I'm betraying our soldiers who are out there fighting this very minute."

"It's not like you've abandoned them, Alexis. We're here for a reason."

Of course, we were. This stop hadn't been for personal reasons, to 'go home again.' We couldn't afford such luxuries. The Captiva Island colony needed a visit from leadership. They needed a morale boost, and since this was the place I still liked to call home, who better than royalty herself to make the visit? I hadn't come alone, of course. Besides Tristan and Dorian, we had a whole entourage— Blossom, Jax, Charlotte, Owen, Sheree, and Vanessa had joined us. They'd all gone on over to Captiva, Blossom and Jax to check out her house, Charlotte and Sheree to the safe house, and Owen and Vanessa to the condo the Amadis had bought for him, my protector, a lifetime ago. So much had changed since then . . .

"Yes, we're here for a reason. We should get our butts over to the safe house sooner rather than later."

Tristan blew out a breath. "Will you at least let me enjoy the sunset? Do you know how long it's been?"

I did. Because although I'd 'seen' many sunsets from the Amadis Island, I hadn't really *seen* them. I hadn't stopped to appreciate their beauty, to admire God's artistic talent, to be reminded of their meaning, that we'd made it through another day. And this had always meant a lot to Tristan, so I sat there with him, trying to embrace what he'd said about needing to remember what we fought for—this beautiful planet and the people on it.

His lips peppered the skin on my neck and shoulder as the sun descended, and I did allow myself to enjoy that for a few minutes. Our time alone for intimacy had become so rare. But as soon as the sun had disappeared behind the horizon, my conscience was nagging at me. Blossom had telepathically told me that she was picking up Dorian and Sasha and taking them to the safe house, and I knew we needed to get there, too.

"We should go," I said, my voice husky and my body filled with desire.

Tristan gathered me into his arms and flashed. We didn't appear at the safe house, though. Instead, we stood in our bedroom.

"I'd like some time with my wife first." His eyes sparked, his mouth lifted in a sublime and inviting grin, and I succumbed.

Night had fallen completely by the time we did arrive at the safe house. I'd already sensed the depressed mind signatures in the colony as soon as we'd come close enough, but seeing everyone's faces really drove it home. Most of those who remained here weren't fighters. They were our weaker members, staying behind and close together, while their spouses, parents, and children went off to fight the Daemoni and protect human souls. I spoke with each of them, telling them what I knew about their loved ones and reminding them that if we all stayed strong and united, we'd beat the Daemoni. And then I gave a lame rally speech to the entire group, promising them what I promised everyone.

"I will personally kill Lucas," I said to them, my voice as fierce as ever. "And we will destroy the Daemoni from top to bottom and everywhere in between."

My speech was met with applause, but I still sensed defeat as a thin veil hovering over the colony.

"They need something more," Sheree, one my favorite Weres, said after my core group had gathered in my office, filling it to capacity. I sat behind my desk with Tristan standing beside me, and the rest had scattered themselves around the room.

"I have an idea," Blossom said from her perch on the side of my desk. She faced the group at first, but then she turned toward me with a glint in her hazel eyes, twisting her blond hair around a finger. "This week is Thanksgiving. How about we stay and prepare a real Thanksgiving dinner for the entire colony?"

"Like we have so much to be thankful for," Vanessa muttered, rolling her ice-blue eyes and tossing her white-blond hair. I couldn't help but agree with the vampire's sarcasm.

"We still have lots," Blossom said defiantly.

"We do," Sheree agreed, "and a coming together like this and sharing it with everyone will remind them that we do."

I peered around the room, gauging everyone's expressions for their reactions so I wouldn't have to tap into their minds. I tried not to invade privacy when I didn't have to. Charlotte looked to her son and to Vanessa, then at me. She smiled but it didn't reach her eyes.

"We do have some things," she agreed, though I could hear the reluctance in her voice. We'd lost so much, both of us . . . all of us. She knew that's what I was thinking.

Jax, another favorite Were, cleared his throat. "I think your 'thanksgiving' is a tad different than Australia's. What's the big deal?"

Blossom explained the American Thanksgiving tradition of turkey, stuffing, and all the trimmings, watching or playing football, and eating yourself into a food coma.

"You don't give thanks for anythin'?" Jax asked as he rubbed his bald head.

"Well, yeah, silly," Blossom said, lightly punching his thick arm. "We do that before we eat, but really the whole day is about spending time with family and friends and celebrating all that we have to be grateful for."

"Well, it sounds all right to me," the were-croc said. "Why not?"

Everyone's eyes came to me then, filled with expectation. I inwardly grimaced, the part of me that rebelled against having to be the decision-maker all the time rising. But I no longer had a choice. And this decision was pretty easy. As nice as a real Thanksgiving dinner sounded, we just couldn't afford to take that time out.

"We can't stay here that long," I said, and I looked to Tristan, who was always my voice of reason. He'd surely back me up.

He cocked his head. "Weren't we just talking about how we needed to stop to appreciate what we're fighting for?"

I stared at him for a long minute with annoyance. *Argh. Is he ever wrong?*

"*Not often,*" he silently replied, and I glared at him. "*Let's give this to them, ma lykita. They deserve it—your team as much as anyone.*"

My eyes swept over the group once more. Owen, who leaned against the bookshelves, shrugged. He, too, knew how I felt, and he, too, would rather be fighting. He was a warlock, after all. But I also knew he, too, would enjoy a respite, especially a break from having to guard me so closely. His job had become more important than ever.

Sheree and Blossom both begged me with their eyes. How I loved their optimism and generosity. But they hadn't experienced the recent sense of loss as I had. As Tristan, Charlotte, Owen, and Dorian had. Not at the same magnitude. They also didn't have the same drive to fight. They were the weights that balanced the rest of us. And maybe this time they were right.

"You really think we can prepare a Thanksgiving feast for all of these people on such short notice?" I asked, and Blossom's eyes lit up.

"I'm a witch, Alexis," she said. "We can be quite resourceful."

I looked again at Tristan, and he nodded.

"All right," I said with a sigh of resignation. "We'll stay for Thanksgiving and give the colony a boost of happiness. But first thing Friday morning, we're on our way. These aren't the only people who need us. Our troops are literally dying for us."

Everyone gave a somber nod, then Blossom excitedly rattled off some menu and decorating ideas, her mind going a hundred-miles-an-hour like it always did, and everyone else began jumping in. Before long, the office sounded as though it held a large crowd with all of the chatter about favorite dishes and family traditions. Nobody could forget that in a few days we'd have to return to the war, but for now, everyone obviously liked the idea of having something good to focus on.

If only it could last.

Chapter 2

My eyes peeled open the next morning to sunshine pouring through the curtained window, and it took me a moment to realize I lay in my own bed in my own home. Part of me wanted to enjoy this luxury, but a bigger part of me squirmed inwardly with guilt. I stretched and rolled over, right into Tristan's waiting arms. A beautiful grin stretched across his face before he planted a kiss on my forehead.

"Good morning, *ma lykita*."

"Morning," I answered, and I snuggled into him, wishing his strong arms could push away the ever present feeling of dread.

Even when things were relatively quiet, like they had been for the last couple of weeks, I couldn't shake the feeling that anything could happen at any moment. Small battles with the Daemoni waged all over the world as they increased the frequency of their attacks, but it was only a matter of time before it all escalated into a major war. Of course, the timing of it could possibly be up to us. I was sure Lucas and the Ancients waited for the Amadis to respond to their last devastating attack. Although we were building up for it, we simply didn't have the numbers that our enemy did. And I didn't think Lucas would wait too long to be on the defensive. Soon enough, he would go on the offensive again. I just hoped our people were ready when he did.

"*Alexis, are you up?*" Blossom's voice said in my head. I didn't have to search far for her mind signature.

"Did you know Blossom's in our kitchen?" I asked Tristan.

"I heard Dorian let her in a few minutes ago."

"And you weren't going to say anything?"

"Oh, I was about to. I felt you tensing up with whatever is going on in your head. She'll be a good distraction for you."

"I don't need a *distraction*. If anything, I need to focus more. People's lives depend on us, and here we are planning some stupid—"

"Lex, do you really think any of us would have agreed to this Thanksgiving idea if people's lives were at stake?"

I pushed myself up on my elbows and glared at him. "They're always at stake, Tristan! The Normans' souls are in danger every day with the Daemoni running around like they are."

"And we have people out there."

"Exactly. Fighting while we're sleeping in our nice, comfortable bed and planning a party."

He pushed a lock of hair behind my ear. "We all do our share, *ma lykita*, especially you and the rest of us here. Everyone deserves a break, even us."

"*Alexis?*"

Ugh. Yeah, Blossom, I'm up. What do you need?

"*I kind of hoped you'd go grocery shopping with me.*"

My eyes narrowed as I returned my attention to my husband. "Blossom wants me to go to the market with her, Tristan. To the market! And the day before yesterday I was covered in blood from a vampire attack."

"And so was she. She needs this, Lex. They all do, or they'll start getting sloppy. You can't leave without protection, so if you try to go back to the fight, you're putting even more lives in danger. Blossom's and Owen's and Charlotte's. Sheree's and Jax's—"

I blew out a breath. "All right, all right, I get it."

As I rolled out of bed, I silently told Blossom that I'd be ready in an hour, and she'd better have a protector lined up for us. I waited for her to leave the house, taking Dorian with her, and I pulled Tristan into the bathroom with me for a quickie in the shower.

Two hours later, Blossom, Charlotte—our protector for the day—and I were off island, pretending like we were perfectly Norman at the grocery store. Blossom tore her list in thirds and handed a part to Charlotte and one to me. The warlock eyed the witch.

"I'm not leaving Alexis's side," Char said.

"Oh, right. Of course not," Blossom said, taking the paper from Charlotte.

"I'll be fine," I groaned, snatching the slip from the witch and handing it back to Char. "All of the mind signatures here are Norman, so just put up a shield over the store, and we'll *all* be fine. Then we can get this done faster and get out of here sooner."

Charlotte pierced me with her sapphire blue eyes. "And how do I know you won't go running out of the store to jump into the middle of something you don't belong in?"

I pressed my lips together, unable to answer her. I kind of had the reputation of diving into situations that were over my head. It's not that I didn't give it enough thought each time. I just can't seem to help myself, especially when someone's life or soul is in danger. My purpose was to defend souls, and I'd been told over and over to take that purpose seriously, so I did. Regardless of what that meant for me . . . or those responsible for protecting me.

"I promised Tristan and my son that I wouldn't leave your side," Charlotte said. "And I owe it to your mother."

With no answer to that, I relented, and we grabbed our shopping carts. Blossom went one way, and Charlotte and I went the other. Within no time, we met Blossom at the front of the store with three carts full of seven turkeys, four hams, several ten-pound bags of potatoes, more bags of sweet potatoes, bread for stuffing, cans of cranberry sauce, pumpkin pie filling, flour and milk for gravy, and all kinds of baking ingredients that would keep Blossom happy for days.

"So you're good with supervising the cooking part of things while I do the baking?" Blossom asked me once we'd loaded Tristan's truck with enough food to feed a crowd—which was exactly what we expected. Although Vanessa and Owen were currently handing out the invitations back on the island, we expected all seventy-something Amadis who remained in the colony to show up.

"Yeah, Tristan and I can handle it."

"If it gets to be too much, just let me know," the witch said as we climbed into the truck. Charlotte sat in the driver's seat, knowing how much I hated driving the monster of a thing, and I let Blossom have shotgun while I took the backseat. "A touch of magic can always help."

I barely registered her words, though, as a tingle scurried along the back of my neck. Something felt . . . wrong. I opened my mind and skimmed through the mind signatures in the vicinity, searching for Daemoni. None came on my radar, though. Only Normans, all of them in relatively good spirits as they, too, prepared for the holiday: moms and grandmas doing the food shopping and preparing for Black Friday madness, children anxious for the short school week to end, men thinking about the upcoming marathon of football games. Normal thoughts for normal humans. So why did that odd feeling linger?

Right as we headed for the bridge that crossed the causeway to Sanibel Island, it hit me. Dark wave after dark wave coming from the area of Fort Myers Beach.

"Charlotte, we need to turn around," I said, my voice full of alarm. I shared with her what my mind picked up.

"Screw that. I need to get you back." The warlock stomped the accelerator down harder.

"No, Char!" I protested. "They're attacking the Normans. We can't abandon them!"

"Alexis, I'm not taking you into battle with just the three of us. Give it up."

I turned in my seat, as though I could see the attack through the back window. But all I saw was blue sky and bright sunrays shining on the palm trees and now on the water as we crossed the bridge.

"I can let the others know," I said. "They can flash there and meet us."

Blossom groaned. "All I wanted was a normal, all-American holiday just this once," she muttered.

"We're not going to fight," Char said. "Not now. We have people—"

"They need our help!" Not planning to argue with her a moment longer, I reached out for Tristan, sharing with him what I had with Charlotte.

"*Don't we have people there already?*" he asked, saying what I hadn't allowed Char to finish.

I didn't answer him at first, though, as my eyes grew wide. A dark cloud of . . . something strange . . . headed our way, skimming over the land and trees on the far side of the sound.

"Um, Char," I said, "you better drive faster or be ready to fight."

Charlotte looked in the rearview mirror. "What the hell is that?"

"I don't know," I said, "but it feels evil."

"*Lex, what's going on?*" Tristan asked me, "hearing" the trouble through my mind.

I'm not quite sure, but it's not good.

"Oh, my God," Blossom whispered. Her large hazel eyes were wider than ever as she stared over my shoulder.

The cloud had grown bigger. And darker.

I focused my eyesight and could see now what it was: Daemoni.

"*Get home, Alexis!*" Tristan shouted in my mind.

"Get home, Alexis!" Charlotte shouted out loud.

"I'm not leaving you," I shouted back.

"We're going, too!" She cranked the wheel and the back of the truck fishtailed as she pulled into a church parking lot on Sanibel Island. "Come on, let's get out of here!"

Leaving all of that food behind, the three of us flashed to Captiva, appearing near the safe house. Tristan, Owen, Sheree, and Vanessa already stood outside on the steps, and I ran for them.

"Where's Dorian?" I demanded.

"Safe inside with the mages," Tristan answered.

"We need to go," I said. "Stave them off before they get here."

"Um, Alexis," Sheree said, her voice soft yet edged with . . . was that fear or awe? Her brown eyes stared to the southeast. I turned to follow her gaze, but I already knew what was coming. I could feel their mind signatures, sense their evil intentions.

The Daemoni had followed us. Swarms of mages and were-creatures flew through the air, while vampires trampled through the islands. It was more than the bloodsucker nest that had taken over Fort Myers Beach. This was an all-out attack directed at us.

They had dared to come here, what had once been a safe haven for the local Amadis. I had brought them here.

"Looks like we fight," I said through a clenched jaw. "Prepare for battle."

Chapter 3

Sheree exploded into her tiger form, and Jax followed, taking his alternate form as a white crocodile. Owen threw a shield over me and another over Tristan. We usually waged our own mini-battle before the real one, because everyone wanted me tucked away, coordinating the battle with my mind from a safe distance. But I always refused to leave Tristan, refused to watch helplessly through everyone else's eyes as I had done the day I'd lost him. We usually ended up compromising—as long as there was a shield over Tristan, I would agree to remain hidden, but not far away.

Today, however, we wouldn't argue. We didn't have time, nor near enough soldiers to fight. They needed me out here, too, our second most powerful fighter after Tristan. Dorian was much too close for my comfort, but when I tried to search for his mind signature, I was barely able to find it, he was hidden so well behind a powerful wall of magic. The Daemoni wouldn't be able to sense him. I hoped.

As the Daemoni approached, I realized the black cloud was not made up by the creatures themselves, but by the dark energy they were producing. They marched on, plowing through trees and the water, destroying anything and everything in their way, which was mostly property belonging to Normans. Boats, cars, even houses exploded with a blast of magic or a powerful punch. If we survived this, we'd have a lot of repairs to make and memories to wipe. If we didn't survive . . . well, God help those Norman souls. They wouldn't be alive, or at least not Norman, for long.

Some of the Amadis from the colony had gathered outside with us. They weren't our best fighters, but they knew they had to step up when necessary. Everyone's eyes fell on me, waiting for the order. I looked over at Tristan one last time, and he gave my hand a squeeze with his own.

"*Let's do this*," he said.

As the official leader of our army, the actual command came from me. I silently called it out, ordering Owen and Charlotte to cloak everyone while sending small groups in different directions, using guerrilla warfare to counter the Daemoni's head-on attack. Thanks to Tristan, I'd been learning all kinds of war strategies, but I never let our mental connection break during a fight, even when I had to mind-speak with others. His logic and strategic planning countered my impulsive tendencies. In other words, he ensured I didn't screw up.

My core group, sworn to protect royalty—aka, me—stayed near my side. I swiped my finger over the amethyst embedded in my dagger and the knife showed itself on my hip, where it always hung. I unsheathed it while scanning the Amadis mind signatures, then the Daemoni's, then back to the Amadis. When our soldiers were in place and everything seemed to be going as planned, we charged. Owen and Charlotte lifted the cloaks only at the last second.

The element of surprise worked to our advantage, but not for long. I shot electricity out of my left hand while swinging my dagger with my right, pushing Amadis power through the blade at the same time. Most of my foes retreated, as much afraid of the Amadis power as the electrical current that could fry them to ashes. But they didn't go far and returned from a different angle. I sliced through them with the silver blade, and they cried out in pain, but they didn't relent. Not until I blasted them so hard, they had no choice but to flash away.

Tristan fought with brute strength, paralyzing the enemy before crushing them with a blow from his fist. But as more began to swarm on him, he also began using his unique power, blasting them many yards away. Except then they would find whoever was closest and attack. Owen and Charlotte fought hard with their magic, their green and blue lights shooting everywhere while other mages' retaliated with orange and red spell streaks. Sheree and Jax focused on the were-creatures, and Vanessa on the vampires. The other Amadis used whatever advantage they could get.

But we were so outnumbered.

The Daemoni continued their forward momentum, and we were unable to thwart it. For every push forward we could get them away from the safe house, they pushed us back twice as far. Normans screamed from the beach, from houses and cars, and they scurried for cover indoors. Our mages ensured they remained safe as the Daemoni warlocks tried to blast the houses to kill the people inside. They may have been gaining ground on us, but so far anyway, we hadn't lost a soul—not an Amadis one, nor a human's. Seeing that we wouldn't stop protecting the Normans, the Daemoni turned their full focus on us.

"*Annihilate the entire Amadis colony, then you can take the Normans. Spare no one, not even royalty.*" The same voice, same words echoed through the Daemoni's minds as I scanned over them, an order they must have received earlier as they prepared their attack. And the voice was familiar, icy, one that sent chills down my spine. It belonged to Lucas, my sperm donor. So much for wanting to bring Tristan, Dorian, and me to his side. He had to have known we were here—why else make the comment about royalty—and he obviously wanted us dead.

In a rare show of unity and cooperation, the Daemoni came together and focused all efforts on us. Their Weres stopped running the beach, their vampires stopped attacking any Normans that remained outside, and their mages ceased throwing magic randomly at houses and Normans' property. They directed all weapons, whether fangs or claws or magic spells, on the Amadis.

We continued to fight hard and smart, but their sheer numbers had us constantly backing up.

"*Alexis!*" Sheree mind-shouted at me. "*The safe house.*"

I know. I clenched my teeth to ground out the words, although they came silently. We'd reached the safe house. If we couldn't hold the Daemoni off and finish this battle, everyone inside would be in danger. Including my son. *Tristan, what do we do?*

"*Fight!*" was his only answer.

The Daemoni suddenly seemed like they hadn't even been really trying before. Dark energy surged through them as they redoubled their efforts. Snapping jaws and swinging fists came at me. I slashed at them with my dagger. Zapped them with electricity. Pushed Amadis power into them, their screams making my blood curdle.

Light-spells blasted all around us. Tree branches snapped and fell. Vampire limbs soared through the air after being snapped off the creatures. The sounds of crashing stones reverberated all around us. Several fires burnt, darkening the sky with their smoke and making my nose twinge.

And we still fought on.

My heart pounded in my ears as I soared for a Daemoni vampire, arcing my silver blade down and into her shoulder, severing her arm. Her red eyes glowed as she glared at me with violent anger before charging at me. I gathered a large bubble of Amadis power within me and pushed it out at her. Her whole body—well, minus the arm—writhed and convulsed. I sent an electric current at her, not relenting even as her pale skin turned purple and an acrid smoke arose. She was barely able to grab her arm before disappearing in a flash.

The fight carried on into the night. Although the Daemoni had numbers on their side, we had more determination, more passion, more heart and soul. We were not only fighting for the Normans, but this time we were also protecting our loved ones and our safe haven. We had more to fight for. Eventually we dwindled their numbers down. We could see victory on the horizon. Maybe it would rise with the sun.

But then . . . bright yellow light streaked through the sky. An explosive blast shook the ground and made my ears ring. A plume of flames and smoke shot into the air.

"Tristan!" I yelled.

The safe house. It'd been hit. Hard. And our boy was inside.

I searched for Dorian's mind signature even as I ran for the mansion. Tristan ran after me while aiming his palm skyward. Then

I saw what he had—a Daemoni mage who exuded powerful magic, possibly even a sorcerer, hovering in the sky. Before Tristan could blast his power, though, another shadowy form shot through the dark and plowed into the first.

"Oh, my God," I whispered, and then I screamed, "Dorian! No!"

He could fly, but we didn't know what other powers he possessed. Besides self-healing, no others had manifested yet. He had unusual strength and speed—but only unusual compared to Normans. There was no way he could stand up against a Daemoni yet, especially not a mage as powerful as this one.

"Owen," I called, "he needs *you!*"

Owen ran and leapt, soaring through the air as he blasted a spell at the flying mage. My heart stopped for a moment when I thought it was going to hit Dorian, but my boy twisted in mid-air, and the spell missed him. The blue light smashed into the Daemoni warlock-slash-sorcerer. The form fell to the ground. Owen shot a series of several spells, not relenting until the mage disappeared with a loud *pop*.

The few Daemoni who still remained on the grounds let out a collective gasp. Tristan spun around and hit each of them with his power. They all *popped* away.

My hand flew to my mouth as I stared at the safe house engulfed in flames. Those who had fought were now running inside and pulling people out while mages directed water from the gulf through the air and to the mansion. Dorian landed next to me with a soft swoosh. I pulled him into a tight hug, but I couldn't tear my eyes away from the destruction all around us. From what I could see with my inhuman vision, even in the darkness, the whole island had practically been destroyed. All of the houses, mansions, condos, and businesses appeared to be nothing but piles of rubble.

And I had no idea how many lives had been lost in the end.

Chapter 4

By the time the sun rose, all of the fires had been extinguished, but devastation surrounded us. The island looked even worse in the morning light than what I'd feared in the dark. It appeared as though a hurricane had blown through. Trees lay on the ground, either uprooted or snapped in half. Every building had suffered damage, with caved-in roofs, shattered windows, and large objects such as cars and boats smashed into them. Some were nothing more than big piles of charred rubble. Bicycles hung in trees, and sand buried the streets.

I'd sat on the safe house's front lawn, still wiping at the tears that wouldn't stop, holding Dorian and Tristan for what felt like hours. But the Amadis needed me, so I eventually had to push myself up and tend to their needs. Owen, Charlotte, and Blossom gathered up some of our more powerful mages and set off for the Normans. They fixed what was unexplainable, then altered the Normans' memories before sending them on their way off-island. The good thing about this being a holiday week was that many of the regular Normans were away, spending the holidays with their families up north.

"There's just so much in ruins," I said to Tristan after ensuring that a pair of Were siblings had found each other. "Not even Owen can repair all of this before some Norman starts demanding answers."

"The Amadis have their ways. We'll figure it out, *ma lykita*."

I pushed my hand through my hair and turned to stare at the ruins of the safe house once again. It had suffered the worst damage, and Owen wasn't sure he'd be able to put it back. Too many of the stones it was built from had disintegrated from the magical explosion.

"*Alexis?*" Blossom's voice came as a whisper in my mind. "*We're at your house. You, uh, might want to see this . . . or maybe not.*"

My breath caught, and I looked up at Tristan for just a moment before flashing to our house on Sanibel.

"Oh, my God," I choked out, and more tears sprang to my eyes. Our house—our beautiful little house on the beach—was gone. Leveled. Another of our homes decimated by the Daemoni.

Tristan appeared by my side and pulled me into his arms. "It's just stuff, my love. The important parts of this home are okay."

I nodded, my head rubbing against his chest, but I still couldn't help the flow of tears. This house had been our little sanctuary, away from the demands and controls of the council, a place of our own. We'd bought it knowing life would be tough but hoping we'd always have this place for ourselves, for our family. The extra bedroom held our hope for a daughter to come into our lives. Blossom and I had painted for the first time here, making it into something that was *ours*. Something I'd hoped would be a permanent structure in our lives. But nothing was permanent for us. When would I learn that?

A hand too small to be Tristan's landed on my back and rubbed up and down. I looked over my shoulder at Blossom, who gave me a sad smile.

"My house is gone, too," she said, her voice heavy. "But we're all okay, and that's what matters."

"We've finished counting heads," Owen said as he strode up behind her. "All Amadis and Normans accounted for."

"Injuries?" I asked as I swiped at my eyes and nose.

"A few," Charlotte said. "Nothing Tristan can't help heal."

We spent the remainder of the day fixing people up, then the mages worked on shelters for everyone for the night. Owen and Char put up a shield and cloak over the entire island to give us at least one more night and day before Norman authorities caught on that anything had happened here. That night, as we lay in a tent on the beach, Tristan and I discussed how we should handle those authorities. Times were changing, and we had to be careful, but we couldn't simply run and hide from them. Not with the war waging around the world. The local authorities needed to understand that they were not immune to the attacks.

I didn't know how I managed to fall asleep, but my body must have forced me to so it could regenerate. I awoke with the sun shining through our tent's walls and a chorus of excited voices outside. When I stepped out of the tent with my hand on my forehead and my eyes squinting against the bright vision in front of me, Blossom came running over the sand to me.

"We're still having Thanksgiving!" she squealed.

My brows pushed together. "Um . . . *what?*"

"Aunt Sylvie brought her whole coven, and Christina, a warlock, came, too, to protect them, and they've all been working hard on preparing a feast for us!" Blossom continued her gushing. "Isn't it wonderful? It was so thoughtful of them to come all the way from Daytona, and they found our food that we left in the truck, so they're working their magic. After everything that happened—"

My eyes widened, and my jaw dropped. "After everything that happened, I think this is the *last* thing we should be doing."

"What? We don't deserve a victory party?" Owen asked, sauntering up from behind our tent with Vanessa at his side.

"A victory party?" I repeated in disbelief.

"Yeah, we still won," Jax said as he draped an arm over Blossom's shoulder.

"And the food's practically ready. Everyone's pretty excited for it," Charlotte said, walking up to join us.

"*Excited?*" I blinked. My mouth gaped, closed, gaped again, like a fish. Sure, we'd run the Daemoni off, but what exactly had we won? "They want to *celebrate?*"

"Why not?" Tristan asked as he stepped through the tent's door and stood by my side. "They deserve it, Lex."

"There's so much to be grateful for," Sheree agreed, the last of my core group to join us.

My head snapped toward the ruins of the safe house—the one place everyone here had relied on for security. Now it was gone. I lifted my arms and swept my hands out, gesturing to all of the destruction. My house, Blossom's house, Owen's condo, everywhere the Amadis people had lived and worked had been damaged or even destroyed.

"What could they be thankful for?" I whispered, the question more to myself than anyone else.

"Well, I'm thankful we still have our strongest warlocks to keep us protected," Vanessa answered anyway as she took Owen's hand in one of hers and Charlotte's in the other.

"I'm thankful for a chance at friendship . . . and something more," Jax said, tightening his hold on Blossom.

"Me, too," the witch replied to him before her gaze skimmed over all of us. "I'm thankful for *all* of you."

"I'm thankful for second chances and people who really care," Sheree said. She moved up to stand between Blossom and me and took each of our hands into hers.

"I'm thankful for you and Dad and Sasha," Dorian declared as he and the lykora ran up to us. He threw his arms around Tristan and me.

Tears stung my eyes by now.

"I'm thankful for a strong leader who brought us to victory," Tristan said as he pulled me into his arms.

"Here, here!" cheered a crowd of Amadis that had gathered around, including Blossom's Aunt Sylvie and several witches and wizards I'd never met yet.

My heart swelled as emotions crashed over me. My mind, always alert these days, listened as everyone mentally counted their blessings.

"*I'm thankful for an excellent leadership team*," one thought. Although many others' echoed hers, I searched this one's out. A warlock I didn't know yet, but the one Blossom had called Christina, tall with light brown hair and brown eyes deeply focused on Tristan. Maybe it was the mischievous little smirk on her face and in her voice that caught my attention. "*I'm especially thankful to set my eyes on this man. He's so lickalicious.*"

I couldn't help the giggle as I looked up at my husband. He *was* lickalicious. But licking would have to wait.

"What are you thankful for, Mom?" Dorian asked as he studied both of us.

A grin stretched across my face, and I lifted my arm to indicate everyone, although my eyes never left Tristan's hazel ones that sparkled beautifully. "For *all* of you!"

Then I wrapped my arm around my son and the other around my husband and pulled them both into a group hug.

Especially for my men, I thought to both of them.

"So we can have our Thanksgiving?" Blossom asked, hope overflowing in her question.

I looked around at all of the faces, young and old, some magical humans, others were-animals and vampires, all of them full of gratitude and love. We may have lost everything material—our homes, our belongings, even our safe house—but we still had what mattered more than anything: our lives and our loved ones.

"Who am I to stop you?" I asked with a smile, and the crowd erupted in cheers.

So we ate, drank, and were merry with a Thanksgiving feast like no other spread out on the beach of Captiva Island. Blossom had worked so hard with the others on decorations that were now ashes. She didn't get to bake the twelve cakes she'd had planned. Tristan and I didn't get to spend hours in the kitchen together cooking up a storm like old times. But the food was delicious and the company extra special.

"Best Thanksgiving ever!" Dorian exclaimed at one point, and everyone lifted their glasses to toast their agreement.

Later that night, just before ducking into our tent for bed, Tristan whispered something to Owen. The warlock nodded and flicked his hand toward our tent, before calling Dorian over to him. He took our son and walked down the beach toward his own tent. I looked at Tristan and tilted my head with curiosity. He grabbed my hand and pulled me into the tent. As soon as he zipped it closed, all of the sounds outside fell away.

"Owen muffled our tent?" I asked as excitement zinged through me.

Tristan gave me his most sublime grin. "Since today's all about counting our blessings, I thought it only right to show what I'm most grateful for."

"Oh, yeah?" I gave him a teasing smile. "And what is that?"

He yanked me closer to him and bent his head so his lips grazed my neck. "My wife," he murmured, and in a flurry of movement, he had me undressed. "And her naked body."

"Mmm . . . " was all I could muster as his lips and hands explored, and my body immediately reacted. But before he brought me down on knocking knees, I tore off his clothes as quickly as he'd done mine. "And I'm thankful for this lickaliciousness."

He pulled away and gave me a strange look. "This what?"

"Nothing," I said with a giggle as I pulled him down on top of me. "Now show me how grateful you can be."

And he did. And all night we shouted out our thanks as we counted multiple blessings together. It really was the best Thanksgiving ever.

Recipes

Recipes for you to try this Thanksgiving—or whenever—submitted by me and members of my street team, Kristie's Warriors. I hope you enjoy them!

Jewels' Human Dip

Submitted by Wendy Jahnke

This is a dip Jewels might enjoy on Thanksgiving in Amity.

Ingredients:
 8 oz Braunschweiger
 4 or 5 Tbsp. Sour Cream

1. Take Braunschweiger and cut in to cubes place in bowl.

2. Add sour cream and blend well. Serve with crackers.

Sundae's Pack Stew

Submitted by Heather Wakefield

My mom always made the delicious, warm chicken and dumplings that made the house smell so good. Since wolves eat chicken and my mom gave me the middle name Sundae, this seems like the perfect stew Sundae the werewolf would make for her pack.

<u>Ingredients:</u>
- Whole fryer chicken
- 1 medium onion, chopped
- 3-4 celery sticks, cut into chunky bits (bite size)
- 4 large carrots, cut into bite-size pieces
- 3 cloves garlic, smashed enough to break open
- Parsley (pinch of dry or handful of fresh)

1. Cut the chicken, and put it into large pot. Boil with salt until meat pulls easily away from the bone. Skim foam off the top when it boils.

2. After boiling the chicken for about 30 minutes but before it is done, add the carrots and garlic, as well as other seasonings you like, such as paprika, chili powder, and cumin. Continue boiling for another 10-15 minutes, then add onion and celery, a few pinches of dry parsley or a small handful of fresh parsley. Let all of that simmer while you do the dumplings.

For the Dumplings

About 2 cups of all-purpose flour, seasoned with your favorite spice(s) for better dumplings
2/3 cup milk
1-2 eggs

3. Mix eggs and milk first, then slowly add flour. Make a ball with the dough then turn out onto floured surface and roll out. At this point, you can use a knife to create noodle like shapes, or you can use a cookie cutter. (Take note that less flour will give you softer dumplings. If the dough is thicker and easier to handle, then the dumplings will be firmer and a bit chewy. Both ways are good, so adjust to your textural liking. If you use a cookie cutter to create shapes it's easier when the dough is firmer.)

4. Pull the bulk of the chicken out (at this time, you can debone your soup if you choose to). You need the cauldron to be at a slow boil, then drop some dumplings in. When they float, they are done. Keep adding more and using a big spoon to push the cooked ones out of the way until all the dumplings are done.

Blossom's Oh So Tender Turkey!

Submitted by Heather Brandt

I imagine Blossom making her Thanksgiving turkey this way in the story Gratitude.

Ingredients:

One Butterball turkey 15lbs-20lbs (never had it turn out right unless I use Butterball)

Butter to coat turkey with

Your choice of stuffing (I prefer Mrs. Cubbisons)

1. This turkey will cook all night long on 200 degrees. You don't have to preheat, but you're welcome to preheat oven to 200 degrees if you'd like. First thing I do is clean my turkey out, rinse and place in turkey pan.

2. Next I mix the stuffing. The amount of stuffing will depend on the size of your turkey. I overfill as much as possible, since that's my favorite part.

3. After stuffing is made and turkey is stuffed to your liking, butter the outside of your turkey.

4. Lastly cover turkey completely with foil and place in oven. I usually have my turkey in the oven between 8 P.M. - 9 P.M., and it's done by 10 A.M. - 11 A.M. the next morning. You can also use a roaster to cook. I have had the same delicious results with either. You'll wake to your whole house smelling of turkey and never worry about your turkey not being done on time!

Mindy's Homemade Stuffing Craving

Submitted by Sue VanNort and Shelly Fenner

For Mindy's craving for human food at Thanksgiving.

Ingredients:

    Loaf of day-old bread, any kind you like, or pre-seasoned stuffing mix

    1 stick butter or margarine

    24 oz chicken broth

    3 stalks celery, finely chopped

    1 medium size onion, finely chopped

    1 lb. ground sausage, browned

    1 tsp sage

    salt and pepper to taste

1. Melt butter in frying pan, add celery and onion. Stir continuously until softened.

2. Remove from heat. Mix all ingredients together. Be sure that the bread is completely moistened. I put mine inside the bird and cook it slowly at 325 degrees. It can also be placed in a baking dish and baked.

3. Be sure to cover and stir occasionally.

4. Inside the bird, stuffing is done when the bird is done. Baked separately in a baking dish, it's done in about an hour at the same oven temperature as the bird.

Mindy's Fake It 'Til You Make It Thanksgiving Casserole – My Grandma's Spin On the Traditional Green Bean Casserole

Submitted by Christina Silcox

Ingredients:

1 1-lb package frozen California vegetables (broccoli, cauliflower, carrots)

1 can cream of mushroom soup

1 ½ cups shredded Swiss cheese

¾ cups milk

1 ½ cups French-fried onions

salt & pepper to taste

1. Mix cream of mushroom soup and milk in a large mixing bowl.

2. Stir in veggies, 1/2 cup of swiss cheese, 1/2 cup of French-fried onions, and salt and pepper. Pour into prepared baking dish.

3. Top with remaining Swiss cheese and French-fried onions.

4. Bake at 350 for 35 minutes, or until golden brown and heated through.

Blood on Snow Almond Fudge and White Chocolate Cranberry

Submitted by Zee Hayat

Ingredients:

    1 cup white chocolate bits
    ½ cup slivered almonds
    ½ cup cranberries
    ¾ cup Condensed Milk
    1 Tbsp. lemon zest
    1 Tbsp. of butter

1. On a baking sheet, grease the foil with butter and set aside.

2. On medium heat, melt the white chocolate bits.

3. Stir in the condensed milk.

4. Pour in the cranberries, lemon zest and almonds and stir in.

5. Pour onto baking sheet and refrigerate for 2 hours.

6. Cut into squares and serve with fruits or as stand-alone dessert.

Sasha's Delights – Dog Cookies

Submitted by Felicia Semmler

I love Sasha. She reminds me of my Pebbles, and Pebbles loves these cookies. She goes crazy for them, and they are better for the animals than store-bought animal treats. Even birds love them, and they're safe. Sasha would enjoy these while her people ate Thanksgiving dessert.

Ingredients:
- 2 cups flour
- ¾ cup oats
- ½ cup peanut butter
- 1 ¼ cups hot water
- 2 drops liquid imitation butter

1. Preheat oven to 350 degrees.

2. Mix flour and oats together then mix in water, imitation butter, and peanut butter (mix in more flour if it's too sticky).

3. Knead the dough and roll out until it's about ¼-inch thick.

4. Cut the dough into shapes with cookie cutters or cut into squares.

5. Bake on a lightly greased cookie sheet for 40 minutes or until they reach desired texture.

6. Store in an airtight container at room temperature for 1 week, in the fridge for 3 weeks, or freezer for 6 months.

Christmas Stories & Recipes

Joy

This first short story for Christmas, *Joy*, gives us a peek into how the Daemoni "celebrate" the birth of their enemy. We meet new characters that may or may not show up again in future Soul Savers stories, but know for sure that the events in this story have nothing to do with the actual series itself. I hope you enjoy this little fantasy.

Chapter 1

Christmas Eve day began with a clear dawn as the sun rose brightly in the sky and shone down on the city below, making everyone with high hopes of a white Christmas groan. Claire, however, grinned, reveling in their disappointment. After all, her magic kept the clouds away. Just barely, though. Even a warlock like her wasn't powerful enough to completely change the weather, but she could at least ruin their expectations for a good part of the day, as long as nothing distracted her from her spell.

She'd had to start the magic at the top of the tallest building, but now she'd been able to move down to the fourth-floor apartment she shared with a couple of other Daemoni warlocks. The three attended the same university, where they used their magic to help the local vampire nest gain access to the students. With school closed for the break between semesters, the warlocks had other havoc to wreak.

Claire's curly brown hair blew around her face as she stood on the balcony, taking in the scene below. Children ran excitedly up and down the sidewalk, laughing or even singing. Normans, loaded down with bags of gifts or food, smiled and tipped their heads at each other, wishing everyone they saw a Merry Christmas.

Claire frowned. Her plan hadn't worked. The Normans kept their Christmas cheer even as the sun baked down on them.

"It takes more than weather to ruin this holiday," said Inga, one of her roommates, who'd stepped outside with her. "Watch this."

Inga's index finger tapped on the balcony's railing. Below, a child who'd been sitting on the edge of the sidewalk suddenly kicked out his leg. A woman who could barely see around the stack of boxes she carried tripped over his foot and hurtled into a man hauling a Christmas tree. As the man went to catch the woman, he threw the tree, which flew through the air and crashed into the windshield of a car, setting off its alarm. The woman's boxes apparently held cakes and pies because she and the man were both covered in whipped cream, various colors of frosting, and fruit filling. Almost everyone nearby started yelling at someone else, pointing fingers and slewing profanities as they blamed each other for the fiasco and demanded remuneration for whatever harm they endured. Even those who'd only been bystanders were forced into the arguments as witnesses.

"Now *that* ruined a few people's days," Inga said, and both girls burst into laughter, their petite bodies doubled over.

"What are you two up to?" asked Kath, their other roommate, as she joined them on the balcony. She glanced to the street below and knew immediately what had happened. She chuckled but rolled her eyes. "That's just child's play. We have much bigger problems to cause. Are you two coming?"

Kath referred to the Daemoni celebration of anti-Christmas, as the older generations preferred to call it. Their generation called it Random Acts of Evil—the opposite of how their enemy's leadership celebrated the holiday. Regardless of their name for it, all Daemoni hated the Norman Christmas more than any other holiday, because it marked the worst day of their lord's immeasurable life. In reverence to him, they carried on their own traditions of destroying the faith and spirit of as many people as they possibly could. They did things that made Normans hate the holiday as much as they did or forced them to question how their God could allow such things to happen. Things like homes burning down, presents getting stolen, and loved ones being taken away forever.

"I wouldn't miss it," Inga said, her turquoise eyes practically glowing with anticipation. The warlock descended from a long line of witches on one side and warlocks on the other. Someone had once said she was named after her ancestor who had been Jordan's mistress, the witch who tried to steal him away from Eris. The original Inga wasn't exactly revered by the Daemoni because of everything that happened, so this Inga vehemently denied the relation or namesake. Daemoni were known liars, though, and Claire didn't know whom to believe. She didn't really care. In fact, she kind of envied all of the scandal surrounding Inga, whether it was true or not, because it seemed to make her even more Daemoni than average, at least in Claire's eyes.

Kath peered through her own curly brown hair at Claire — the two mages looked so much alike, some people swore they were twins—waiting expectantly for her answer.

"Yeah, I guess," she said with a shrug, and she turned away, back toward the street. She stared at the Normans still arguing and cleaning up below as her fingers played out a rhythm on the railing. The clouds she'd been holding at bay suddenly closed in, graying out the sun. The air temperature dropped drastically, and rain began to fall. The humans below cursed some more, making Claire feel a little better. But something bothered her inside.

"What do you mean, *you guess?*" Kath demanded. Claire didn't have to look to know her roommate stood with her hands on her hips and one leg jutted out. "We *have* to. It's part of our Daemoni duty."

"Isn't that kind of ironic?" Claire asked as she turned back to her roommates. "We're Daemoni. We're supposed to be able to do whatever we want to. But we're always doing what *they* demand."

Kath's brows pushed together, and she squinted her eyes. "But . . . don't you *want* to do all of this?"

"It's so much fun!" Inga agreed, clapping her hands together.

Claire blinked at them, not knowing how to answer. She'd been having this debate with herself for months now. On the one hand, she did enjoy her "job" of leading Normans to the vamps so they could be turned, or simply be dinner. She had fun with Random Acts of Evil antics and other ways the Daemoni asked her to use her magic to ruin human lives or, better yet, those of the Amadis. So she did kind of do what she wanted. But on the other hand, that made her a perfect little sheep, following orders, doing exactly as the higher-ups commanded. She was tired of doing everything everyone else wanted. What kind of Daemoni did that make her?

She tried to explain this conundrum to her roommates.

As she'd feared, Kath laughed. "There you go again, overanalyzing everything. You are so daft."

"Mental," Inga agreed, but then her head tilted as she studied her roommate for a few seconds. "Unless you're talking about those horrible women you call mother and grandmother. And that dickhead Barry."

"You mean Dingle-Barry?" Kath said with a laugh.

Claire snorted at their favorite nickname for the warlock her mother and grandmother insisted she marry when the time came. His douche-bagginess out-douched every Daemoni warlock they knew. And that was saying a lot. Claire couldn't imagine being with him for one night, let alone life, which stretched out longer than normal for them. She'd grown tired of her mother's comments about him being perfect for her because he was far from it.

"Yeah, they're definitely not a barrel of laughs," Kath said. "But don't worry. We'll make sure you have to have nothing to do with them tonight. We'll keep you far away from them."

"There you go," Inga said conclusively, glad to have found a solution. "You won't have to deal with them. We promise. So you're good, right?"

Claire didn't answer. Her mother and grandmother weren't the only ones who tried to control her life, and for once she wanted *full* control. But her roommates obviously weren't getting it.

"Of course she is," Kath said. "They're the only problem. Because, come on, we have it made. In the end, we always get to do what we want."

"Always?" Claire countered. "You just said yourself that anti-Christmas is a *duty*."

"So sometimes we have to follow commands," Kath said, throwing her hands up. "So what? It's fun stuff. That's all that matters, right?"

Claire pressed her lips together, and blew a huff through her nose. But as always, she acquiesced in the end and nodded. "Yes, of course. I was just being stupid."

"So you're coming tonight?" Kath asked, her excitement renewed.

"Of course," Claire answered with the best smile she could offer.

She went into her room to dress, and the heavy, cold rain pounded against her window. As she pulled on her knee-high, black leather boots over her tight, black jeans, she imagined herself by a lake at night, snow falling around her. She knew exactly where the lake was—far up north where she'd found escape after fighting some Amadis last winter—and the thought of flashing there right this very minute made her stomach tingle with giddiness. *The freedom*, she thought and wished for, *to do something for myself just once.*

She'd be violating direct orders, though, and the potential consequences frightened her. What would the Daemoni leaders do if she didn't show up tonight? If she didn't participate in the "family" tradition? Would they punish her for doing exactly what they preached—taking control of her own life and doing whatever the hell she wanted? Times were changing, of course, so they might. She chewed on her lip until a banging on her door made her jump.

"Claire, let's go!" Kath yelled through the door.

The warlock gathered her black leather trench coat and pulled it on as she followed her roommates out of the apartment. Not wanting to draw attention to themselves quite yet, they walked through the city with umbrellas, although they could have easily manifested bubbles around themselves to stay dry. By the time they reached the city park, a small crowd of other Daemoni had gathered in the dark cover of the trees. Vampires, were-creatures, and other mages milled around, waiting for the leaders to announce what kind of mayhem they would cause tonight.

When the leaders arrived, the Daemoni pushed tighter together, encircling them. Claire stayed back, on the outer edge of the group even as Inga and Kath moved in closer. As she listened to the coven, nest, and pack leaders share their wicked plans that would destroy Norman property and even some lives, the image of the lake once again popped into Claire's head. Did she dare? Would anyone notice?

She took two steps back, away from the group. Not a single eye seemed to have tracked her. Two more steps brought her into her own space, an obvious distance from the rest of the crowd. Still, no one seemed to notice.

Again she thought about how she'd always followed orders, performed exactly as expected, and did everything she was told to do. Once more, she considered how her perfect service to everyone else felt like it made her less . . . bad. How could she terrorize others when she was too terrified herself? Too scared to break the rules, although they weren't supposed to even have rules. That was the whole point of being Daemoni!

"It's time to enjoy my so-called freedom," she muttered to herself. "Time to take what I've always been promised."

And without further thought, she envisioned the lake and flashed away.

Chapter 2

The lake looked like a black hole in the white mounds surrounding it. The water hadn't frozen completely yet, so the falling snowflakes liquefied as soon as they touched the surface. All around the body of water, however, the snow began accumulating on the hills and evergreens, creating what the Normans would call a perfect Christmas scene.

Although the thought of Christmas usually made Claire cringe, she didn't mind it at the moment. She could appreciate the beauty around her and even the peacefulness. Was it so wrong to want a break from all the ruckus and chaos the Daemoni loved? If sorcerers could get away with being hermits for centuries, surely she could spend a few hours by herself in this peaceful place. Of course, maybe tonight wasn't the best night to indulge herself. The guilt of abandoning her friends and people warred with the giddiness of doing her own thing for once. She hated the guilt—she wasn't supposed to have a conscience, damn it!—and let the giddiness win.

She tied her trench coat tighter around her body and walked along the lake's shore, her boots sinking into the thick snow. With a flick of her finger, her footprints immediately disappeared, leaving no trace of her path. She practically skipped alongside the water's edge, and then danced and twirled, holding her arms out to her side, hanging her head back and sticking her tongue out to catch the big flakes. The only sound that could be heard was her own breath. She felt freer than she'd ever had before.

Fuck you, Mother and Grandmother, she thought. *And you, too, Lucas. Screw the Amadis and the Normans. Tonight is mine!*

She'd barely made it a hundred yards around the lake when the snow began falling faster, sticking to her hair and eyelashes.

She enjoyed every bit of it. Even when she reached the far side and found herself in a full-blown blizzard.

The wind howled and blew the snow sideways, and the warlock could barely see more than two feet in front of her. Normans could easily become lost in such a blinding storm, but being a mage had its advantages. Obviously, Claire could flash away and return to the city and the anti-Christmas festivities, but that was too easy and too boring. Instead, she created a bubble around herself so she could at least keep the snow from falling in her eyes. She heated the air within, too, to counter the falling temperatures the storm had brought along with it. Then she continued her stroll around the lake as she considered what to do next.

A yellowish glow in the distance provided her answer. A light that came in and out of sight as the snow fell heavily and gusts of wind stirred up more from the ground. Claire headed for the light, but even with her protective bubble, she found it more and more difficult to walk as she leaned against the wind. Finally, the cabin with the glow in its windows came into view, and Claire made her way around a large truck and found the cabin's back entrance.

She paused on the porch and used a spell to listen through the door. She wanted to stay here for the night, so the people inside had to go. Four Normans—two adults and two young children—talked about drinking hot cocoa, making popcorn, and singing carols by the fire. Claire nearly gagged on the saccharine sweetness of their conversation, but when the youngest child, a small girl, started asking about opening presents, a smile grew on the warlock's lips. A perfect opportunity for a Random Act of Evil had presented itself.

Claire considered a variety of spells she could perform to cause the cabin to be hers for the night. The most obvious was to kill them all, but she couldn't bring herself to do so. She always had trouble going to such extremes, especially when young children were involved. She justified her softness by saying that those children could become Daemoni in the future, but it was really her conscience acting up again. She needed to do something about that. Although, by not killing them, she was doing things the way *she* wanted to. Rebelling in her own way.

Rebelling against the rebels? What side does that even put me on? She blew out a sigh. *This is all so confusing.*

She wanted to be bad in her own way, so she mentally flipped through her other options until she found one that was her own flavor of fun: she would scare the Normans out by making them think the cabin was haunted. With a twist of her hands, a cabinet door in the empty kitchen swung open and banged shut, and her work began. She started by creating noises in the kitchen, bathroom, and upstairs loft while the Normans sat in the main room of the small cabin. The children squealed with each bang of a door or drawer at first, but as their fear rose, they began to cry. The parents tried to remain cool as they scurried around the cabin searching for a source of the noises, but Claire could sense their anxiety building when they couldn't find the cause. They didn't start talking about leaving, though, until the warlock became more persistent.

She caused the lights to blink on and off by themselves, then moved objects right in front of their eyes. The mother yelled at the father, accusing him of ruining Christmas because he'd brought them to this haunted cabin in the middle of nowhere, and she begged him to take them home. He argued back that the snowstorm made the roads too treacherous to drive on, and she countered that the four-wheel-drive had been his reason for buying the late model truck that sat outside. Their argument exploded, punctuated by the children's sobs and screams.

Claire realized she needed to make the decision for them. With a flick of a finger, she magically tossed the biggest present under the tree through the front window. The shattering glass silenced the parents' fight. Claire sent more presents outside, then made them pile into the bed of the pickup.

"See! Even the presents want to get the hell out of here," the mother exclaimed, and Claire nearly burst into laughter at the ridiculous statement.

"Let's go, Daddy. Please," the little girl begged, and she ran outside.

The rest of the family followed at the same time Claire caused the falling snow to slow. She couldn't hold the spell for long—this storm was too strong for her powers—but hopefully long enough to convince the father it was safe. He glanced up at the sky.

"The blizzard has slowed," the mother said as she scooped up the little girl into her arms. "Let's go while we can!"

"I don't know," the man said as he contemplated the heavy clouds in the dark sky above.

Claire had the interior of the house banging and clattering as though it belonged in a B-rated horror movie, but she thought she might have to go to her last resort—throw embers out of the fireplace, lighting the cabin up. She'd rather not, though, because she couldn't magically fix the destruction a fire would cause, not when the only remains would be ashes. And if the flames grew out of control, her whole purpose for driving the family away would be for nothing.

The family, clad only in pajamas and robes, huddled in the space between the cabin's front door and their truck while the father still stared at the sky. The boy, about seven years old, tugged on his dad's sleeve and pointed toward the woods behind the cabin. The air in Claire's lungs became trapped as she thought she'd been caught. But all eight eyeballs stared beyond her, doubled in size. Their mouths fell open, and their fragile bodies quaked.

Claire spun around, ready to fight whatever had them more frightened than the inexplicable happenings inside their cabin.

A monster bounded out of the trees and down the hill, all teeth, claws, and glowing red eyes. No, not really a monster. Claire let out a bit of air. Just a grizzly bear that roared at the family as it barreled toward them. The father wrapped an arm around the boy and lifted him off the ground. Without any more debate, the parents ran for the truck and practically threw their children in the backseat before jumping inside the front. The engine cranked over, and the truck's back tires threw snow ten feet into the air as the father tried to get them out of there as fast as possible. With a fishtail of its back end, the truck disappeared around the corner, and the cabin fell silent as Claire stood completely still.

The bear turned on her. Its jaw opened wide, baring all of its teeth, including fangs longer than Claire's fingers. It roared again as it ambled toward the warlock. She studied it for a long moment, then relaxed and nodded as she released the trapped air from her lungs.

"Thank you for that," she said.

The bear growled in response. Its eyes glowed brighter. He dared to challenge her! Claire lifted a brow while settling her hands on her hips. She glared back at the beast.

"You know I'll win," she said. "You're no match for a warlock."

The bear growled again, but then its whole form began to shrink.

"What the fuck did you do that for?" the man who'd replaced the bear snapped at the warlock.

Chapter 3

Claire couldn't help staring. Standing way over six feet tall, with black, disheveled hair, dark eyes, tanned skin that stood out against the snow, and a hard body that was all mounds of muscle and no fat, the man was a glorious beast. Every bit of him was big and powerful. Intimidating. Even the not-a-bit of him that hung between his legs.

Claire blinked, then flicked her hands, covering the were-bear with pants. He strode toward her, the amazing muscles of his upper body rolling and rippling, and she was glad she hadn't given him a shirt.

"You ruined my dinner," he growled, his eyes still glowing an angry red.

Claire slowly licked her lips before sticking the bottom one out.

"Sorry," she said as she looked up at him through her lashes.

"*Sorry?*" he barked.

She shrugged. "I need a place to stay during this storm."

Saying the word reminded her of her spell, and she broke it. The snow began falling harder again, and the wind whipped at them.

The man narrowed his eyes. "You could have done anything. Why here? You ruined my plans."

Claire cocked her head. "And what plans were those?"

"Do my Random Act of Evil, maybe eat someone for dinner, then hibernate in their cabin for a few days."

"Well, sorry. The cabin is mine now." Without touching the knob, Claire opened the door, and turning her back on the Were, she stepped inside.

"You mages are unbelievable!" the Were snarled. "Especially you cocky-ass warlocks. I don't care how hot *you* are, you're all the same inside. You think you can do whatever you want to *who*ever you want, even your own kind."

Claire spun, ready to show him exactly what she could do to him and to remind him that he was *not* her kind. Although she knew what he meant—they were both Daemoni—her mother and grandmother had ingrained in her that mages were nothing like the Weres. Warlocks, especially, were far better than the beasts. But it was this thought that stopped her. She'd wanted to do whatever she felt like doing. She'd wanted to break the rules that shouldn't exist. And she definitely wanted to know what this man felt like under her . . . inside her. Had he really called her hot?

A slew of sexy thoughts ran through her mind, and following through on them would be the ultimate crime in her mother and grandmother's eyes. They didn't care about her—only about their bloodline. In fact, if it were up to them, Claire would have been married to Dingle-Barry when she was fifteen years old. *He* had the right blood and upbringing. They'd throw an absolute Daemoni fit if she did anything more than kick this Were out into the cold. And if she slept with him . . . ?

A grin spread across Claire's face as she once again eyed the beautiful man before her. "I can't offer you dinner, but you're more than welcome to come inside."

His gaze raked over the warlock, and as if his eyes requested it, her coat magically fell open, exposing the tight black sweater that stretched across her not-so-little breasts. Her legs quivered when his eyes slowed over the swell of her hips and stopped at her thighs. She was tiny. He was not. Thoughts of all the ways he could take her soared through Claire's mind. She bit her lip as she waited for his response.

The next growl that came out of the man had changed. This one was full of lust, not threat.

When he didn't immediately stride inside and sweep her into his arms, Claire removed her coat, turned her back, and swayed her hips as she entered the cabin more deeply. As she'd hoped, he followed her inside, closing the door behind him.

"Claire," the warlock said over her shoulder to introduce herself.

"Tony," the were-bear replied as they entered the kitchen.

Claire flicked her hand to repair the little bit of damage she'd caused while running off the Normans, then she glanced around the kitchen. Hot homemade cocoa still steamed from a pot on the two-burner stove, and the supplies to cook popcorn over the fire sat on the counter. Claire waved a finger toward the refrigerator, and the door opened.

"Help yourself," she said. "Not any Norman meat in there, of course, but surely you can find something to your liking."

Tony leaned over to poke his head into the tiny fridge, his large frame nearly blocking out the light inside. Claire stared unabashedly until he straightened up with nothing in his hands, although plenty of food sat on the shelves.

"I'm not hungry for anything in there," he said as he turned to face her. The weight of his full gaze fell on her, and his black eyes smoldered, making her weak. She'd never felt such magnetic attraction to a man before, nor such sexual tension hanging in the air. But still he remained on the other side of the kitchen. Claire turned her back on him and poured herself some cocoa. She made him a mug, too, and tossed some mini-marshmallows on top, then she gathered the pan, oil, and popcorn and went into the family room.

The small room could only hold a single sofa and a wooden coffee table that sat in front of the fireplace, stockings hanging from the mantle. In the corner, a Christmas tree still twinkled with little colorful lights, although the presents were all gone. A bearskin rug lay on the wooden planked floor between the table and hearth. With a silent spell, Claire turned the rug into what appeared to be a simple shag before Tony could see it. She didn't want to know what his reaction would be—for all she knew, that could have been one of his relatives. And she certainly didn't want to ruin tonight's prospects because of a stupid rug.

She knelt in front of the fireplace, poured the oil into the pan followed by the popcorn kernels, and then arranged the pot on the pile of burning logs. Tony came in and set their mugs of hot cocoa on the coffee table, and sat on the sofa, watching her intently.

"This . . . drinking cocoa, making popcorn on a fire, you . . . this is not exactly how I expected to spend this evening," he said.

Claire chuckled. "No, me neither. But what can you do when there's a blizzard like the one outside?"

"Keep warm any way you can." His voice held all kinds of promises that sent Claire's heart into a gallop. She swallowed, her throat suddenly dry, as she leaned into the fire to give the pot a shake. She could feel Tony's eyes on her ass. "But you have all kinds of ways to stay warm, so why are you here?"

The warlock leaned back on her heels and stared at the fire. "I'm exactly where I want to be tonight, so why bother using magic to be somewhere else?" She looked over her shoulder at him. "And I could say the same about you. Surely you have a home or even a den and your own fur coat to keep you warm."

"My home's far away." He paused, then added, "And I'm exactly where I want to be tonight, too."

With a small smile playing on her lips, Claire pulled the pot off the fire and placed it on the table, its lid sitting sideways as big puffs of white popcorn pushed it upwards. She stood and grabbed the blanket off the arm of the sofa, sat down next to Tony—but not too close—and wrapped the fuzzy cover over her before picking up a handful of popcorn and her mug. When she sat back, an arm landed heavily on the back of the couch behind her. She pretended not to notice and ate her snack.

Wind howled outside, and the snowdrifts grew larger, blocking out the bottom panes of the window next to the fireplace. Claire snuggled deeper under her blanket and sipped on her cocoa while watching the flames dance in the hearth. She didn't even mind the

Christmas tree, and Tony didn't seem to either. Sitting here as they did in this cozy little cabin while the snow fell outside and the fire popped and sizzled almost made her understand Normans and their love for this holiday. There certainly was a sense of peace that she could appreciate.

The arm behind her fell across her shoulder. When she didn't wiggle away, Tony pulled her closer.

"I guess I was wrong about all warlocks," he murmured, his mouth very close to her ear. "You're definitely not like the others."

Claire suppressed a chuckle. If he only knew exactly why she'd invited him inside with her. She may not be exactly like the others—like her mother and grandmother and everyone else so concerned about their bloodlines that they never had any fun—but that didn't make her any better. In fact, her whole goal tonight was to be bad. Bad in every way that felt good. Sitting here so warm and contentedly definitely felt good, but she had much more in mind.

At the same moment she twisted in her seat to face Tony, he turned toward her. Their faces were only inches apart, and his warm breath fell on her lips. She looked into his deep, black eyes and saw the same primal need in him that she felt in herself. He lifted a large hand to the side of her head, which she tilted into his palm as he stroked her cheek with his thumb. She'd never imagined a Were being so gentle, especially one as big and feral as a bear. She wasn't sure she wanted gentle.

Their gazes locked, he leaned in. She licked her lips, readying them, then closed her eyes and opened her mouth slightly. Her heart beat once as she waited. Again. She was about to open her eyes when she felt him. But right when his lips touched hers, two *pops* sounded in the room.

Claire's eyes flew open to find the new arrivals standing in front of the door to the kitchen. Tony jumped off the couch with surprise, fur already rising on his arms and his teeth elongating. He crouched for the change as he stared at the two women, both dressed in long, wool cloaks and knee-high boots.

"Shit," Claire swore under her breath. "Why didn't I think to shield and cloak the place?"

"Because you're not letting your *brain* do your thinking," said the younger of the two women.

Claire clenched her jaw against the voice that sounded to her like fingernails on a chalkboard.

"Hello, Mother," she said through gritted teeth. "Grandmother."

Chapter 4

Tony shot up straight, and his gaze flew to Claire then back to the new arrivals.

"What do you think you're doing with this *beast*?" Claire's grandmother demanded, her haughty voice as grating as her daughter's.

Although he'd gained control over the change, Tony let out a growl. Claire's grandmother simply turned her piercing blue eyes on him and lifted a silver eyebrow. One side of his lip lifted, but he repressed the snarl. Claire stepped in front of him.

"What are you doing here?" she asked, her gaze bouncing between the other two warlocks. As usual, their hair was pulled back into tight buns, but little curls sprang free at their temples. Her mother's was still the same brown as Claire's with only a few streaks of gray, but her grandmother's was as silver as a teapot. Both were petite, as small as Claire, but much more intimidating.

"I can ask you the same thing," her mother said, placing a hand on her hip. She glanced around the tiny cabin and sniffed with disgust. "I don't know what you're trying to pull here but your absence tonight was noticed. You disgrace the entire family for *this*?"

Her mother's glare landed on Tony with the last word. Claire swallowed, and her chest tightened. She didn't know how to respond. As much as she hated it, guilt and shame began to push away the contempt that had been driving her all day long. That had given her more courage—and more freedom—than she'd ever experienced before. And it could have led to many regrets, regrets worse than the ones she already had.

"Let's go, Claire," her mother said. "Come home with us before you make an unimaginable mistake."

Guilt may have been trying to slide its way in, but the back of Claire's neck prickled at this comment. Her eyes slid over her shoulder to Tony, who studied her closely, waiting to see what she would do. She remembered the welcome feeling in her stomach when his breath had mixed with hers. The tingle along her skin when he touched her. The way his eyes made her thighs clench. Was being with him really an unimaginable mistake?

"*Claire*," her grandmother snapped. "Listen to your mother. It's time to go, child. Do as you're told."

The younger warlock's head tilted as that prickle on her neck became more like a needle in a nerve. Her nostrils flared. She stood to her full height and stared directly into her grandmother's eyes.

"I am *not* a child," she seethed. "And I will do what *I* want to do."

"Do you know how childish *that* sounds?" her mother demanded.

Claire squared her shoulders and took a step toward her mother. She turned her full gaze on her. "No, Mother, it doesn't, because I am making a decision for myself for once. I will suffer the consequences, but staying here is *my* choice."

Her mother rolled her eyes and held her hand out. "That's enough. We can discuss this later. Right now, people are waiting for you."

"Like who, Mother? Nobody cares what I'm doing right now."

"Like your friends Inga and Kath."

Claire snorted. "They're so wrapped up in having their own fun, they don't give a shit what I'm doing. They're doing what they want to do, and so am I, for once. Besides, they're more than happy to keep me far away from *you*."

Claire's mother's eyes narrowed as her gaze cut to Tony then back to Claire, and her jaw clenched. "At least do what you want with your own kind. Think of Barry!"

Tony let out a huff in the corner. Claire gave a slight shake of her head, her only way at the moment to tell him that he had no need to worry about Barry. Then she let out a sarcastic laugh.

"Barry is *your* kind, Mother! Cruel, controlling, and a pompous ass. Since you like him so much, why don't *you* hook up with him?"

She took another step toward her mother and grandmother. "Better yet, make a threesome of it. I don't really give a shit. All I care about right now is that you both get the hell out of here and leave me alone once and for all. Stop trying to run my life!"

She lifted her hand toward them, and the other warlocks saw the threat. Their eyes grew wide as they stared at Claire daring to challenge them to a fight.

"Now go." Claire pointed her finger toward the front door, which swung open at her silent command. Wind gusted and blew snow inside.

"Claire—" her grandmother started.

"I said to GO!" The youngest warlock bellowed. Her hand began to glow a bright orange as she prepared to launch a blast of magic at them. "If you don't flash this very second, I'll send you out myself."

Both women's heads tilted, and their eyes narrowed. Claire wiggled her fingers in a wave. Her mother and grandmother gasped as their bodies flew out the door and landed in a drift of snow. A small avalanche fell on top of them, and only their eyes, wide as grapefruits and shooting daggers, could be seen. After two faint *pops* hissed in the otherwise quiet night, the eyes disappeared, and Claire slammed the door shut. She spun to face Tony.

"I'm . . . um . . . so sorry," she said, nearly breathless. She couldn't believe what she'd just done. She'd kicked her own mother and grandmother out of her life! But she couldn't believe they'd actually shown up here and made a complete ass out of her. She hoped they'd learned to stop sticking their noses where they didn't belong, but she doubted it. They probably didn't even take her seriously about leaving her alone for good. But at least she'd have tonight. Or did she?

"Maybe this isn't such a great idea," Tony said, his voice laced with apprehension. His teeth, hands, and the rest of him, including his voice, were back to normal, with no traces of the bear inside him.

Claire breathed in and out several times, wondering if she should agree with him. Wondering if she should just let him go, if that's what he really wanted. But when he didn't move so much as a muscle to leave, her insecurities vanished. She threw up a cloak over the cabin—she wasn't making that mistake again—and without a word, she strode the three paces over to his place in the corner of the room, grasped his unruly hair tightly in her fist, and placed her other hand over his package and squeezed.

"This is a fan-fucking-tastic idea," she breathed before slamming her mouth over his. He immediately grew hard in agreement.

Their lips parted, and their tongues intertwined. He tasted like berries and something erotically wild that Claire couldn't get enough of. One of his hands cradled her head while the other clamped down on her ass. She continued stroking him, and he groaned into her mouth. Then in one swift moment, he spun her around, tore off her sweater, wrapped a hand around both of her wrists, and lifted her arms above her head. With his hips pressing against her, he backed her against the wall. Her heart pounded as he dove for her neck, and she moaned when his mouth found her breast. Within minutes, no shred of clothes remained on either of their bodies, and Tony held Claire's hips, her legs wrapped around his waist and her back pressed against the wall as he pushed inside her. They both cried out . . . several times as their passion built.

Claire had never experienced anything like this were-bear. He was beast and man at the same time. Wild yet considerate. Powerful yet gentle. He let her explore every bit of his muscular build with both her hands and her mouth as long as she let him do the same. His touch, whether his fingers or his lips or tongue, was so hot, and even the slightest caress made her body vibrate. The way he moved her, the things he did to her . . . she'd never had such an erotic night.

Morning had come, although it was still dark outside, when they finally collapsed in each other's arms on the rug in front of the fireplace. They spooned together, Tony's fingers stroking lightly over Claire's skin, down her ribs, over her hip, to her thigh, as they watched the sky turn pink through the window. The snowy scene outside went from gray to blue to dazzling white. A blanket of snow reached as far as their eyes could see, completely covering the lake and everything around it.

"Looks like the storm has passed," Tony murmured in Claire's ear. "I'm sure you'll want to take off soon."

Claire turned to look up at him, a smile dancing on her lips. "You know as well as I do that the storm wasn't what kept me here. Just as it wasn't what kept you here."

"Didn't you get what you wanted, though?" he asked, his voice cocky as he smirked at her. He traced his fingers over her cheek before kissing her forehead.

"Mmm . . . yes, I did," she answered, her eyelids becoming heavy as she stroked a hand over his hard chest and down his abs. "But I think . . . " Her hand moved lower, and Tony's eyes widened as he throbbed against her. "I think I haven't had quite enough."

He let out a growl while grinning at the same time. And then he devoured her . . . well, devoured her body in every way she'd let him.

"Had enough yet?" he asked a few hours later.

"Not sure . . . " Claire drifted off to sleep, and they both dozed for a while. When they awoke, it was snowing again. "Oh, damn. Looks like we're stuck here for another night."

"You are insatiable," Tony said with a husky chuckle.

"I have a lot of being good to make up for."

His chuckle turned into a full-out laugh. "Show me how bad you can be."

"Are you sure that's what you want?" she asked, her voice full of mischief.

He gathered her curls into his hand and pulled on her hair, lifting her head so she'd look at him. "I want whatever you want."

She smiled. "Good answer."

So Claire did what she wanted, and so did Tony, because they both wanted the same thing—each other. As many times as possible. And they both agreed on a twist to what the Normans preached on this holiday: It was better to give than to receive . . . but it was always best when both happened at the same time.

Miracle: A Vampire's First Christmas

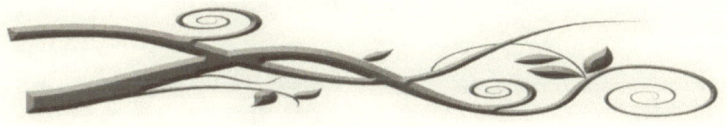

In this next story, *Miracle*, we get to know a secondary character from the Soul Savers Series, but in a whole new context. If you're caught up with the series, you may find this story confusing if you try to fit it in somewhere in the timeline. If you're new to the series or not quite caught up, you may think as you start reading this that you've been spoiled. I wouldn't do that to you! I ask that you not worry about how these events and characters' actions relate to the main series. They don't. Many things here make no sense in the context of the main series. So I ask that you think of this as a parallel universe to the real one in the primary series. Yes, I just said that—the "real" one. Just go with it. Try not to read too much between the lines, and simply allow yourself to enjoy the miracles of Christmas.

Chapter 1

The blood-red card sat like a tent on the antique table in my suite, looking deceptively beautiful and innocent. No picture adorned the front, though. Only a flourish of script in black ink that reminded me of my pre-vampire days. None of this typed text of today's world, or worse, the sloppy and shaky handwriting of someone who can't be bothered to write cursive with a pen except when they have to. This was old school and gorgeous, like calligraphy.

"To Vanessa"

Curiosity didn't just kill the proverbial cat—it had nearly killed the very real me numerous times, and it got me again. I snatched the card off the table and opened it, only to find:

"I'm watching you."

"What?" I snarled at it. "What the hell does that mean?"

I looked around the room, but I knew that these walls may not have eyes, but this mansion did have ears. Actually, minds—ones that could hear others' thoughts. Was this a threat from Katerina or Alexis? A reminder? Or did it come from someone else? A tingle ran down my spine, and I hated tingles with a passion. They signaled something was about to go wrong.

I stomped down the stairs and followed my nose to the grand kitchen, where I knew I'd find someone by the smells and sounds of it. The witch wasn't exactly the one I'd expected to find—she was centuries younger and blond—but she might have been even better than Ophelia, the mansion's head servant, to give me answers.

"I know I'm not exactly welcome here," I said as I stopped at the butcher-block island, "but this is really uncalled for."

Blossom stood on the other side of the island, messing with some kind of dough. She looked up at me with a raised brow, and I threw the card down in front of her.

"Who would do such a thing?" I demanded as she wiped her hands on her apron and picked up the card to investigate it.

"Well, it could be anybody," Blossom mused as she studied the inside. "Even Ms. Katerina, for all we know."

My eyes narrowed. "I doubt the matriarch would stoop to this level. She and everyone else have pretty much said to my face how they feel about me being here, and that they're watching me."

"Really?" Blossom asked, her tone curious but I sensed skepticism. She turned her back to me to pull something out of the oven. "That's what they said?"

My body wanted to squirm, but I only shrugged and picked at a piece of dough stuck to the counter. "Well, not exactly. They were nicer about it. You know how the Amadis are." I looked back up at her. "Which means this did not come from Katerina or Sophia. Maybe Alexis, but she *does* say it to my face every chance she gets, so I doubt it's her. Some asshole has access to my suite and left me a threatening note, and I don't like it!"

"Threatening?" Blossom sounded genuinely perplexed as she placed a metal sheet full of freshly baked cookies on the counter. "I wouldn't call it threatening."

My eyes widened. "Then what the hell *would* you call it?"

"Oh, come on, it's kind of fun, don't you think?"

"*Fun?*" No other words came to me, and I stood there staring at her, my mouth opening and closing.

"Oh, my God, you don't get it, do you?" Blossom's lips twitched, and then she giggled.

"What?" I demanded.

"It's a game, Vanessa. Christmas merry-making." She held out the card to me and pointed at a line of script that I had missed:

"From your Secret Santa"

"It's like how the Norman parents tell their kids that Santa is always watching them to know if they've been naughty or nice," Blossom explained. "Your secret one is watching you."

My hands went to my hips. "I have a Secret Santa?"

"It looks like it. So stop worrying. It's going to be fun." She picked up a spatula and started scooping cookies off the sheet and sliding them onto a plate. I watched her while mulling over this news.

"I don't like this Secret Santa thing," I finally said. "It feels like a set-up."

Blossom's big, hazel eyes rolled up to look at me. She'd finished removing the baked cookies, and now she dropped mounds of dough on a clean sheet. "You need to relax."

"Easy for you to say," I grumbled. "I'm trying to remember why I'm here. Trying to be good. And not be selfish. But how am I supposed to return the favor to this Secret Santa if I don't even know who the hell he or she is?"

The witch tilted her head. "You could pay it forward, you know, give something to someone else. That's kind of what Christmas is all about: giving, not receiving."

My stomach dropped. I was so not going to be good at this Christmas thing. Giving and not receiving? I'd been working hard at learning how to give, but I *loved* to receive. In fact, I loved to receive so much, that I pretty much always simply took whatever I wanted. I wasn't supposed to like any of that anymore, though, so I'd resolved to never receive any gifts again. At least, not without giving in return. And now this whole Secret Santa scheme made everything so confusing.

"I'm so going to suck at this Christmas thing," I grumbled.

"You'll be fine. Why don't you help me decorate these?" Blossom picked up the plate of white cookies and took it over to the table where bowls of colored frosting and all kinds of decorations sat. "It's a very Christmas-y thing to do, and people love to eat them. It makes them very happy."

I blew out a sigh and followed her over to the table. This was me: giving. Making people happy in return for nothing.

I picked up a cookie in an odd shape.

"I might have used my magic to create some new shapes," Blossom admitted. "A trick Aunt Sylvie taught me when I was little. We used to make all kinds of cookies together throughout the Christmas season. She would make it so much fun! I took me a few years to learn how to use magic without screwing up the whole recipe." Blossom paused when she saw my blank expression while I still held my cookie in the air. "Anyway, that one can be a face. See the nose and the chin? You can make it whoever you want."

I wasn't an artist, and I wasn't magic. Making it whomever I wanted was impossible. So I did my best in at least making it resemble a face while Blossom told me stories of baking and decorating cookies with her aunt.

"Um, that's, well, interesting," Blossom said a few minutes later after looking over at my cookie.

Her tone made my brows push together, and I frowned at my artwork. "It's not very Christmas-like, is it?"

"Well, the blood is kind of . . . no, not really."

I dropped it on the table. "I told you! I'm hopeless!"

"Relax. Just eat it and try on another one."

I didn't really want to eat it, but I didn't want to disappoint Blossom any further after she'd been so nice to me. I could eat normal food, and my body could sort of digest it—my blood basically disintegrated it into nothing, kind of like acid does—but it always tasted bland and dry to me. Remembering I had a bottle of blood in the wine rack, I poured myself a glass.

"Oh my God, Vanessa," Blossom shrieked as she jumped up from the table. The oven's timer was buzzing, but she simply stood there, staring at my cookie with her nose wrinkled. "That's so disgusting!"

I glanced at the cookie that was now stained red. Without realizing I was doing it, I'd dunked it in my glass of blood. Red juiciness ran down my hand, and I licked it up.

"Ewwwww." Blossom shuddered and gagged before hurrying over to the oven. "Are you . . . are you sure you don't want a cup of milk?"

I popped the blood-soaked sweet in my mouth, and it tasted delicious. When I turned down the milk and Blossom frowned at me, I knew I'd screwed up again. I couldn't even enjoy a simple Christmas cookie the normal way.

"I told you I suck at this." I pushed away from the table and stood.

"I have an idea," Blossom said. "Sheree's in the media room, watching all those sappy Christmas movies. Why don't you go join her? You could learn all kinds of things, so you won't suck at it."

She was probably just trying to get rid of me before I ruined anymore of her cookies, but maybe she actually cared about trying to make things better for me, too. Regardless, I followed her suggestion and left the kitchen, in search of the media room.

Chapter 2

After wandering around for several minutes, I found the media room at the end of a long hall on the first floor and discovered that this old stone mansion hadn't been completely left in the 19th century. I'd learned long ago to accept change, even if I didn't exactly love everything about modern day technology. And some things just made more sense than the old ways. Like overhead lights, for example. Why were there so many fire sconces in this place instead of normal electric lamps? I was always afraid my hair would catch when I passed by one and light me up like a bloody torch. The media room had overhead lights, as well as computers and a wall full of several television screens.

All but the largest screen, which hung in the middle of the vast wall, were black at the moment. The center one showed a little boy dressed in a snowsuit with his tongue stuck to a light pole and a group of kids surrounding him laughing. I walked around the row of theater-style seats and found Sheree curled up in one with a blanket over her legs and a bowl of popcorn in her lap.

"Hey, Vanessa," she said without tearing her eyes from the screen. "Want to watch movies with me?"

I shrugged as I fell into the seat next to her. "Blossom says it'll teach me all about Christmas and put me in the spirit."

"Oh, that's a great idea! This one I'm watching right now is a fun one."

With nothing else to do anyway, I sat back in the recliner and watched as a boy tried to convince all the adults in his life to get him a BB gun for Christmas.

"I don't get it," I said after a while, opening my mouth wide in a pretend yawn.

"It's a fun, timeless story about family and love and Christmas. It kind of reminds me of my family . . . before . . . " Sheree frowned and pushed a hand through her dark brown hair. "Okay, I guess if you don't have anything to base it off of, it's not the best way for you to understand. I'll put something else on."

"Oh, don't change it on my account. I'll just find something else to do." I began to stand up. See, I could be giving. Not that sitting here mindlessly staring at a screen was much to be giving up.

"No, it's okay. I've seen it a million times."

My butt planted back in my seat as I stared at her. Was she serious?

She shrugged. "We used to watch all of these movies when I was a kid. Every year starting on Thanksgiving and all the way to Christmas, my brothers and sisters and I would pile on the couch with blankets and pillows and popcorn and watch every Christmas movie we could find. This was one of my favorites. But here—" She pressed a couple of buttons on the remote control and the screen showed a black-and-white film. "It's a Wonderful Life is perfect for you!"

Sheree cried at the end while I was still trying to figure out what the stupid knob on the bannister had to do with anything. She put in another "classic," Miracle on 34th Street, and cried at the end of that one, too, but I'd missed half the storyline, my mind going back to the 1930s and the havoc I'd been wreaking at the time. She put in another that totally lost me.

The only thing I noticed that was interesting was a guy hanging mistletoe in a doorway and grabbing kisses from all the ladies that passed through. I couldn't help but daydream about where I'd hang mistletoe—in the hallway in front of Owen's door. Then he'd have to kiss me every time he went in and out of his room. I longed to feel his arms around me . . . to taste his lips . . . to see something real in his bright blue eyes, so much deeper than my light blue ones. Mistletoe wouldn't get him to care about me, though. I'd seen glimpses of it, but I didn't know if he could really care about anyone ever again.

"Vanessa?" Sheree's voice sounded distant at first, and I realized I'd drifted off into a vamp-doze. Not really sleeping because I didn't need to, but not quite conscious either. "You didn't like that one, did you?"

I didn't really like any of them, to be honest, but I couldn't tell her that. "How come they all take place in the '30s and '40s? Not exactly my favorite time of my life."

Sheree made a face. "Sorry. I didn't think of that. Here, maybe you'll like this one."

When it showed what looked like Victorian England, I growled quietly. Definitely not a happy time of my life. In fact, in my two-hundred-odd years, I didn't really have any good memories to focus on. At least in the 1930s I was enjoying myself, even if I was being evil.

"Give it a chance. It's got ghosts and stuff."

Well, that sounded interesting. But it wasn't the ghosts that pulled me into the story.

"I really like this Scrooge guy," I said after a while, before any ghosts had shown up.

Sheree groaned. "You would."

"Am I not supposed to?"

"Well, at the end you are."

By the end, though, I'd lost my admiration for him. "What a wuss."

"No, he's not! Being kind and generous doesn't make him a wuss."

"Then what would you call it?"

"He changed for the better, just like Tristan. Like you."

I rolled my eyes and stood up. "Not just like Tristan and me. This dork changed overnight because of his dumb dreams. Not exactly realistic."

"It's just a story," Sheree said. "A good Christmas story about a mean old guy who saw his wrongs and became a good person. I thought you'd like it."

"Yeah, well, I did until it got stupid. Overdone, like all of these movies. In real life, this guy would have gone back to his old stingy self the very next day. That's how people are, aren't they? So is that what Christmas is about? Faking generosity for a day so everyone will adore you and forget that you're an asshole the other 364 days of the year? I don't get it, Sheree. I don't think I ever will."

Sheree stared at me with bewilderment written all over her face. She opened her mouth a couple of times, but apparently didn't know what to say. I strode for the door. Sheree called after me, but I didn't go back. I instantly felt bad for leaving her like that, when she'd been trying to help me. She and Blossom thought the movies would do me good, but all they did was prove even more that I sucked at Christmas.

Not wanting to face anyone else in the mansion, I flashed to the village on the other side of the island. You'd think people would be used to my presence by now, but not all were. As I meandered through the crowded main street, people's expressions ranged from mild shock to total distrust. I tried to ignore them and focused instead on the shops. One particular window display drew me inside, where I might have found vampire heaven.

Packaged in what looked like wine bottles with pretty labels was blood of every type imaginable, including lots of mage blood. A particular bottle with a red label and the Amadis symbol stamped in silver on it grabbed my attention. I picked up the bottle and fingered the symbol's shape. "Heavy with the essence of regeneration from one of our rarest sources." Remembering the time I'd tasted such essence myself, my mouth watered at the thought of the bottle's contents.

"It's not for sale," a deep voice from behind the counter said. Once dark-skinned but now that pale-ashy color of vamps of African descent, he leaned casually against the shelves behind him. "It's reserved for warriors and the severely injured only."

"Then what's it doing here?" I asked, curiosity once again getting to me.

"It brings our kind into the shop. Don't tell me you couldn't smell it from outside." He grinned, his teeth brightly white against his darker lips.

I gave a small smile in agreement. I definitely had smelled it from down the street, drawn to it like a bear to honey. That particular bottle had a unique—and delicious—fragrance. One I knew personally. One I'd probably never get to taste again.

After the blood shop, I visited the store next door, which sold what might look like silly little knickknacks to the Normans, but those of us in our world knew they actually served as spell-binders for the mages—objects they could attach spells to for future use. They only worked for certain kinds of spells, but for some of them, the mage didn't even have to be present for the spell to activate. Of course, I wasn't a mage and had no use for these things, but since I didn't have anything else to do, I browsed through the store and admired all of the shiny silver, which at one time had been the bane of my existence. I stopped close to the back and picked up a music box.

"A nifty little thing that is," said the witch-shopkeeper as she came in from the back room. Her eyes flitted over me, and she pursed her lips as she walked right on past me with her nose lifted. "Our items are only for mages, though."

"What does this one do?" I asked, partly out of curiosity but mostly to piss her off for wasting her time. If she'd been Daemoni, she would have thrown me out on my ass, but she was Amadis. She'd be as courteous as she could stand.

"When the music plays, a two-way portal will open. Of course, only the most powerful warlocks can make it work."

"Of course," I muttered as I put it back. Not too many Amadis warlocks possessed enough powerful magic to create a portal, and a two-way one was almost unheard of.

I took my time studying other objects until I couldn't stand the weight of her annoyed gaze any longer. After wasting more time in the village, I eventually sucked it up and flashed back to the mansion. Only to land on top of a tree log lying in the foyer.

"What the hell?" I muttered. Annoyed that someone must have left it there and forgotten about it—probably that old witch Ophelia—I picked it up, took it into the parlor and tossed it into the fireplace. The low flames already in the hearth caught it immediately and burst into a giant fire with a whoosh.

"Did you get your shopping done?" Blossom asked as she came into the parlor, a bunch of boxes hovering in the air in front of her. She placed the boxes on the ground and looked around with her brows pinched together as if she'd lost something.

"Shopping?" I asked, as confused as she looked.

"I thought you went to the village to do your Christmas shopping." She stepped through the doorway to look into the foyer and then turned back to me with her hands on her hips.

Shit. I'd passed through every shop in that village and not once did I think about buying anyone a present.

"Do you know if Ophelia did something with the tree?" Blossom asked, but at the same time realization slammed into me, her gaze slid over to the fireplace. "Oh, my God. Alexis, Tristan, and Dorian searched for that one for hours!"

"Are we ready to decorate?" Sheree asked as she skipped into the parlor. Her mouth fell open when she saw the tree—the mother effin' Christmas tree!—being devoured by flames. She immediately turned to me, her normally brown eyes glaring at me with the yellow irises of a tiger.

"I'm . . . I'm so sorry," I muttered. "I thought . . . "

I couldn't finish. It didn't matter what I thought. I'd been too caught up in my own selfishness that I hadn't stopped to think that the log in the foyer might have been more than just a log. Too self-centered to think about anyone but myself while I was at the village.

Without another word, I bolted upstairs to my suite. Anger consumed me. Anger at myself for even thinking that I could do this Christmas thing. Or even this Amadis thing. I didn't belong here. I was nothing like them, and I never would be. My door slammed against the wall when I threw it open and slammed again into its jamb when I shut it. I wanted to throw things. To have an all-out Daemoni style tantrum.

Then I saw the black bottle with the red label embossed with silver sitting on my table where the notecard had been this morning.

I fell silent as I stared at it. Then I stomped over to the table and picked up the note accompanying the bottle:

"Use it wisely. There's more where this came from, if you're good. Your Secret Santa."

I threw my head back and screamed with frustration.

"I don't know how to be good!" I yelled at the ceiling. I stomped my foot and yanked on my hair as I glared at the bottle as if it had been the one to offend me. "And what am I supposed to do with this? I can't drink it! I can't accept it! I can't even say fucking thank you!"

I grabbed the bottle and threw it. It stopped in mid-air instead of crashing against the wall.

"Sure you can," said a voice from the doorway, and my mood immediately changed.

Chapter 3

I spun around and couldn't help the smile on my face when I saw Owen, his tall frame leaning against my doorway. Blossom and Sheree had been nice enough, but I felt like Owen understood me better than anyone. He'd become an outcast, too, and neither of us really knew where we belonged anymore. At least he had some idea about how to live in this strange Amadis world.

I picked up the note and waved it at him. "I have a Secret Santa. How stupid is that? And how, pray tell, do I tell him or her thank you for something I can't even have?"

His bright blue gaze, the color of the ocean, landed on the bottle, then came back to my face. "I don't think your Secret Santa would give you something you can't have."

"Unless it's a test," I said. "You know—see if I can pass the temptation."

He shrugged. "I guess it could be, but I doubt it. Secret Santas are cool. Not jerks."

I placed my hands on the table behind me and leaned back. "Okay, let's say it's a real gift. I'll still be good and wait for the perfect time to drink it. But how on Earth do you suggest I return the kindness, since you think you're so smart?"

The corner of his mouth lifted in a crooked grin. My early daydream of mistletoe and kissing popped into my mind. I shoved it out before such thoughts got me into more trouble.

"And while you're at it," I said before he could answer, "tell me how to make up for all the problems I caused downstairs. I kind of blew it. Bad."

He gave me a full smile now. "Ah, I think you're already forgiven for the tree. Blossom and I took care of it before anyone but Sheree even knew. But I do have an idea."

I hesitated with the twinkle in his eye.

"What?" I asked, skepticism heavy in my voice.

"You can return the kindness by showing that you're really appreciative. You do that by doing something for others."

"Pay it forward. Blossom already said that."

"Blossom's a smart witch. And I have a perfect opportunity for you. I need an elf."

I lifted an eyebrow. "An elf?"

"Yes, an elf. Tristan and Alexis have gone off, starting a few days early on their Random Acts of Kindness thing—"

I couldn't help the snort because I was trying to suppress a chuckle.

"What?" Owen asked.

I shook my head. "Irony. Ever since Sophia started that tradition with little-girl Alexis, I'd kind of started one on the Daemoni side. Random Acts of Evil. It's become an anti-Christmas tradition." I paused then quickly added, "Not that I'm proud of it or anything."

The warlock stared at me for a moment, then shook his head. "Well, now you really need to make up for it by doing something nice and not evil. Like being my elf."

"*Your* elf?"

"Yeah. There are some kids who need a visit from Old Saint Nick."

As ludicrous as his proposal sounded, I couldn't say no to Owen. I'd probably never win him over, but I couldn't help trying. An hour later, as we walked through the hospital corridor, I'd already started to regret it. Because of my weakness when it came to him, I looked like a green bean in a dress. While he wore a long robe with scenes beautifully embroidered into it and a hat with a tip that folded over and hung to his shoulder, a flick of his hand put me in dark green tights, a short red dress with fake fur on its hem, and clown shoes with toes that curled over and bells that jangled with every step I took. They matched the absurd hat on my head. To make it all worse, his face was covered with a beautiful beard that reached to his chest and long hair whiter than mine (although I already missed the disheveled straw-colored hair that he normally had), and I had nothing to mask my face. I was exposed to the world in all of my ridiculousness.

"What are you?" a boy demanded of me as soon as we strode into the room where a group of children had been gathered.

Some sat in wheelchairs, others walked around in pajamas, almost all had tubes and wires coming out of their bodies and tying them to machines. The emergency room and surgical wings could have been too much for me with all of the blood that spilled there, but this ward brought no temptation at all. Not when I could smell the cancer and disease running through these children's veins.

"I'm an elf," I said, trying to keep the biting sarcasm out of my voice. I didn't think I succeeded.

"You're too tall to be an elf," he said.

"Yeah, elves are short," said the girl who sat next to him.

I looked over at Owen, at a loss for words. I had no idea what their vision of elves was. Had he set me up to look like a fool? When I tilted my head and the tip of my hat hit me in the cheek with another jangle, I knew that was a stupid question. Of course I looked like a fool.

"I brought my biggest and strongest elf today," Owen said in explanation, his voice sounding deeper and older than usual.

"She doesn't look very strong," said a kid from a wheelchair on the other side of the room.

"She just looks silly," another girl said.

"I think she's pretty," said a tiny bald girl from right next to me. I nearly jerked away when she wrapped her little hand around mine, but I suppressed the impulse and put on a smile. "I want to be like her when I grow up."

My stomach flipped. Oh, no, she didn't. She had no idea what she was saying.

"No, she's silly. This whole thing is silly." A boy, probably ten or eleven years old and the tallest and oldest in the group, stood in the corner, leaning against the wall, his arms folded over his chest. "You really expect us to believe you're Saint Nick and she's an elf? We're all dying in here. We're not even going to grow up! I think we can handle the truth about Santa."

"Tim . . . " warned an adult who stood by the door. She was dressed in hospital scrubs, so probably an employee.

Owen ignored the boy and already began handing out presents. The smaller children squealed with excitement, but Tim scowled harder.

"What?" he said. "This is bullshit."

"Tim!" the woman admonished.

"It's stupid! We're dying like old people but you treat us like babies." He stood up straight, his hands balled into fists by his side. "Why can't you tell them the truth? There's no such thing as magic. They should know that Santa isn't—"

I didn't know what came over me, except that I knew Owen was trying to make these sick children happy, and I wasn't about to let this brat ruin it. I flew across the room, grabbed the boy by the shoulders and pinned him against the wall several inches off the ground. His brown eyes grew so wide that white showed all around his irises. And that familiar smell of fear that had once made my mouth water poured out of his flesh.

"You're . . . you're not an elf," he croaked as his eyes looked into mine. Did mine still glow Daemoni red? I didn't know, but judging by the way this boy looked at me, I knew they showed something that terrified him.

"You don't want to know what I really am," I snarled, and although my voice was nothing more than a whisper, he obviously heard the threat in it.

Several of the children gasped.

"Vanessa," Owen said calmly, although I knew it was a warning.

"Wow, she really is strong," said one of the smaller boys who'd made fun of me earlier.

With a low growl, I let Tim go. And when I turned, I found all the faces of the children in the room staring at me. Shock and fear had made them still as stone. My breath caught, and my hand flew to my mouth. My fangs hadn't let out fully, but my tongue felt the extra sharp tip of one.

"I'm so sorry," I whispered behind my palm, and then I hurried out of the room.

Shit! What had I done now? I strode several paces down the corridor, then pressed my back against the wall and slid to the floor. I yanked the hat off my head and dropped my face into my hands. My eyes burned. Tears! Fucking tears! I. Didn't. Cry. Not in decades anyway.

"I hate to say it, but it's kind of comforting to see an elf having a bad day."

My head snapped up at the Norman's voice. She stood next to me, a little plump in her yoga pants and t-shirt, her hair pulled into a sloppy ponytail and her face haggard. Tired. No, utterly exhausted. She was probably only in her thirties, but she looked as though she'd been awake for centuries.

"I . . . I'm sorry?" I stammered as I rose to my feet.

"My days have been shit for three years now, since my little Loraleigh was diagnosed with leukemia. The holidays are really hard, seeing everyone else so happy and hopeful. Even the families in here at least get to see each other. Ours is hundreds of miles away, and they have no way of getting here. We won't even see them for Christmas, and that's all she wanted." She sighed and looked away as she swiped the tear under her eye with a thumb. She drew in a shaky breath and blew it out. "I'm sorry. I know I shouldn't be happy for your sorrow. Is there anything I can do for you?"

I jerked back, dumbfounded. I didn't fully understand love yet, but I had learned enough. Experienced enough. I'd felt a broken heart before, and I knew this Norman woman's heart was being broken by a disease that was killing her child. And she was asking what *she* could do for *me*? Me, a worthless Daemoni vampire who had murdered people who had once been someone's child! How could she even be thinking about me?!

I shook my head, fighting the urge to run far away and wallow in my shame, but then I paused as an idea occurred to me.

"Where is your daughter?" I dared to ask.

The woman turned toward the room I'd just run from. The door opened and children came out of it, big smiles on their faces.

"Did you see that?" one of the boys said excitedly.

"It just appeared in my lap out of nowhere!" said another as he pushed the wheels on his wheelchair. A toy sat in his lap.

"There she is," said the woman next to me as Owen, still dressed as Saint Nick, came out of the room with a little girl holding his hand. The little bald girl who'd called me pretty. My eyes cut to the woman's face. She'd plastered on a smile when her little girl saw her and ran for her. The smile became real and filled the woman's eyes as she scooped her daughter into an embrace.

"Mommy, Santa said I could be his elf when I grow up," Loraleigh said, her little voice practically a squeal. "Just like this pretty one!"

She looked at me with those big brown eyes. The cancer in her bones and blood smelled rank. I wasn't an expert or anything, but the odor was so strong, I didn't know if she'd even make it to this Christmas, let alone see any in the future. Days. I'd had centuries already, and this little angel only had days left.

"Owen, we need to find Tristan," I said.

Chapter 4

"Tristan can't heal her," Owen said as soon as we were out of earshot of Loraleigh's mother.

"Why not?" I demanded as we strode down the hallway to the storage room, where we'd flash.

"For one, she's Norman and a teeny-tiny one at that. The potency of his blood could kill her. For two, we don't know exactly how it works except that his DNA heals injured cells. For all we know, it could give more power to cancer cells, especially if they've been hit with radiation. We *don't* know what will happen because, for three, Tristan couldn't possibly go around trying to heal everyone in this world who has cancer, which is where this could lead."

"I'm not talking about everyone. I'm talking about this one little girl."

Owen placed a hand on my shoulder, stopping me in my tracks. He turned me to face him, and his blue eyes pierced into mine. "Why?"

"Why what?"

"Why her?" His voice softened. "What makes her more special than any of those other kids in that room today? So special that big, bad Vanessa even wants to help her."

I frowned. "I don't know. I'm new to these emotions. I don't know where they come from or why. I just know I have to do something for that girl and her mother. They don't deserve this. They've been fighting for so long. They deserve peace and happiness. And Loraleigh—that's her name, I know her *name*—she's not gonna make it, Owen. And her mother's going to be left behind!"

Owen's hand moved from my shoulder to my cheek.

"Then they'll have their peace," he said quietly. I jerked my face away from him and shook my head. "It's God's will, Vanessa."

"How?" I asked. "How could God will this? I thought He was merciful. Or has Sheree been feeding me a bunch of bullshit?"

"There's a reason for everything, even when we don't understand what it is."

I shook my head harder. "No. I don't believe it." I placed a hand on my hip and jutted my chin out. "You and everyone else talk about there being a reason for everything. Well, maybe there's a reason I met Loraleigh and her mother today. Maybe I'm supposed to do something for them. Help them somehow."

His eyebrows jumped and a smile twitched on his lips. "Okay. I'm game. So what are you going to do?"

I blinked. I didn't know that answer. What *could* I do? I could turn her, but that wouldn't be doing her any favors. Nor her mother. She was too young anyway, but even if she were older, giving her an eternity as a vampire was no gift at all. If Tristan's blood couldn't heal her, then mine definitely couldn't. So what *did* I have to offer this girl and her mother?

"There must be something I can do. Something I can give them. They only have a short time together, and there's nothing I can do about that, Owen!" Tears stung my eyes. Again. I turned my back so he wouldn't see and opened the storage room door.

"Maybe not, but maybe you can make it last as long as possible. Get them through Christmas, at least. Make it the best Christmas they've ever had . . . "

I spun back around and threw my hands in the air. "How does that help? In the end, Loraleigh still dies and her mother is left with nothing."

"Not nothing. She'll have memories to hang onto. Good ones. That's all we really want, isn't it? Good memories with our loved ones. That's what life is all about."

I thought about baking cookies with Blossom and the happy memories she shared of previous Christmases. I recalled all of the movies Sheree made me watch, while she reminisced about watching them with her family. Trees and Secret Santas and Random Acts of Kindness . . . All of it had been about traditions. Remembering old memories and making new ones. Owen and I were dressed like Christmas freaks right now because he wanted to create good memories for kids who needed them.

"That's what Christmas is all about," I murmured as the truth hit me.

"So what are you going to do?" Owen asked at the same moment an idea occurred to me.

"We've gotta go!"

And with that, I flashed my way back to the shield around the Amadis Island, and then swam at vampire speed. Water still dripped from my clothes when I entered the trinket shop. The snooty witch from earlier waved her wand to dry my clothes, then glared at me for daring to return.

"I'd like to buy the music box," I said, hoping Owen would work with me to cast the appropriate spell. Hopefully, he was strong enough—the Amadis didn't have a more powerful mage.

"I'm sorry. It's been sold."

"*What?*" I stomped to the back of the store, thinking she was lying to me because she simply didn't want me to have it. But it was gone. Shit. There went my plan.

Without a word, I flashed to the mansion and hurried to my suite before anyone saw me. Or, more accurately, saw the tears that were about to spill. Damn, I was turning into Alexis.

Just as I had earlier, I threw the door open and stomped inside . . . and stopped. Another present from my Secret Santa: the silver music box.

"I take it you thought of something," Owen said from behind me.

I turned to find him leaning against the doorframe again. "You're my Secret Santa, aren't you?"

He laughed. "I'm not that sneaky."

"Yes, you are."

"Okay, I can be," he said with a shrug. "But no, it's not me."

I didn't know if he told the truth or not—he didn't smell like he was lying but a mage could cover that—but I didn't have time to worry about it right now. Loraleigh's life was ticking away. I picked up the music box and handed it to him.

"Can you make it work? The way it's supposed to?" I asked.

"Sure," he said easily. "Where do you want the portal to go?"

I shared my plan with him, and we made our way back to the hospital. It was the middle of the night here and visiting hours were over. Owen threw a cloak over us, and we snuck upstairs to Loraleigh's room. Her mother slept in a cot in the corner, but the little girl didn't. She stared at us from her bed as if she could actually see us.

"I knew you'd come back to see me," she whispered. "You're so shimmery now, though. Am I dreaming?"

I looked at Owen, but he shrugged. I uncorked the blood bottle.

"Just a few drops," Owen said, his voice only loud enough for my vampire ears to hear.

I nodded, and then dipped my finger into the bottle. With it covered in blood, I held my finger over Loraleigh's mouth. She licked her lips when the blood dropped on them, then swallowed.

"That will make you strong," I said, keeping my voice low.

"Like you?" she asked.

"Maybe. But it will only last for a few days. When you get bigger, though, you'll be very strong, too."

She gave me a sleepy smile, then dozed off. Owen set the music box on the table next to her bed and cast his spell.

We remained cloaked right outside the room as we waited for Loraleigh and her mother to wake up. As soon as they did, they must have seen the music box and opened it because the melody flowed through the room. The little tune was immediately drowned out by gasps and squeals and laughter in a variety of voices as their family came through the portal.

"Loraleigh, where did this music box come from?" her mother asked, amazement in her voice.

"From Santa and his elf," the little girl replied. "They brought me the best Christmas ever!"

Of course, her mother would never believe her. The door to her room opened, and the woman stuck her head out to look up and down the hall. Not able to see us, she went back in, shaking her head as she shut the door.

Owen put a muffle over the door before we left.

"That was a great thing you did," he said when we were back at the mansion. He took my hand and pulled me into the parlor. "They'll never know it was you, though. Nobody will ever believe her."

I shrugged. "That's exactly how I want it. We were her Secret Santa and gave her the best Christmas ever. That's all she wanted."

"Sounds like someone doesn't suck at Christmas anymore," Blossom said as she entered the room.

"You get it now, don't you?" Sheree asked, following the witch in.

"Yeah, yeah, I get it," I said with an eye roll. "But don't tell anyone. I have a reputation to maintain."

"We wouldn't want anyone to know Vanessa has a warm spot in her heart," Owen chided.

"Exactly," I said as my eyes flitted to movement outside the doorway.

"Don't you want to know who your Secret Santa is?" Blossom asked.

Katerina Ames, the Amadis matriarch, the woman who had been my enemy my entire life, stood outside the door, wearing a green silk gown. She peeked in at me with a knowing look in her doe-like brown eyes, and everything made sense. Only two people in the world could have heard my thoughts while I was browsing in the village and either of those people could have supplied the blood in that bottle, but only one really believed in me. Only one would have gone through this much trouble to prove that I was worthy—to myself more than anyone.

"Nah," I said in answer to Blossom's question although I didn't break the hold Katerina had on me. "It's not the who or what that matters, right? It's what we can do for others to pay forward the original gift of this holiday."

Everyone in the room stared at me, and I could feel their disbelief. But still my gaze remained locked on the woman in the foyer.

"*Very good, Vanessa,*" Katerina spoke in my mind. "*Not everyone discovers the real meaning of Christmas so quickly. I do think you are where you belong.*"

I gave her the slightest of nods, although I wasn't so sure about that last part. "Belonging" could take time, but I felt that I'd made real progress.

"I'm not sure I like you so sappy," Sheree said.

"Yeah, it's kind of weird," Blossom agreed.

I turned to look at them, then at Owen. He made a face. "It doesn't really suit you," he said, but he followed it with a wink.

"Don't worry, it's not permanent," I snapped at them all. "And if you tell Alexis I've gone weak, I'll bite each and every one of you until you beg me for mercy." My eyes darted to Sheree, and I shuddered. "Except you. That's disgusting."

They all thought that was hilarious, but I was completely serious. Especially about biting Owen. In fact, I'd take whatever excuse I could get to do that. Maybe now, just maybe, he'd let me. A girl could always hope for a miracle. It was Christmas after all. And after doing what I'd done for a Norman girl I'd never met before, I was walking proof that miracles do happen.

Presence

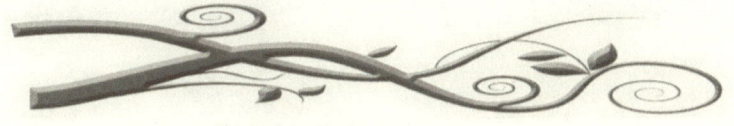

Now, we get to peek in on Tristan and Alexis in this final story of the Christmas collection, *Presence*. Once again, I ask that you try not to fit this anywhere in the main series. It *won't* fit. It's a lovely and romantic—and steamy—piece simply for you to enjoy with a scene readers have been begging me for. But don't worry if you think you'll be spoiled because you're not caught up: it's just made up stuff (as compared to the main series, which, you know, is real. . .)

Chapter 1

A curtain of coppery hair fell over my face as the woman of my dreams leaned over and pressed her mouth against mine. Soft and supple and, as always, tasting like brown sugar. I couldn't have asked for a better way to wake up, and if my long life ended this second, I'd die a happy man. My tongue pressed against her lips, urging them to part, but I felt her pulling away instead. So I wrapped my arms around her petite body, caging her in, and rolled over on the bed, flipping her to her back. I braced myself on my forearms to support most of my weight as I lay on top of her.

"Tristan," she admonished, her brown eyes bright and full of fake outrage. "I have to go."

Noticing that she was fully dressed in black jeans and a purple sweater while I was still in bed, I frowned.

"Do you really think I'd let you go with a simple peck?" I asked before leaning in and nuzzling my face in her neck. I inhaled her sweet scent before hovering my mouth over her ear and flicking the lobe with my tongue before sucking it. She let out a gasp that sounded like a mix between a giggle and a moan. I instantly grew aroused at the sound. When I pulled back to look at her, she wore the same dazzling smile that stole my heart the first time I ever saw her—as an adult, anyway. "I think you need a proper goodbye."

I dove down again, this time my mouth on hers, my lips pulling her full ones open.

"My . . . mom . . . is . . . waiting," she said between kisses, while at the same time tightening her arms around my neck and pulling me closer. I shifted my weight onto one arm, slipped my free hand under her sweater, and grasped her waist. I deepened the kiss, and she indulged me as my thumb slid over her ribs and grazed the bottom of her perfectly round, perfectly soft tit.

The next thing I knew, I was on my back staring up at her. She'd flipped me over and now straddled my hips. I groaned when she rubbed against me, and her eyes widened while she popped up on her knees.

"Sorry," she gasped although that smile played on her lips.

"You're such a tease," I grumbled. I lifted a hand to that coppery hair and twisted my finger into a lock of it.

"You know I can't. Not now . . . with all these people around who can *hear* us." She used air quotes around *hear*, because she didn't mean hear with their ears, but hear when she blasted our best moments into their minds. The Angels had given her one of the most powerful gifts they could give her—telepathy—but it really messed with our sex life, especially when we were at Rina's mansion on the Amadis Island. The matriarch's home was buzzing with extra activity right now with Christmas only days away.

"So where are you off to?" I asked, trying to put my thoughts on a different track than what they were on now—the feel of her naked body against mine. Thoughts that didn't help my hard-on.

She smiled with a mischievous twinkle in her eye. "Not for you to know until Christmas Eve." She leaned over to give me another kiss, pressing those perfect tits against my chest, before jumping off the bed. "See you this afternoon."

"Alexis," I said as she opened the door, "is there anything special you want for Christmas?"

She looked over her shoulder, and her gaze slid from my face down to the foot of the bed and back up again.

"You. Just like that." She gave me a smile so sexy, I nearly sprang off the bed and tackled her, but she disappeared in a flash before I could move. "*But in a place where I can do something about it,*" she added from her new location on the first floor of the mansion.

I looked down at the "it" she referred to under the tented sheet and groaned while thumping my fist against the bed. What kind of answer was that? She could have me anytime she wanted. She knew that. Once I could stand without discomfort, I made my way to the bathroom, thinking about the part she'd added telepathically: A place where we could do something about it. For the first time in weeks, I had a viable idea for what to do for her for Christmas.

An hour later, the door to Rina's office opened as soon as I approached.

"What can I do for you, Tristan?" she asked as she held her arm out to welcome me into her office. The matriarch must have sensed me, because she apparently hadn't invaded my thoughts to know I was there. She wore a dark green ball gown, and rubies around her neck and wrists glinted in the light as she closed the door.

"I've been trying to think of something special to give to Alexis for Christmas," I began.

"That should not be hard for you, considering you always know the best solutions," she said as she sat in one of the wingback chairs by the fire.

"Yes, you would think," I agreed, taking a seat on the antique leather sofa next to her, "but when it comes to presents for women, the best answer changes every five minutes. Alexis is especially hard, because of her rules."

Rina smiled, understanding my point. "Oh, yes, the tradition Sophia began. It is a quite lovely idea, giving gifts that either you own and want to give to the other person or that you have made yourself."

"I've already given her a piece of my heart, though. Topping that is proving . . . difficult."

"Tristan, darling, you do not need to top it, as you say. Our Alexis would be fine with anything you give her."

Rina was probably right—Alexis's answer this morning was proof—but I had a need to do more than just "anything." My wife deserved the best I could give her.

I hesitated before asking my next question. "Would a night alone, in a private place, fall within their rules?"

Rina smiled knowingly. Also a telepath, she knew exactly the problems Alexis and I faced. "I believe it would be a perfect gift. Do you have specific plans?"

"I was thinking our beach house in the Keys."

"Do you think it is safe?"

"We'll be fine for a night."

Rina pressed her lips tightly before finally nodding. "Shall I check if the jet is available?"

"That would be appreciated." I leaned my elbows on my knees as she closed her eyes and fell silent for a moment.

"Hmm . . . there is time to take you to Florida tomorrow, Christmas Eve, but it would not be able to retrieve you for three days."

"We need to be back by Christmas morning for Dorian," I said as I did the calculations in my head. "With warlock speed there and back, we'd only need the jet for about ten hours on Christmas Eve. It can be back here by four in the morning Christmas Day, if that's okay."

Rina lifted a brow. "That is not much time alone."

No, not at all, I thought, but I shrugged. "We'll take what we can get."

"Very well. We can do that. I wish I could give you more time."

I stood. "I appreciate this. Hopefully, Alexis will, too."

I'd barely left Rina's office before more plans started running through my mind. I had several phone calls to make to Miami and the Keys to prepare for this perfect night. We'd only get about four hours alone, but I'd make those the best four hours for Alexis that I could. Before diving into those calls, I swung by the kitchen for breakfast and found Blossom busy baking, her blond hair piled on top of her head and flour smudged under her big, hazel eyes.

"Hey, Tristan," she greeted with her usual bubbly self. "Guess what? Jax says he might take me to Australia. Isn't that cool? I've never been to Australia. Well, actually, I've never been out of the United States, except for now, of course, but this island barely counts since it's only Amadis, and we haven't seen any of Greece or the rest of Europe, which you know, is fine, I'm just happy to be here with you guys for Christmas, but if we could get off-island and go to Australia, that would be incredible. We'd only get like four or five days, but still, I'd love to see the Outback where Jax is from and all the animals—" She paused, seemingly to take a breath, but she tilted her head. "Alexis didn't like the animals, did she? Didn't something happen to her?"

I chuckled at the memory of my wife with the kangaroo. If Alexis were here, she would have hit me.

"I don't think Australia is exactly her favorite place on the planet," I said as I opened the refrigerator and dug around for food. Ophelia, who made an amazing breakfast, must have been busy with other work since it was past normal breakfast time. Or maybe Blossom had run the older witch off with all her babbling.

"Hopefully Jax and I will have a much better time, and I can tell her all about it, and maybe she'll want to give it another chance." Blossom handed me a plate of cinnamon buns and cookies she'd apparently been baking.

"Maybe," I said as I stuffed a bun in my mouth, grabbed a cookie, and headed for the door. I gave her a wave and ducked out before she started rambling about something else. Blossom had a huge heart, but her brain ran non-stop, as did her mouth. I didn't have time for a chat if I was going to prepare this special gift for Alexis.

I went to the media room, the only place in the mansion with electricity and anything 21st-century like telephones, to make my calls.

"G'day, mate," Jax, the were-crocodile, said from his place in front of one of the computers. "You got a minute? I don't know how to run this damn thing." He held a mouse in his hand and pointed it at the screen like a TV remote. "I can't even get this whirly-gig to work."

He'd only left the Outback recently after forty years of isolation, and he was a proud old boy, but I couldn't help but laugh. "You're going to break something. What the hell are you trying to do?"

"Trying to get to Australia," he said, his voice full of frustration. "I made a bit of a promise to Blossom and don't know that I can keep it."

"Ah." Knowing the frustration of trying to impress a lady, I felt bad for teasing him. I sat down next to him and took over the computer, looking at flights from Athens to Sydney.

He let out a low whistle when I told him the price. "They're proud of their flights, are they? I don't exactly have millions sittin' around in my shack."

I clicked a few buttons on the website and redid the search. "It's not as expensive if you wait until after the holidays."

"I think we'll have to get back to Amadis business after the holidays." Jax rubbed his bald head. "It's all right, mate. I'll figure somethin' else to do for the lass."

I'd just heard Blossom talk non-stop about the trip. The disappointment would flatten her. "Let me do it for you. I have the money. She doesn't even have to know."

Jax's head popped up, and his dark eyes were wide. "Hell, no. Nice of you to offer, but I don't take charity."

"It's not charity—"

The were-croc jumped to his feet and was at the door. "No worries, mate."

I hurried out the door after him and convinced him to follow me to Rina's office. He would never ask her permission to use the Amadis jet, but I would.

"I am sorry, Tristan, but tomorrow was the only time the jet was available, and you have already reserved it," she said.

Jax clapped his hand on my shoulder and said, "Like I said, no worries, mate. I appreciate you tryin' though."

He strode down the dark hallway for the main part of the house. I looked at Rina and pushed my hands through my hair, then blew out a breath.

"Give them our reservation," I said. "He doesn't have anything else to give her for Christmas."

"Are you certain, Tristan?" Rina asked. "And your gift for Alexis?"

"I'll figure something else out."

Chapter 2

I still hadn't thought of what to do for Alexis when she returned in the early afternoon from her off-island trip with Sophia.

"Did you have a good morning?" I asked her as she sat down for a late lunch with me. I hoped she'd drop some hints of what she was getting me so that maybe it would provide some ideas of what to do for her.

"Do you remember our honeymoon?" she asked out of the blue. "So peaceful, just you and me on the beach, hardly any cares in the world . . . "

I grinned. "I remember it quite well."

She scowled. "Well, it was nothing like that. The Norman world is a madhouse with everyone running around shopping for last minute gifts. People are *crazy*. And then Sheree and Vanessa came with us for protection and about drove me insane. They were both looking for just the right gift for Owen, that dog, and they seem to think they'll be getting something terribly romantic from him, but I know Owen—"

"They said that in front of each other?" I asked, curiosity getting the best of me.

She laughed. "No. Their freakin' thoughts were so loud and excited, I couldn't help but hear them even when I wasn't trying." She massaged her temples for a moment, then looked at me with those mesmerizing brown eyes. "You know what I wish existed? A faerie stone that calmed everyone the eff down."

I rubbed her shoulder for a while as a new plan formed in my mind. I'd given up our opportunity for a mini-retreat to our honeymoon spot by letting Jax and Blossom use the jet, but if she wanted a faerie stone, that was something I might be able to provide.

"I need to go," I said before kissing her goodbye.

"Where?"

I tweaked her chin and repeated her words back to her. "You'll find out Christmas Eve."

She tilted her head, but I only winked before darting out of the room.

I flashed to the village, and then contacted Bree the way she had shown me.

"I need to ask you something," I said when she appeared in front of me at the end of the pier that jutted out into the Aegean Sea, and I told her my idea for Alexis's present.

When I finished, Bree looked at me with a golden eyebrow raised. "You ask a faerie for a favor?"

I narrowed my eyes. "If that's what it takes."

I'd hoped for special privileges, but should have known better. It didn't matter, though. Alexis's happiness—and peace—would be worth it.

Bree smiled warmly. "I won't charge you, but if we run into any faeries in the Otherworld, I can't guarantee anything."

I nodded. "Of course."

Bree turned toward me, placed her hands on my head and her thumbs over my eyes, forcing me to close them. The air shuddered around us, and she released me. Although it seemed as though we still stood on the pier at the Amadis village, we weren't really there anymore. She'd brought us through the veil. I knew we'd entered the Otherworld immediately—my chest squeezed painfully.

"What do we need to do?" I asked, pressing my hand to my chest as I followed her off the pier. We didn't sink into the ocean, but, rather, traversed the Otherworld. Breathing became more and more difficult. "I'd forgotten how much it hurts to be here."

"That's the human part of you that knows it's not supposed to be here yet," Bree said, tossing her golden hair over her shoulder to look at me. "We need to—"

She wasn't able to finish her sentence. A creature with bat wings, horns, and a body like a human heavyweight boxer—a female boxer—flew at me with a sword raised. A demon.

"You attract them like an angel," Bree said with dismay.

I didn't have the same defenses in the Otherworld as I did in the Earthly realm. When the demon swung her sword at me, it sliced through my skin like butter. I bit back a howl of pain and charged. Her wings beat at the air, but I grabbed onto her hoof before she rose too high, then climbed up her trunk-like legs and wrestled her to the ground. She fought back, digging her claws into me and snapping her jaw full of needles too close to my face for comfort.

"I've fought worse demons than you," I growled. Nothing was worse than the demons inside. Of course, Alexis had helped me beat the one that used to control me. Just the thought of her now—of our love, of leaving her if this demon won—gave me the boost of strength I needed.

My power had a lesser effect on the beast, but I blasted it at her anyway. It didn't paralyze her, but her movements slowed. With a feint here and a perfectly placed kick there, I was able to steal her sword even as my lungs seized painfully. Pushing through the agony, I swung the blade upwards and sliced it across her neck. My ears nearly exploded with the sound she made as she picked up her head and disappeared. Demons couldn't be killed in the Otherworld, but hopefully I'd deterred her from coming back—and any others from attacking.

"Let's hurry," Bree whispered.

Traveling through the Otherworld was disorienting. The farther away we moved from the veil, the farther Earth fell away, as though we ascended through the atmosphere, but we didn't rise into the Heavens. From what Bree had told me, only the Angels could rise into the Heavens. The faeries occupied a different part of the Otherworld that somewhat resembled Earth, but . . . wasn't. We followed a path, presumably toward their city, but it never came into view. When we entered a meadow of wildflowers, Bree stopped, fell to her knees, and dug her hands into the ground. They eventually emerged, producing a yellow stone that looked like citrine the size of a walnut. She closed her hands around the stone and murmured something in fae, then she held the stone out to me.

"I have given it the quality of peace," she said. As soon as I took it from her, two familiar faeries popped into the meadow.

"Oh! Wot is this?" asked the purple-haired one who I'd met before in England. In the Earthly realm, she went by the name Debbie.

"This is a delight for the eyes," Stacey, the pink-haired fae, answered. She danced around me, and a long-nailed finger stroked my cheek. Her Yorkshire, England, accent was less apparent in this realm. "Did you miss us? Needed to come for a visit?"

"I need the faerie stone," I said matter-of-factly, not wanting to get involved in their faerie antics. "For my *wife*."

Both faeries scowled at the reminder of my love. They didn't have the same effect on me because of it, which apparently annoyed them. They deserved to be annoyed for all the trouble the fae caused for everyone else, but an unhappy faerie wasn't a good thing.

"And why should we do anything for you?" asked a third familiar voice. Jessica, another purple-haired faerie, had appeared.

"What will you do for us?" demanded her sister, Lisa, tossing her blue hair. She and her sister had also lost the heavy twang of their accents—Southern U.S. when they were on Earth.

"He doesn't have to do anything," Bree said, standing by my side. "He's—"

"We know who he is," Debbie said. "*What* he is."

"Doesn't matter," Stacey added.

"He doesn't get special treatment," Jessica agreed.

"What do you want?" I asked. There was no use arguing with them, and I needed to get out of here. After the fight with the demon, not only my chest ached, but so did the rest of my body.

Lisa twirled a lock of her blue hair around her finger. "We'll let you know when the time comes."

"Beware," said Jessica, "if you take that stone, you will *owe* us."

I bowed my head and said through gritted teeth, "I understand."

Those two words bound the contract more tightly than any written one on Earth, and as soon as I said them, Bree took us out of the Otherworld. We appeared in the woods near the matriarch's mansion, and I gasped like a fish out of water. I fell to my hands and knees, struggling for a deep breath. Minutes passed before I could finally breathe normally. By then, my injuries had also healed. Only the rips in my clothes showed any evidence of the fight with the demon, but when I rose to my feet, I still rolled my neck and shoulders and shook out my limbs, making sure I was truly free of the pain.

"You're okay?" Bree asked, and I nodded. "I hope this does what you desire."

She gave me a quick and awkward hug before disappearing. Although the pain was gone, I still felt stiff as I made my way past the training gym and to the mansion. I reached for the handle when the wooden door flew open.

"Men," Vanessa snarled as she nearly mowed me down. She blurred off for the beach.

As soon as I entered the foyer, Sheree stomped past me.

"Men," she growled around elongated teeth as she headed for the back of the building.

Owen stood at the bottom of the stairs, his blond hair standing in all directions and his blue eyes wild with confusion.

"What's up, Scarecrow?" I asked.

"Women!" he snapped, and without another word, he disappeared.

I closed the front door and shook my head with bewilderment.

"I told you, they need a calming stone," Alexis said as she strode out of the sitting room and over to me. "If only they existed."

"*They* need one?" I asked as she wrapped her arms around my waist and laid her head against my chest.

She snorted. "Yeah. As many as possible. Crap really hit the fan. I told Owen this would happen, but he never wants to listen to me. Now I'll probably have to clean up his mess." She let out a sigh when I closed my arms around her. "At least I have you to calm me. You've always had that effect on me. Too bad we couldn't bottle it."

My brows pinched together. "I still do that for you?"

She looked up at me and gave me that smile I love. "Always. Thank God. Otherwise, I'd be worse than I already am. Worse than them!"

She laid her cheek against my chest and moved her hands down my back. When she shifted and her hip pressed against mine, she froze for a minute before her hand dove into my pocket.

"I thought you were just glad to see me, but I guess not," she said when she pulled the stone from my pocket. "What is this? It kind of looks like that one ugly birthstone. I was always so glad mine is an amethyst. I couldn't imagine having to wear something like this. What's that yellow one called?"

"Citrine," I muttered, and then I blew out a breath of frustration. "And that's a faerie stone for calm and peace."

A smile broke out on her face. "Really? You got it for them? Oh, Tristan! You should give it to Owen, and then he can give it to them for Christmas. Oh! He can put it in a piece of jewelry like you did for me. They'd never know, but damn, would it make life a little easier for all of us."

Her excitement was contagious, and I couldn't help but return her smile. Her happiness made me happy, but I couldn't exactly say that was supposed to have been *her* Christmas gift. Now what was I going to do? I snatched the stone from her and crushed it in my fist before shoving the pieces into my pocket.

She laced her fingers through my other hand and pulled me toward the stairs.

"Looks like you need to change before dinner," she said. "What happened to your clothes anyway? They're all ripped up."

I grunted, but kept my thoughts clear in case she snooped my mind for the truth. "Nothing, my love. Just a little ramble in the woods. Don't worry about me."

Chapter 3

Sleep evaded me. I stared at the ceiling as Alexis slept in my arms, my mind running through possible gift options and tossing them away as garbage because none of them were just right. Christmas Eve would dawn in a few hours, and I had nothing to give her. How could I let this happen? The more I thought about it, the more worked up I became, and the more likely I'd wake her with my thundering heart. Very carefully, I slipped out of bed without waking her and flashed to the training gym.

I went through my aikido routine as the gray light of dawn filtered through the rafters, hoping to distract myself so my subconscious could work on my problem, but I still had no solution after two hours of practice. After some calming stretches and exercises, I flashed to the village for art supplies and returned to the gym, where I'd have privacy.

When aikido didn't work for me, drawing and painting usually provided the escape I needed. I didn't know what I'd paint when I'd first made the decision to get the supplies, but as soon as I started, I should have known where my inspiration would come from. I began with a painting similar to the drawing I'd done of Alexis when we first met. That sketch had been in pencil, but the color in this painting brought her to life. As I put the finishing touches on her lips, I imagined what they felt like to my fingertips. I tasted them on my own lips.

My stream of consciousness took me to our wedding, and I painted my beautiful bride in her wedding dress. She'd been so self-conscious in it, which had been absurd. No one could look as good in that dress as she did. Stunning. Her coppery hair had been piled on top of her head with loose curls draping around her face. She'd looked so nervous, like she might bolt, until she took my hand. Her mahogany eyes showed so much love as she recited her vows to me. I'd barely been able to focus on my own vows, blown away that she was actually committing herself to me. *Me!* Love had never been in my realm of possibilities until she came into my life, and there she was—taking the Amadis vows of marriage. On the canvas before me, I captured her face against the backdrop of the sunset on the beach as she said her vows.

I couldn't wait to get her to the beach house that night and only stopped at the restaurant to show the monster that once lived inside me who was in control. All I wanted to do was take her and make her *mine*, but if I couldn't restrain my human desires, the monster knew I wouldn't be able to restrain it. So I forced myself down. Waited as patiently as I could manage. Now I painted the joy in her eyes when she looked at the house for the first time—the Caribbean room, especially—and realized I'd done it for her. She'd been so worried about not getting me a wedding present when that adoration on her face was worth more than gold to me.

The memories flowed, and as I painted her, I felt her luscious lips, her soft skin, the vulnerability that poured off her. She was scared, I knew, on a few levels, but she put her trust in our love. In me. I held tightly to my control as I fumbled to take that dress off of her, and nearly lost that hold when I couldn't figure it out. Her lips had tilted with that sweet but sexy smile as she showed me how to take off the top. And fuck if I didn't almost lose it again when those beautiful tits burst free. They were a little smaller then, before the *Ang'dora*, but still perfect. Round, plump, with pinkish-brown tips hard like pebbles.

I moved to another canvas as I remembered the rest of the night. Admiring the perfection that was my Alexis naked. Seeing her flawless olive skin, her curves, the lines of her hips and her thighs and calves, the pink folds between her legs. Feeling her, soft and supple, under my fingers and lips. Tasting her in many places for the first time. Hovering over her and the frightened look in her eyes when my fingers slid inside. She was wet and pulsing, ready for me. Making me throb for her.

"You're so big," she had whispered, and I'd wanted to go all caveman on her. To show her just how much of a man I was. To take possession of her and make her *mine*. But I didn't want to scare her anymore than she already was, because damn, I would have gone mad if she'd shut down on me. Again, though, she showed her love and her trust.

I lost all hold on my conscious mind as soon as I entered her. She wasn't the first woman I'd been with, but nothing had felt like her, on the outside or in. Bliss overcame me. I wanted to go slow and make it last forever if possible, but at the same time, I wanted to pound her hard and hit that explosion with all the force we had building inside us. I was so afraid I'd break her small, human body, though. I didn't know at first that she could have nearly broken me. But I found out quickly. She barely moved, and I almost came right there and then without her, but I didn't want that to be how her first time ended. Somehow, by ensuring that she enjoyed this as much as I did, I held on, stroking her, licking her, sucking and biting, wanting to devour her, pumping and thrusting and rocking together until we both climbed and shouted and exploded with a fierceness more mind-blowing than I could have ever imagined.

And not too long after, the tip of her pink tongue slid over her swollen red lips, and she wanted to do it again.

"Um . . . " The clearing of a throat brought me back to the training gym. Blossom stood in the doorway with her eyes squeezed shut. "My guess is those are for your eyes only?"

I turned to the line of paintings I'd done and really saw them for the first time. I'd captured my Alexis beautifully. Perfectly. Erotically.

"Erm . . . " I didn't know what to say, part of me wanting to show her off, but part of me appalled that anyone else had seen her. Even if it was only Blossom. "Can you hide them?"

With her eyes still shut, she flicked her hand. The canvases went blank, but black rather than beige.

"Did it work?" she asked, barely cracking one eyelid open. When she saw that it had, she opened both eyes completely. "I'm, uh, really sorry. They're really gorgeous, I mean, like *wow* gorgeous, but I'm sure you didn't want . . . I mean, I didn't mean to—"

"Forget about it," I said, the initial shock worn off. It was only Blossom, and although Alexis would be embarrassed if she knew her best friend had seen these, it could have been worse. She could have been Owen or Dorian. How senseless of me to be painting these here. But that's what my woman did to me—made me lose all of my senses.

"I just came to say thank you for letting us use the jet, and, well, Merry Christmas." She threw her arms around me in a hug.

I patted her on the back. "Merry Christmas, Blossom."

"Dad! There you are!" Dorian came running down the path. "I've been looking everywhere for you."

"I need to go," Blossom said. She bent over to give Dorian a hug goodbye, then she looked at me and over my shoulder at the blank canvases. She couldn't lift her spell with Dorian there, but she grabbed my hand and tapped the tips of my fingers in a pattern as her lips moved silently. "Tap the pattern on the bottom left corner of each one to expo—er, see them."

"Thank you."

She gave me a mischievous grin. "I don't know who's luckier—you or her."

I chuckled. "Definitely me."

"Yeah, you're right." She leaned in closer to me, and whispered, "She'll love the gift, though."

I cocked my head as she walked back toward the mansion, not understanding. Because I still didn't have a gift for my wife.

"Dad, I don't have a present for Mom," Dorian said, poking me in the stomach. "Can you help me?"

Apparently our son was in my same situation.

"What were you doing in there anyway?" he asked before I could answer his first question. He looked past me at all the black canvases.

I looked over my shoulder and realized one hadn't been blanked out. The last one—Alexis later in our honeymoon, watching the sunset on the beach. Well, that's where my vision had apparently been headed. Blossom had walked in before I finished it. Seeing it gave me an aha moment. Was this painting the gift Blossom had meant?

"Oh, that's a pretty picture of Mom," Dorian said, but then he frowned. "It's not done, though."

He followed me inside, and we both studied the picture.

"She was pregnant with you then," I said.

"She doesn't look fat."

I laughed. "You were a little thing then, like a tiny bug inside her. So what do you think? Blue or green here?"

I pointed to a part of the sky right behind Alexis, thinking blue and not just any blue but a cornflower blue. Dorian had a bit of artistic talent, too, though, and I wondered what he'd pick.

"This soft, kind of grayish blue," he said, pointing at a color I'd already mixed on my palette. Pretty close to cornflower. He swept his finger over the painting without touching it. "And make the strokes like this."

I handed him the paintbrush. "Why don't you do it?"

We finished the painting together, and Dorian beamed with pride when I praised his talent. His hazel eyes sparkled. When I'd first seen them do that, I'd finally understood what Alexis meant about my own eyes when she said the gold in them sparked or sparkled, depending on my mood.

"We could give this as our present to Mom," Dorian suggested as we admired the painting. "I think she'd love it."

"I think that's a great idea. But it should be from you."

"Do you already have a present for her?"

"I'm working on it."

"She'll like it no matter what, Dad. She likes everything you give her, even if it's just a kiss."

I ruffled his hair and chuckled before taking him back to the house. He might be right, but I would give my wife more than a kiss. Christmas Eve had already blasted to almost noon and I still didn't have a present for her, but I wasn't giving up yet.

"Dude, Tristan, I've been looking all over for you," Owen said as soon as we walked into the kitchen. He grabbed my arm and pushed me back out to the foyer, I assumed to get away from Dorian's ears. He lowered his voice. "Alexis said you have something that could help me?"

I dug in my pocket and pulled out the pieces of faerie stone. "They're all yours if you want the pieces. They have the quality of peace."

"Just what I need." He smacked me on the shoulder. "You're a lifesaver! But, uh, what do I do with them?"

I shrugged. "Take them to the jeweler in the village."

Scarecrow snorted. "You think I should give them jewelry? *Both* of them?"

"Probably not but how else will you get them to wear the stones?"

His brows puckered so that three lines showed between them. "Good point, but what? The last thing I need is to give either of them the wrong idea."

"Scarecrow—"

He held up his hand to stop me. "I get enough grief from your wife. I know I need to do something but not now. Not at Christmas."

I nodded. "You do what you got to do. As for the jewelry, just don't give either of them a ring."

"Right. Chicks read too much into rings. Maybe a necklace? Or earrings?"

"I don't know about earrings, but Vanessa certainly likes necklaces. A bracelet might be safest, though."

"Cool. Thanks, man." He stepped toward the door, then turned back to me. "Since I owe you one . . . " His eyes narrowed, and he got that look when he was sensing for others' presence. He took a step closer to me and lowered his voice to a whisper. "She'll kill me if I tell you, so all I'm going to say is Alexis has something sweet planned for you tonight. Off-island. Just the two of you. She needs me to set a few things up, so if there's anything you might want to have there . . . her present maybe . . . I could take it ahead of time."

Son of a bitch. She'd really gone all out, and I had a perfect opportunity to do the same, but I still had nothing. Or . . . did I?

Chapter 4

Scarecrow didn't let me go to the mysterious location with him, so I gave him specific instructions on how I wanted everything arranged. As specific as possible anyway, considering the only thing he divulged was that we had some kind of place of our own to be alone for the night.

Anticipation built as afternoon became evening. We enjoyed a festive dinner with everyone except Jax and Blossom who had already left for Australia, then we gathered in the sitting room to exchange presents. Although Sophia's tradition was theirs only, and not one for all of the Amadis, everyone who stayed in the mansion had stuck to the rules of giving only something of our own or something we'd made. Pieces of art, baked goods, and knitted scarves were exchanged, along with a few more creative items. Dorian gave me a leather cuff he'd tooled, with some help of course, and a tear rolled down Alexis's cheek when she opened the painting our son gave her.

"*Thank you,*" she said in my head as she smothered Dorian in a hug.

That's Dorian's gift, I said, but she knew he'd had my help.

"*Are you ready for yours?*"

My gaze swept over to the 15-foot Christmas tree. *There are no more gifts.*

She smiled. "*Mine wouldn't fit under there.*"

Mine either. I winked when her eyes came back to my face after she stole a glance at my lap. Her expression glossed over for a moment, her eyes filled with adoration.

She blinked, then stood up so fast, her form was a blur. "Wow, I'm so tired. I think it's time to head upstairs."

"Already?" Dorian asked, and he scowled when he looked at the grandfather clock in the corner. "It's only eight o'clock."

Alexis stretched and forced a yawn. "Really? I'm exhausted."

"Maybe you're getting sick, Mom. You should go to bed. You don't want to be sick on Christmas."

"Yes, little man, I think you're right." She bent over and gave him a peck on the cheek.

"Me, too," I said, quickly rising to my feet. "I'm not feeling well, either."

"Probably because you can't stop kissing Mom," Dorian said, bringing a laugh out of everyone in the room.

"I'll take care of him," Sophia said with a knowing smile.

We made our escape, but instead of going upstairs to our suite, Alexis grabbed my hand and led me into the darkness outside. We flashed to the pier and hopped into one of the speedboats. The stars sped by overhead as we passed through the island's shield, but instead of having us flash, she told me where to navigate the boat. A small island, a dark shadow at first, came into view. Alexis pointed to the boat dock, and then she disappeared. I studied the area while tying up the boat. A house stood on the edge of the beach surrounded by foliage, and I sensed Alexis inside.

"*Stay on the beach,*" she instructed me.

I had no problem with that. I'd found Owen's set-up out there, waiting for me. I adjusted the arrangement of canvases into a semi-circle and tapped the pattern out Blossom had given me to lift her spell. Several renditions of my wife in various states of arousal came into view. With a flick of my fingers, I lit the candles scattered about: pillars on metal stands near the paintings, votives in the sand, and tea lights floating in the water of the quiet cove. As I appraised the scene, a gasp sounded behind me.

"Tristan! I did this for you, and you made it . . . even more perfect."

I turned and sucked in my own breath at the sight of her. She stood in the center of the circle of paintings, her hands over her mouth and her eyes glistening, wearing a dress that looked very much like her wedding dress. She moved closer to the first painting, and I flashed to stand behind her, wrapping my arms around her.

"They're . . . amazing," she breathed as we moved to the next one. She praised each one at first, but grew silent as we proceeded and the paintings became more intimate, more erotic. "Um . . . wow. Do I really look that good when we're doing it?"

I laughed out loud, then leaned in and pressed my lips to her exposed neck. "You are the most beautiful creature in the world," I whispered against her ear, "especially when we're doing it."

She shuddered, then turned to face me. Her hand swept over her dress. "Looks like we were thinking along the same lines." She stood on her toes to deliver a kiss that made my dick jump in my pants, then she took my hands and pulled me inside the house. Into the bedroom, specifically, which appeared to be very similar to our Caribbean room in the Keys. "Owen helped me make it look just right. It's just an illusion, of course."

"It's a perfect gift," I said.

"Oh, this is only the beginning." She pushed me to the edge of the bed, forcing me to sit, then she took two steps backwards, away from me. I reached for her but she shook her head. "Blossom helped me, too. For example, this dress is only an illusion."

"I like it, all of this, reliving our honeymoon."

She giggled. "Not exactly, though. See, I was pretty innocent and naive then. I've grown up quite a bit . . . learned a few things . . . "

With a glint of naughtiness in her eyes, her fingers swirled in the hem, and the dress disappeared. It didn't expose her naked body, though. She suddenly wore a black leather corset, a black thong, and Blossom's hot-pink stilettos. With a snap of her fingers, music filled the room, and a pole appeared.

"This is your real gift," she said.

Her body began to move to the music, and I quickly realized she wasn't dancing randomly, but performing a choreographed routine. As if I wasn't already turned on, I grew hard as a rock watching her work up and down the pole like an expert. Where did this come from? I hoped it wasn't a one-hit wonder. By the time the music stopped and she stood in front of me, the top of her corset was loosened and her thong was gone. With a yank of my finger, the string came away from the first several eyelets, and those magnificent tits sprang free. My hands enclosed her waist, and I jerked her to me, ready to ravage every inch of her body.

"You are so damn sexy," I said against the soft skin between her breasts.

She placed a hand on my chest and pushed me away. She shook her head, and then pointed at my pants. "And you're still dressed. Didn't I tell you what I wanted for Christmas?"

I moved fast, but she was even faster. In a heartbeat, my clothes were on the floor, I was pressed against the headboard with leather straps tying my wrists to each post, and my dick stood hard and tall, at complete attention for my wife. She climbed onto the bed and, slowly, so painfully slowly, she crawled over to me on all fours with a wicked smile that made every muscle in my body jerk toward her. The leather ties dug into my wrists. I could easily break through them, of course, but I played along. For now.

She teased me with her mouth on my jaw, then my throat, to my chest, down my stomach, and back up again. Her tongue thrust into my mouth as she kneeled over me, swirling her hips only centimeters above my cock, making it dance with her, straining to get inside. But instead of lowering herself onto it, she rose to her feet and stood on the bed, towering over me, her tits like soft globes over the top of the corset, her nipples long and hard. Her slit right in front of my face. My fingers twitched, wanting to touch it. My tongue slid over my lips as I gazed at it, yearning for the salty-sweet taste inside.

"Mmm . . . me first," she said, her voice thick and husky and her eyelids hooded. But she didn't mean what I thought.

Again faster than even I could track, she'd spun around and was on her knees in front of me, her fingers wrapped around my shaft. Her fist moved down, and her mouth followed.

"Oh, damn, Lex," I moaned as her tongue swirled around the head and her lips slid farther down, taking me in.

My body began to tremble as she licked and sucked and made love to me with her mouth, all the while her ass bent over right in front of me, divulging all of her wet exquisiteness. Nearing the brink of no return but not wanting to come yet, I jerked my wrists and broke the leather ties. I grabbed her round ass and buried my face, finally tasting the delicacy that was my wife.

Neither of us would last long like that, and she knew it. She flipped around and up, once again straddling my lap. But this time she lowered herself down and around me as she leaned over and covered her mouth with mine. I palmed her breasts as she rode me until she threw her head back and screamed my name while slamming down hard. I bucked against her several times, then flipped her onto her back and pounded into her with all that she would take until we both cried out with the explosion of complete and utter bliss.

I collapsed next to her, both of us panting. She rolled over onto her stomach, her body pressed against mine, and closed her eyes. We drifted off for a few minutes, and when I opened my eyes, she was staring at me with so much love, more than I ever deserved. The corners of her swollen lips lifted in a grin.

"Again?" she asked with a teasing lilt.

"Always," I said.

We made love like we hadn't been able to for weeks, and now that we'd taken the edge off, we were able to keep going for hours until we collapsed once again.

"We should go back soon," she said when we finally rested. "For Dorian."

I pulled her closer with her back to me and buried my face in her hair, inhaling her sugary scent. Her silky skin pressed against mine from ankle to shoulder. My fingers traced lightly over her bare stomach, making it quiver.

"Wish we had forever, though," she added with a sigh.

I kissed the tip of her ear. "We do, my love. Maybe not always like this, but we will do it again."

She squirmed until I loosened my hold and she could turn over to face me. "I don't think I can right now."

I chuckled. "You might kill me if we tried."

She laughed. "You're invincible."

"I'm still a man in many ways."

Her fingers trailed over my chest. "How about New Year's Eve, then?"

I leaned in for a long, languishing kiss that would have to hold us over until then. "Meet me at midnight?"

"Of course."

As if in response, somewhere in the distance, the sound of church bells carried over the water, ringing in midnight.

"It's officially Christmas. Thank you for my presents. The paintings couldn't be more perfect."

"Ah, thank *you*," I said, and I kissed her temple. "You made them perfect. But time with you, being in your presence, especially like this, is always the best gift."

She sighed again, this time the sound one of agreement and content.

"Merry Christmas, my sweet Tristan," she said softly.

"Merry Christmas, *ma lykita*."

Recipes

Were Brownies

Submitted by Kelly Victorine

This is for Tony, who just stuck with me. This recipe is my husband's that he made when he was a child, and still makes today, so I thought it was something Tony would like.

Ingredients:
- 4 Eggs (slightly beaten)
- 1 cup Sugar
- ¾ cup Brown Sugar
- 2/3 cup Oil
- ½ cup Cocoa Powder
- 1 ½ cup Flour
- ½ tsp. Salt
- ¼ tsp. Water
- 2 tsp. Vanilla

1. Mix by hand in order given.

2. Bake in 10 x 13 greased pan at 350 degrees for 25 – 30 minutes.

3. Cut while warm. Enjoy!

Vanessa's Old Time Oyster Stew

Submitted by Wendy Jahnke

A favorite stew at Christmas time, so perfect for Vanessa's Miracle story.

<u>Ingredients:</u>
  1 gallon milk
  ¾ stick butter
  ½ tsp. pepper
  2 small cans oysters

1. Pour milk and both cans of oysters into pot.

2. Once milk is warm, add butter and pepper. Stir until boiling.

3. Remove from heat and cover for 15 minutes.

Enjoy!

Vanessa's Sweet as Blood Meatballs

Submitted by Heather Brandt

A delicious, blood-like sauce that Vanessa would love in Miracle.

<u>Ingredients:</u>
     1 lb. uncooked ground beef
     1 egg
     1 ¼ cups bread crumbs
     2 tsp. allspice
     2 tsp. ground cloves
     1 can pineapple chunks or rings
     24-oz bottle ketchup
     1 cup of brown sugar

1. In a mixing bowl, add ground beef, egg, allspice, ground cloves, breadcrumbs, and quarter of pineapple juice (save rest of pineapple juice for later). I usually mix by hand, but you may do this however you like. Add more breadcrumbs, if necessary, to make sure meat will stick together for meatballs.

2. After everything is mixed, spray pan with cooking spray. Make meatballs to desired sizes and cook on medium heat until outsides are completely brown.

3. While meatballs are cooking you will make the sauce. In another mixing bowl, pour the rest of the pineapple juice, brown sugar, and ketchup. Mix together and add brown sugar or ketchup as necessary to achieve your preferred sweetness in sauce.

4. Once meatballs are cooked on the outside, add sauce to pan and let simmer for 15-20 minutes, covered. This should cook the meatballs the rest of the way on the inside.

I normally serve this with beef rice, corn, and sweet Hawaiian rolls.

Snow Dusted Poffertjes (Tiny Pancakes)

Submitted by Jessie deSchepper

These are a yummy treat that are sold on street corners here in the Netherlands to warm you up during the Christmas season, or something lovely to come home to after a day of shopping. Dorian would love them.

Ingredients:
>   ½ cup self-raising flour
>   2 eggs
>   ¾ cup milk
>   salt
>   dairy butter
>   1 Tbsp. vanilla sugar
>   Icing sugar (powdered sugar)

1. Mix the flour, eggs, sugar, milk and a little salt to a smooth batter

2. Put the pancakes cast iron pan (poffertjespan) on the stove slowly, to warm up. If this is done too fast, the plate will not be uniformly heated, making for poor baking results.

3. When the pan reaches normal operating temperature, you place in each cup a little melted butter, then you can pour batter in it.

4. Bake the poffertjes until brown and then flip.

5. On each serving of about 10 pieces, add a knob of butter, and lay thick dust of icing sugar.

Vanessa's Veggie Treat

Submitted by Debbie Poole (the faerie)

A vegetable side dish for a Christmas meal. This is an alternative to vegetables with a meal.

Ingredients:
   Large cabbage leaves, green cabbage is best (2 per person)
   Other vegetables you enjoy

1. If using carrots or sprouts, boil for 5 minutes first. I use parboiled carrots and sprouts with sweet corn in one parcel, and broccoli and cauliflower in the other. The choice is yours.

2. Put enough vegetables in each cabbage leaf to make a fat parcel without it splitting.

3. Fold in the top and bottom then the sides. Secure with cocktail sticks.

4. Steam the parcels for 7 minutes if you like your vegetables with a crunch, 10 minutes for softer veggies.

5. Remove the cocktail sticks and serve.

To make a little difference, you can add spices/herbs to the parcels before steaming.

I have had them with curried sprouts. Very nice.

Blossom's Magical Christmas Jam Pop Up's

Submitted by Char Wilcoxson

These delicious flaky pastries have always been my favorite thing to look forward to at Christmas. My sister would always make sure to make plenty of apricot and raspberry filled ones just for me. I figured that since Blossom was the baker, these would be a fitting cookie for her to make for the family. They pop up like magical tasty treats!

Ingredients (can be doubled to make more):
    1 cup real butter
    1 ½ cups flour
    ½ cup sour cream
    Favorite jams

1. Cut butter into the flour with a pastry cutter or two knifes. Add sour cream and mix.

2. Divide in half to form two balls. Wrap them in wax paper and let chill in the refrigerator for at least 8 hours.

3. Remove from wax paper and roll out one ball at a time onto a floured cutting board. Cut into circles. (If batter becomes too sticky, return to fridge to chill for a little bit). Place circles on cookie sheet.

4. Next ,cut more circles, only this time use something smaller to cut another circle within the circle to form a ring.

5. Mix 3 Tbsp. sugar and 1 Tbsp. water to make a sugar paste. Brush this paste onto the circles that are on the cookie sheet then place the ring on top. Put one spoonful of your favorite jam into the ring.

6. Bake at 375 degrees for 20 to 25 minutes then remove and let cool.

Owen's Quick Farmhouse Fruit Cake

Submitted by Katherine Murphy

<u>Ingredients:</u>
- 8 oz self-raising flour
- 2 oz caster sugar
- 2 oz brown sugar
- 6 oz dried fruit
- 4 oz butter
- 2 eggs
- 6 Tbsp. milk
- 1 tsp. mixed spice
- Little extra sugar

1. Mix all the ingredients in a bowl.

2. Put into a cake tin and sprinkle with a little extra brown sugar (or white).

3. Pop in oven and cook till golden brown and when you poke in a knife it comes out clean.

Claire's Wonderful Winter Christmas Cake

Submitted by Claire Downes

This is a super easy Christmas cake that has been used by my family for decades. It keeps Kath and Inga distracted, leaving me time to escape and create my own kind of havoc.

<u>Ingredients:</u>

- 2 cups Self-Raising Flour
- 1 tsp. Mixed Spice
- 1 cup Margerine or butter
- 3 Tbsp. Brandy
- 2 cups Dark Muscavado Sugar
- ½ tsp. Vanilla essence
- 4 eggs
- 2 cups bag mixed dried fruit
- 2 cups glace Cherries
- Grated rind of 1 orange
- 1 Tbsp. Syrup

1. Preheat oven to 275 degrees F. Sift the flour and spice into a large bowl. Add 1 Tbsp. brandy and all of the remaining ingredients. Beat with a wooden spoon for 3–4 minutes. It helps the magic if you ask your Daemoni brethren to have a stir as well.

3. Spoon the mix into an 8-inch round, lined tin and spread level. Bake for 2-2 ½ hours.

4. Remove from oven when a stick inserted in the middle of the cake comes out clean.

5. Pour the rest of the brandy over the hot cake and leave to cool.

This cake will keep for up to 3 months, but never lasts that long! Ice when needed.

Claire and Tony's Cuddle Up Anti-Christmas Casserole

Submitted by Claire Downes

Who has loads of time for cooking? I know we have far better things to do than spend hours stood at the stove. This spicy Christmassy casserole is perfect served in bowls with a big chunk of crusty bread, and guaranteed to satisfy the biggest bear's appetite! Snuggle up and enjoy!

Ingredients:

Good quality beef, cut into large cubes (you can vary the amount depending on how many you want to feed)

2 Onions

3 cups mushrooms, cut in half

1 cup carrots, cubed

1 cup swede (rutabaga), cubed

A dash of Worcester Sauce

2 cups red wine

1 beef stock cube

1 Tbsp. English mustard powder

1 tsp. mixed herbs

2 Tbsp. Demerara (or brown) sugar

3 garlic cloves chopped

2 Tbsp. oil

Salt and pepper

2 red chiles

A handful of small potatoes, chopped in half

1. Coat the beef in the flour and some salt and pepper. Brown off in a pan with the oil.

2. Put beef and all the other ingredients in a crockpot/slow cooker or large casserole dish and cook on low for 8 hours. Use the 8 hours wisely, do something naughty!

3. Serve in bowls with a large dollop of horseradish sauce, English mustard, and a large chunk of bread on the side. Yummy. Curl up on the sofa with the man of your dreams and enjoy!

Claire's Warlock Cookies

Submitted by Claire Downes

I know, cookies you ask. What is a powerful warlock doing baking cookies? Well, these are truly magical, and are bound to enchant anyone who tastes them. I've lost count of how many of these I've made. The smarties can be substituted with anything.

Ingredients:
- ½ cup butter
- ½ cup Light muscavado (or brown) sugar
- ½ cup all-purpose flour
- ½ cup smarties (or any other sweets, chocolate, or dried fruit)

1. Heat oven to 350 degrees F.

2. Beat butter and sugar together then beat in syrup. Work in half of the flour.

3. Stir in the smarties/sweets/dried fruit and remaining flour.

4. Work together with your fingers.

5. Divide into 14 balls.

6. Place well apart on a lined baking sheet and bake for 12 minutes.

7. Take out of oven and cool on a wire rack.

Blossom's Sassy Spice Cookies

Submitted by Felicia Semmler

Soft gooey cookies that just warm the heart. They remind me of Blossom because she is always so sweet but has a spicy side that comes out. In Miracle, she was in the kitchen yet again.

Ingredients:

    2 cups of flour
    1 tsp. baking soda
    1 tsp. cinnamon
    1 tsp. cloves
    1 tsp. ginger
    ¼ tsp. salt
    ¾ cups butter
    1 cup sugar
    1 egg
    ¼ cup molasses

1. Preheat oven to 325 degrees.

2. Sift flour, baking soda, cloves, cinnamon, ginger, and salt.

3. Cream together butter and sugar then beat in egg and molasses until light and fluffy.

4. Stir in dry ingredients.

5. Shape into balls and roll in sugar.

6. Bake on a greased cookie sheet for 12-15 minutes or until done.

It Sucks To Be a Vampire Brownies

Submitted by Michele Luker

<u>Ingredients:</u>
    1 box chocolate cake mix
    1 box chocolate pudding
    1 bag of Chocolate chips

1. Make the pudding as instructed on the pudding mix.

2. Add this and the dry cake mix together.

3. Add in the whole bag of chocolate chips.

4. Bake in a pan 350 degrees for 50 minutes.

That is it. Best brownies EVER.

Dingle–Barrys: Chocolate-Dipped Peanut Butter Balls With a Kick

Submitted by Christina Silcox

Ingredients:
- 1 ½ cups creamy peanut butter
- 6 cups powdered sugar
- 1 cup butter
- 1 tsp. ground cayenne pepper
- 1 pkg. semi-sweet chocolate chips

1. Mix peanut butter, butter, powdered sugar, and cayenne pepper together in a large mixing bowl.

2. Form into 1-inch balls and place on cookie sheet lined with wax paper.

3. Chill in refrigerator for at least one hour.

4. Melt chocolate chips in a double boiler over medium heat.

5. Dip the chilled peanut butter balls completely into the melted chocolate, drain, and place on a wax paper lined cookie sheet until chocolate hardens.

Pinwheel Cookies Recipe

Submitted by Zee Hayat

Ingredients:

    ½ cup or 100g Butter

    ½ cups or 100g Granulated sugar

    2 Eggs beaten

    1 Tbsp. of vanilla extract and banana extract

    3 Tbsp. milk

    2 cups Wheat flour (all-purpose flour)

    ¼ tsp. baking powder

    4 Tbsp. cocoa powder

    2 drops of any food coloring you want

1. Preheat oven to 350 degrees. Beat the butter and sugar in a medium-sized mixing bowl until light and fluffy.

2. Divide the Mixture in Step 1 above into 2 equal parts. Add the vanilla extract into one of the halves and maybe food color if you want. Mix thoroughly then gradually stir in 1 cup of the flour mixture until evenly blended. Mix into a semi-hard dough. Make sure the dough doesn't stick to the sides of the bowl.

3. Add the cocoa powder and banana extract into the second half. Mix thoroughly, and add 1 cup of flour into the mix and make a semi-hard dough.

4. Place each dough in separate plastic bags and roll out.

5. Once rolled out individually, cut open the sides of the plastic bags with a scissors or knife and place the rolled out chocolate colored dough on top of the plain dough making sure they are perfectly

aligned on all sides. Lightly press the dough on top so it aligns with the one at the bottom.

6. Beginning on one edge, gently roll the dough into a log, so the two colors spiral inside each other. Wrap in another bag and cool in a refrigerator for about 45 - 60 minutes.

7. After the 45 - 60 minutes is up, take the log out of the refrigerator and slice to about ¼ thickness with a sharp knife.

8. Lightly grease a baking sheet, and place the sliced pinwheel dough on a baking sheet lined with parchment paper and bake in a oven for about 15 - 20 minutes.

9. Watch carefully to prevent edges from browning.

10. Remove from oven, and cool on racks.

Sheree's People Chow

Submitted by Kristie Cook

My sister-in-law Sheree was the best at making sweet treats. She loved children, especially her own and her nieces and nephews, and enjoyed the smiles they gave her when she whipped up something yummy. She's greatly missed, but she left me with many family-favorite recipes, including this one for what's usually called Puppy Chow. Sheree the were-tiger has a big heart (just like her namesake) and would probably be happy to make treats for the wolves. However, I think she would more likely call this People Chow and make this for Dorian so he could have a snack with Sasha at Christmas time.

Ingredients:
    1 stick butter
    1 box Crispix or Rice Chex cereal
    1 cup peanut butter
    1 pkg. chocolate chips
    Powdered sugar

1. Pour cereal in a large mixing bowl. Set aside.

2. Melt butter, peanut butter, and chocolate chips on stove over low heat or in microwave. Pour over cereal. Carefully mix to coat each piece of cereal without breaking them.

3. Spread pieces out on wax paper to cool.

4. Place pieces in large plastic bag and dust with powdered sugar. Shake in bag to coat.

BEVERAGES

Fairies Faithful Hot Chocolate to Hit the Spot

Submitted by Stacey Nixon

Since I love hot chocolate at Christmas and I'm a naughty faerie, I thought I'd put my fave things together.

1 large shot of Bailey's Irish Cream
A little over 5 oz (or150 mls) of heavenly Cadburys or Suchards Hot Chocolate
Topped with lots of Whipped Cream

Sprinkle the top with chocolate shavings, and maybe a flake for good measure.

Daemoni Christmas Morning Punch

Submitted by Stacey Nixon

In a flute, pour 1 shot of vodka, add cranberry juice, then champagne or cava to the top. Add a little sprig of mint.

Vanessa's Blood Red Drink

Submitted by Sue VanNort and Shelly Fenner

Vanessa may very well need this after her attempts at trying to figure out Christmas and her "secret admirer." This is very Christmassy because of the coloring and people really need a drink after dealing with shopping!

Ingredients:

    1 gallon Hawaiian Punch Fruit Juicy Red

    2 liters of 7-Up

    ½ of a fifth of vodka or whatever strength you like your fruity mixed drinks!

    Any sliced fruit you like in it

1. Mix liquids together and add fruit.

2. Allow to chill before serving.

Peanut Butter Sasha Snacks (Dog Treats)

Submitted by Jill Cruz

Tips:

Spray your spoon/spatula with Pam to keep the peanut butter from sticking to it.

Store your treats in the fridge to extend their shelf life. They also freeze well.

Recipe can be halved easily.

Ingredients:

    2 cups wheat flour

    1 cup chunky peanut butter

    1 cup 1% milk or non-fat milk

    1 tsp. baking powder

1. In a large bowl, combine flour and baking powder.

2. Add in the milk, then peanut butter.

3. Knead all ingredients together in bowl.

4. On a floured surface, roll out the mixture until about ¼-inch thick.

5. Cut out shapes using cookie cutters or cut into strips.

6. Place on ungreased baking sheet and bake at 375 degrees for about 20 minutes, or until golden brown.

New Year's Stories & Recipes

Resolutions

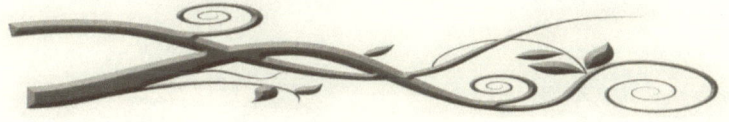

This first short story for New Year's, *Resolutions*, is a silly little tale giving a glimpse into the lives of witches on both sides of the Good and Evil line. There are a couple of characters you'll recognize from other holiday stories, but otherwise, these are new to the Soul Savers world. It was written with tongue-in-cheek, something fun and pointless to get you in the celebratory mood. It has absolutely no place in the main series.

Chapter 1

Christina stared out the apartment window, where a naked tree stood covered in snow, but she didn't see it. The city bustled below, car horns honking and people yelling "Happy New Year" at each other, but she didn't hear it. Her mind was elsewhere: Back on a warm, sunny beach in Florida where she'd had the pleasure of celebrating Thanksgiving with part of the royal family. The food had been great and the company amazing—thinking of Tristan made her lick her lips—but her mind had been stuck ever since on one little thing. Miss Alexis had referred to her as a warlock.

She was a witch.

She tapped the pen against her lip, her elbows on the table in the dining area of the apartment she shared with another witch, and contemplated why Miss Alexis would think she was a warlock. Her magic was strong, but she descended straight from the Salem witches, one of the strongest covens in the world. Her family had converted to Amadis in the centuries since then, but their magic never weakened. Did Miss Alexis sense her strong power and assume that made her a warlock?

"It certainly wasn't my fighting ability," Christina muttered out loud. That day had been the first time she'd ever truly fought the Daemoni, and she wasn't exactly the greatest warrior. She'd never been trained to use magic as a weapon. That's what warlocks did, not witches and wizards. Warlocks were the fighters, and she most certainly wasn't one. So why did Miss Alexis believe she was?

That had been the question on her mind for over a month, and she couldn't help but wonder if Miss Alexis saw something in her that she'd never seen in herself. She'd always avoided conflict in the past. She'd only jumped in that day because everyone else had been fighting for their lives, and she couldn't simply stand back and watch.

She'd used instinct and the bit of knowledge she had to defend herself and the other Amadis. But what if she could have done more?

War with the Daemoni was coming, Christina knew, and the Amadis needed all the soldiers they could get. Could she be a soldier? Is that what Miss Alexis saw in her? Could she be more than a bystander in this war? Few Amadis would be able to get away with no fighting at all. The coming war would require them all to contribute, but Christina had always imagined she and Kate, her roommate, and the rest of their coven would be more involved behind the scenes. Doing things like enchanting weapons and protective gear, helping with communications, concocting potions and special brews—those things that kept you safely off the battlefield. She'd never imagined herself on the front lines.

But what if she could be?

"What are you doing?" Kate asked from the doorway into her room. She leaned against the frame and detangled her dirty blond hair with her fingers as she studied her roommate.

"Writing my New Year's Resolutions," Christina answered.

"Oh! That sounds like fun," Kate said, and she bounded over to Christina's bed and plopped onto it. "So what are they?"

Christina made a face as she looked down at her paper. "Um . . . well . . . "

Kate sprang to her feet and crossed the room to stand behind Christina and look over her shoulder. "Well, those should be easy to accomplish. At least you're not setting yourself up for failure."

The page remained blank. Christina thought about saying she used invisible ink so no one could see them—weren't resolutions supposed to be kept private otherwise they wouldn't come true? Wait, those were birthday wishes. She was pretty sure you were actually supposed to share your resolutions so someone could hold you accountable. And if she couldn't trust Kate, a close friend and her roomie for three years, who could she trust?

"So do you want to lose weight and get into shape?" Kate asked as she moved back to the bed.

Christina spun around in her chair and shot daggers at her roommate from her brown eyes. "Are you calling me fat?"

Kate's blue eyes widened. "Oh, no. Sorry. I was just trying to think what resolutions the Normans usually make. Isn't that one of them? You need ideas, right?"

"Yeah, but . . . not like that."

She hadn't told Kate about Miss Alexis thinking she was a warlock and how her thoughts always went back to that day on the beach, but she finally spilled. She told her all about the battle and even how a thrill had run through her belly when she went one-on-one with a Daemoni wizard and beat him.

"I want to learn to fight," she finished.

Kate's face brightened up. "It's about time! I've been wanting to do the same but . . . " She trailed off, her attention suddenly diverted to something on her jeans. Her fingers picked at it for a long moment before she finally looked back up at Christina. "I was kind of afraid to do it on my own. Our coven hasn't been into that for over a century."

"Some of them had seen enough violence during the trials," Christina defended before adding, "But war is coming. It's time we remembered who we are."

She felt more empowered already simply by sharing her true feelings with someone else. And Kate's reaction had certainly helped.

Her roommate straightened her back and nodded. "So what do we need to know to be Amadis soldiers?"

"Well, of course, we need to learn the best spells to use in a fight."

"Obviously." Kate flicked her hand toward the paper in front of Christina. "Write that down."

The pen lifted and began scrawling across the paper on its own.

"We need to look for potential converts," Kate said. "That's part of being a soldier—getting Daemoni to convert, right?"

Christina nodded, and the pen wrote out that resolution.

"We need to stop avoiding conflict all the time and depending on others like the vamps to defend us," she said. "We need to be willing to stand up and fight whenever and wherever."

"But we need to learn the fine line of mercy, too," Kate added. "That's the Amadis way."

"Right."

The girls reviewed their list of resolutions.

"We can add to it if we think of anything," Christina said. "It's not quite New Year's yet."

Kate glanced at the clock. "Seven hours and three minutes to go. Plenty of time to help me decorate for the party."

"I can't believe you waited until the last minute," Christina grumbled as she pulled her light brown hair into a ponytail.

"Oh, please. It's only five o'clock. Eight fifty-nine would be the last minute."

Christina followed Kate out the door, and they walked down the block and onto the university campus where they both attended Norman college. It was important, their elders said, for them to learn all about Norman ways, especially people in their generation. They had to know who they protected and why. So after many years in mage school, here they were, taking more classes they didn't need while learning how to blend in and live among the Normans.

They weren't the only mages—or Supernaturals—to attend college there. And not all who did were on the good side.

"Maybe we should invite those witches from chemistry class," Christina suggested as they entered the student union where Kate's party would be held. "Kath and Inga, I think their names are."

"The *Daemoni* witches?" Kate asked, her voice a bit screechy, which happened when she freaked out. "Are you crazy?"

"Aren't you the one who said we needed to learn mercy? And I think it was also you who said we need to look for potential converts."

"It's not the New Year yet," Kate pointed out.

Christina peered at her friend. "Are you serious about all of this? Are you going to do it with me or not?"

Kate blew out a breath, sending a stray lock of hair up into the air. "All right, all right. Fine. We'll invite them to the party."

"They can't be all bad anyway, right? I mean, they go to *college*. If they were deep into the Daemoni, they wouldn't bother with such mundane stuff, would they?"

"We can only hope."

Chapter 2

Kath pushed one hand through her brown curls as she paged through her spell book, looking for something interesting. She didn't know what, just . . . something. Interesting. She was bored out of her damn mind and needed a distraction. Her best friend and roommate had disappeared a week ago, on the eve of anti-Christmas. She'd heard from Claire since then, of course, but *what* she'd heard had Kath's insides all twisted up.

"Okay, I admit it. I envy Claire," she said as she slammed the book shut. No potions or spells or other magical mayhem caught her interest.

Inga looked up from the pot of boiling brew on the stove and blew a blond strand out of her face. "Me, too. I want a man like that."

Kath laughed. "Yeah, a sexy one like that were-bear would be just fab. But I envy her boldness, too. How she ignored everyone else and did what she wanted. I want to do more of that!"

Inga stirred her concoction, and Kath thought her other roommate and best friend was ignoring her, but then Inga waved the wooden spoon in the air and pointed it at Kath. "You should make that a resolution."

"A what?"

"A New Year's Resolution. You know, like the Normans do. They make these promises to themselves that they'll be better people, lose weight, manage their money better, blah, blah, blah."

Kath let out an exaggerated yawn. "Sounds utterly boring. Why would I want to do that?"

"You don't have to make yours boring. You do whatever *you* want to do. Whatever you want to accomplish in the New Year."

"So 'do what I want to do more often' is a resolution?"

"Sure. Why not?" Inga dropped the spoon in the pot and opened the junk drawer in the kitchen. She pulled out a scrap piece of paper and a pen and tossed them to Kath. "Here. Write them down so you don't forget. I'll do them with you."

Kath wrote down their first resolution, then a second. "Number two: Find a man who lasts all night."

She read it out loud as she wrote, and Inga snorted.

"All night? Is that realistic?"

"According to the last I heard from Claire, yes, totally realistic. She and Tony apparently can't stop."

Inga let out a sigh. "Life is so unfair." She turned the burner on the stove off, then came around the counter to join Kath at the little round dinette table. "So what's number three?"

"Do a Random Act of Evil at least once a day. They shouldn't be only for anti-Christmas, right?"

"Good one," Inga agreed. "And how about 'torture more Amadis'? We don't give them near enough hell. They dare to hover over us right on our own campus."

"It's not like they've even tried to stop us," Kath pointed out.

"We're just too good at hiding ourselves."

Kath drummed her fingers on the table. "That's part of our problem, you know. We're Daemoni. Claire's right. We need to be more evil, especially with Lucas calling for war. I think he has something big planned, and we need to be ready."

She wrote down "Torture more Amadis" and then added another: "Bring more Normans to the vampire nest."

"It's time to up our game," she explained. "We miss half the house parties around campus where there are prime targets for the vamps. They've already told us they need new recruits to turn. It's the only thing we can do to help boost the Daemoni's numbers."

"We could have babies," Inga suggested, but then she shuddered. "Ugh. I'm so not ready for that."

"I could do it," Kath said, and her eyes glossed over as she fell into a daydream. "I'd be good and grouchy while pregnant. I could get away with casting all kinds of hexes and blame it on hormones. And I'd be the best witch-mother after it was born. I'd teach it magic as soon as it could hold a wand."

Inga chuckled.

"Are you laughing at me?" Kath asked.

"Maybe. Did you hear yourself? We hardly ever use wands. Babies aren't its. And first, you need a man."

"That goes all night," Kath reminded her, and her mind went back to Claire. She missed her other roommate. It was easy to admit her envy because that was something to be proud of. But missing someone meant she was too attached.

"Don't worry," Inga said with a sigh. "I miss her, too. Who cares if it's not very Daemoni like? We can't cut off all our emotions. We're witches, not vamps. We have a lot of human in us."

Kath clucked her tongue. "Don't say such horrid things! We have to overcome that if we're going to be the best damn Daemoni we can be."

"The *best* damn Daemoni?"

"Yes, the best! In fact, *that* should be our resolution. Just that one covers everything."

Inga snatched the scrap paper away before Kath could scratch out their resolutions or ball it up. "These give us ideas on how to do that. Reminders so we stay on track."

She got up and walked over to the refrigerator, where she stuck the resolutions with a magnet. Then she put her hands on her hips, cocked her head and grunted.

"What?" Kath asked.

Inga grabbed the paper off the fridge, scrunched it up and tossed it in the trash can. "I realized just how ridiculously Norman that was. As if we need to be reminded how to be bad."

"It was your idea," Kath said.

"I deserve to be spanked for such stupidity. I wonder if there are any were-bears up for the job?"

"Claire did mention brothers . . . "

Inga spun, her hands still on her hips, and glared at her roommate. "And you didn't say this before because—"

Kath didn't have a chance to boast her selfish tendencies, because an envelope appeared in the air at that moment right in front of her and fell to the table. Inga rushed over as Kath snapped it up and tore it open. Then she let out a howl of laughter before handing the card that was inside to Inga.

The other witch read the writing and broke into laughter, as well.

"Those Amadis witches . . . are inviting . . . *us* . . . to their *party*?" Kath gasped between hoots. "What . . . the hell?"

Inga straightened up and tried to control her giggles as she shook her head with befuddlement. "No idea." Her turquoise eyes widened and a glint of mischief passed through them. "We should go, though."

"Seriously? Can you say *boring*?"

"I bet it won't be. Not if we make it exciting."

Kath bolted upright in her seat. "Oh, I like your thinking! Unless . . . do you think it's a trap?"

Inga tapped the invitation against her lips as she considered this. "It could be, but I doubt it. Knowing them, they probably invited a bunch of Normans, too, so they wouldn't dare blow their cover. But we'll let our vamp nest know, just in case."

"What if they attack the party?"

Inga shrugged then grinned evilly. "What if they do? That will just make it all the more interesting for us."

Chapter 3

"You've been awfully quiet," Christina observed as she and Kate finished decorating the room for the New Year's Eve party. With a little bit of magic, they hadn't taken long to finish, leaving them plenty of time to go home and get ready. "The party will be great. You aren't nervous, are you?"

Kate flicked her hand to hang the last streamer. "I wasn't until you decided to invite the Daemoni witches. What were we thinking, anyway?"

Christina looped her arm around her roommate's and pulled her toward the door. Their jobs here were done. "We were thinking about being better Amadis. It was brave of us to invite them. We could have new converts by the time the clock strikes midnight."

"Or we could have a lot of dead guests."

"They wouldn't!"

Kate tilted her head to peer at her roommate as if she were stupid. "They're Daemoni. Why wouldn't they?"

"Well . . ." Christina sputtered. "Because . . . they have all kinds of opportunities every day, right? So why would the party be any different? I honestly don't think they're like that. They're trying to fit into the Norman world, so maybe they despise being Daemoni."

"Or maybe you're being a little too optimistic," Kate muttered.

The girls stepped outside and immediately tugged their coats tighter around themselves as the icy outdoor air blasted into them. They walked across campus in silence, their bodies bent slightly against the wind. Most students were still home for the semester break, so hardly anyone walked the grounds, making the campus feel a bit like a ghost town.

"They probably won't even show," Christina said once they were on their street. "As cold as it is, we'll be lucky if anyone shows."

"Maybe we should alert our local vamp nest just in case they do come," Kate suggested.

They paused at the front door to their apartment building.

"No," Christina said as she tugged the door open and held it for Kate. "We resolved to be brave, right? To not rely on the vamps to protect us all the time. Besides, we'll be fine. I'm sure of it."

"I changed my mind," Kate said. She stopped on the fifth step and looked over her shoulder, down at her roomie. "You're not overly optimistic. You're freakin' naive!"

Christina rolled her eyes, but as she climbed the stairs to their third-floor apartment, she couldn't help but wonder if Kate had a point. Maybe she'd had a little too much bravado when she sent the invitation. Maybe inviting Daemoni to their party wasn't such a great idea. Actually, the more she thought about it, the more she realized just how stupid the idea was. Memories from the fight on Captiva Island right before Thanksgiving flashed through her mind. She'd been visiting friends when all hell broke loose—literally. Those Daemoni had been fierce. Relentless. Merciless. How could she be stupid enough to believe the witches who went to school here were any better?

Except they weren't relentless or fierce. Christina knew there was a Daemoni vamp nest in the area, Were packs on the outskirts, and a witch coven on the other side of the city. She'd heard stories and rumors about attacks. But the university campus had remained relatively safe—no worse than any other school the size of theirs. She'd never heard of anything extremely unusual that could indicate a Daemoni attack. Normans usually chalked such occurrences up to animal attacks, suicides, runaways, and other logical explanations that their minds could accept, but Christina hadn't even heard of any of those on or near campus. She had to believe that these two witches may have been born Daemoni, but weren't truly evil. And she could even hope they might want to change their allegiances.

She'd nearly had herself convinced that she'd been right about inviting them by the time the party started. And at first, she and Kate seemed to have had nothing to worry about. The Daemoni witches were no-shows. They likely had better plans than spending New Year's Eve at a Norman party hosted by Amadis on school property. Both girls relaxed and began to enjoy the festivities, dancing, eating and drinking, and chatting with classmates.

It wasn't until ten minutes before midnight when chaos began.

☙

"Why don't we go inside?" Kath asked Inga as they huddled outside a window of the student union.

"We will. But this is more fun right now," Inga said. "Watch."

She peered through the window at the party inside, murmured a silent spell, and flicked her hand. All of the soda cans throughout the room exploded, spraying sticky, carbonated liquid like fountains. Kath laughed, then waved her own hand in the air. Every unused chair in the room fell on its back, creating quite a clatter. Everyone inside froze. A couple of Norman girls shrieked. Inga made the lights flash several times before blacking them out for good. More Normans screamed.

The Amadis witches—one with long, dirty-blonde hair and the other with shorter, light brown hair—stood on the dance floor, their eyes searching for the culprits.

"They know we're here," Kath said.

"Well . . . they invited us, didn't they?" Inga asked. "Their mistake."

"And our bonus," said a female voice from behind them.

Kath spun, her heart leaping into her throat. Two of the vampires from the nest they helped stood behind them. Jewels, tall and dark-headed, and Mindy, with short blond hair, also peeked into the window.

"No," Kath whispered. "You guys can't be here."

"Why not?" asked Jewels.

"You'll ruin our cover," Inga pointed out.

"Then maybe you shouldn't have told us about it," Mindy said. She grinned. Her fangs were already completely out. Kath and Inga remembered bringing her to the nest last New Year's Day after finding her at a party she had no business being at. They'd always wondered if the girl would make it as a Daemoni vamp, but the answer now seemed to be clear. "It's my vamp birthday, and I want to celebrate. This looks perfect."

"No!" Inga said, and she blasted a spell at them to ward them off. "We'll keep you out if we have to."

Jewels, who'd flown into a bush ten yards away, jumped to her feet and sauntered back over to them, her eyes flashing angry red. "That's not a good idea, little witch. You know what you're supposed to do. Now get out of our way."

Three more vampires emerged from the shadows surrounding them. A clock in the distance began to chime in the New Year. Kath and Inga exchanged a look.

This wasn't exactly what they'd had planned. They'd hoped to cause a little of their own mayhem and to put those two Amadis bitches in their place. But who were they to argue with the vamps? If they wanted to be real Daemoni—the best damn Daemoni they could be—unleashing vampires on the Amadis party couldn't have been more ideal. They'd start the New Year, and their Resolutions, with a bang.

Chapter 4

Inga and Kath led the way, blasting the doors to the party room open. Normans screamed again. A pink light shot across the room, but Inga raised her hand and blocked the spell. The Amadis witches were ready for a fight. Maybe this had been a trap after all. Letting the vamps in wasn't such a bad idea.

When the vampires tried to attack the Normans, though, they bounced off invisible bubbles surrounding the humans. The witches had shielded them. Inga and Kath shot spells at their Amadis counterparts, and pink and purple lights returned in answer. One blasted into Kath and her curly brown hair went up in flames. A twist of her hand put the fire out but not before it had singed most of her hair.

"Take care of them!" Inga yelled at Jewels, Mindy, and the other vampires.

"They're shielded," Jewels hissed back. "You take care of that, and we'll gladly do our thing."

The Normans all huddled in a corner, their eyes wide, the smell of fear pouring off of them, making the vampires even hungrier. The two Amadis witches stood in front of the Normans in fighting stances. They weren't warlocks, but they obviously weren't going to back down. They really were ready to fight.

Inga and Kath weren't warlocks, either. They'd never really had to fight the Amadis before. Nobody had ever tried to stop their magical antics, so they weren't quite prepared for this. But the vampires were growing angry and excited. Inga could imagine the saliva dripping from their fangs. She and Kath had to do something, or the vamps could easily come after them. The bloodsuckers weren't exactly creatures that could be easily controlled or dominated.

Kath grasped Inga's hand and tightened her grip. "We're the best damn Daemoni we can be. We can do this!"

Inga nodded, and they pooled their power together, preparing to unleash a nasty string of spells on the Amadis and the Normans they protected.

ℭↄ

"Are we going to have mercy on them?" Kate asked when she and Christina saw the two Daemoni witches before them revving up their powers.

"Screw that!" Christina said. "We're going to fight!"

She pushed her hand out and threw a spell at the witches, not waiting to be attacked first. Pink and purple lights zinged across the room, clashing with blue and yellow from the Daemoni witches. Sparks exploded in the air. A blue light soared at Christina. She ducked and rolled, came up on one knee and shot her own spell. Yellow and blue entwined together now and zoomed for Kate. Both Amadis witches deflected it. The spell ricocheted and blasted out a window. The glass shattered, Normans screamed from behind them, and a gust of freezing wind blew in.

The vampires apparently thought this was their sign to attack, but Christina and Kate kept their shields around the Normans. How were they ever going to get them out of this? How stupid to invite evil into their lives like this! Christina vowed to protect the Normans at all costs. That was their number one job.

The vampires encircled them, threatening them, but as long as they kept up the shields, they'd be okay. The Daemoni witches moved in closer. Since they couldn't break the protective bubbles around the Amadis and the Normans, they decided to destroy everything else in sight. Tables and chairs exploded into nothing but splinters of wood. More windows blew out. The very carpet under their feet waved and rolled, knocking the Normans off their feet.

"We need to get them out of here," Christina whispered to Kate, indicating the Normans.

Kate looked at her with a brow raised. "Got any ideas how?"

Christina shook her head, but then an idea occurred to her. "Turn their spells on the vampires. That's how I beat the wizard in Florida—I turned his spells back on him. We can do this!"

They both inhaled a breath and nodded, then focused on the yellow and blue lights flying through the air. Pink and purple intercepted them. The lights exploded in mid-air and more sparks rained down. The Daemoni spells bounced back to the vampires, blasting them in the heads and chests, causing chunks of stony flesh to break and shatter.

"Screw this!" a blond female said as a piece of her shoulder was blasted away. "I'm out of here!"

"You two will pay for this," said another female, dark haired, to the Daemoni witches. She held a piece of her nose in her hand. "Wait for me, Minz!"

The vampires began to run. Soon only the witches remained. Their eyes grew wide as Christina and Kate advanced on them. They shot feeble spells, but Christina easily parried them, causing more explosions of light and sparks. Christina and Kate joined hands, mimicking the move the other two had done earlier to combine their powers. The Daemoni witches looked at each other and shook their heads.

"Should we show mercy now?" Kate asked.

"I don't know that they deserve it," Christina said. "Unless . . . do you two want to convert?"

The witches both scrunched their faces. "Hell, no!" they said in unison.

Christina scrutinized the Daemoni witches in front of her. She'd been wrong about them. She knew now they worked with their own local vamp nest. She wondered how many Normans they'd taken from campus, either to turn or even to feed. She didn't know what she should do at the moment, and, apparently, Kate wasn't quite sure either. Amadis were supposed to show mercy, but what harm would they be allowing if they let these two go?

She sauntered closer to the two witches. "We *have* to have mercy."

"And that will be your downfall," spat one of the Daemoni, the one with the blond hair and freaky turquoise eyes.

"Oh, don't worry," Kate said. "We'll be watching you closely from now on."

"That's right," Christina added. "One wrong move, and we won't be so nice next time."

"For now, you better take the chance we're giving you."

The two Amadis witches raised their hands at their enemies. With another exchanged glance, the Daemoni disappeared.

Christina blew out a breath of relief. She'd done it! She'd stood up to the Daemoni again. She'd taken a huge risk, yes, but that was part of being an Amadis soldier.

"It'll take time, but we'll get this warrior thing down," she said to Kate.

Kate bumped her with her shoulder. "Nicely done."

"Yeah, that was awesome!" yelled one of the Norman guys.

The witches hadn't noticed until now that the Normans had all come out from the corner where they'd been huddled together.

"Nice show," said another girl, clapping her hands together. "I've never seen indoor fireworks like that."

The others broke into applause, too. Christina and Kate stared at the partygoers for a long moment, not believing what they saw. They weren't scared anymore. They didn't even realize their lives had been in danger. They thought the fight had been a performance!

"Um . . . Happy New Year?" Christina said.

"Happy New Year!" Everyone yelled.

Christina and Kate weren't sure what the New Year would bring now, but they did know one thing for certain: They'd better get to work on those resolutions right away if tonight was any indication of the coming year.

Fervor

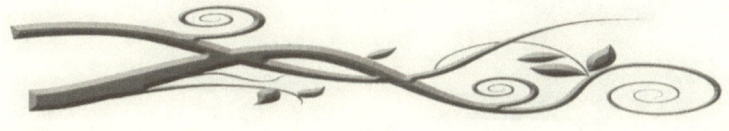

This next tale introduces a couple of new characters and also brings in some you've already met. With a conflict between brain and heart, a dash of faerie mischief, and a masquerade ball like nothing in the earthly realm, this little story is loosely based on a love story familiar to all little girls. I hope you enjoy it as much I loved writing it. This story has nothing to do with the main series, but who knows . . . maybe we'll see Jessie and Jack again in the future.

Chapter 1

Being a were-panther is pretty cool . . . except when you're in love with a werewolf.

That was the story of Jessie's life. At least, her more recent life, since the day some werewolves found her starving in the Georgia woods six months ago. The Daemoni were-panther who had bitten her and caused her change had disappeared long before, leaving her to die at the ripe old age of nineteen. Lucky for her, Sundae's pack took her in and converted her to Amadis. She had a job at Sundae's bar and a place to live, and although she'd never really be part of the pack, she had friends. Or, at least, people who knew and accepted exactly what she was and still let her hang around. Life was better than it'd been a year ago and she'd be forever indebted to Sundae, but it was still far from perfect. Especially when she could never have the only guy who'd ever made her knees tremble and her stomach turn flips.

"Hey, Jack, what are your plans for tonight?" asked Gray, one of the pack members and Sundae's younger brother. He sat at the bar with his new girlfriend, Rissa, who also worked there now. Jessie envied their relationship, but as soon as her mind would wish a wolf had bitten her instead of a panther so she could be a member of the pack, she'd shudder and gag at the thought of being a *dog*.

Her ears perked up to hear Jack's answer. Of course, her ears always turned to him when he was in the room so she wouldn't miss a word. His voice alone sent pleasurable shivers up her spine. Looking at him didn't hurt either, with his dark hair and contrasting blue eyes.

"I don't know yet," Jack answered as he eyed the cue ball on the pool table while leaning on his stick, looking like a model posing in a tight black t-shirt and jeans. Jessie's gaze lingered on his hands—big yet steady and talented. She knew this because he did most of the pack's tattoos. "I haven't heard of any parties this year. Guess everyone has other plans for New Year's Eve."

"Did you get the invite to the big ball?" Gray asked.

Jack chuckled. "I guess there's that party. What's up with that anyway? Who does *balls* these days?"

"Well . . ." Rissa started, and Jessie giggled, knowing where the only other female's mind had gone—straight into the gutter. They were often worse than the guys. That's what she liked about Rissa and Sundae. No girly pretensions about them.

Gray chuckled and shook his head at his girlfriend.

"I love your dirty mind," he said before leaning in to kiss her jaw.

"Seriously, dude," Jack said, ignoring their PDA. "A ball sounds so . . . Cinderella-y."

"It's a faerie thing," Gray said. "You know how they are."

"Which is exactly why I won't be going," Jack said as he bent over the table and made his shot. "It's not safe for single guys."

"Good thing I have Rissa now," Gray said with a sappy grin. "But come on, dude, you never know who you might meet there."

Jack's eyes slid over to Jessie, but jumped away when he saw she was watching him.

"With the faeries, though, you don't know if the vibes you're getting are real or another of their games," he said.

"Not all the girls going are faeries," Rissa said as she twirled a dark lock around her finger. "You'll know they're real if she's not one. You're going, aren't you, Jessie?"

Jessie's eyes widened when the conversation spotlight turned on her. She hadn't expected anyone to care what she was doing to bring in the New Year tonight.

"Um, no, I don't think so," she said as she scrubbed her rag on a non-existent spot on the bar.

"Aw, you should. I need someone sane to keep me company," Rissa said.

Jessie cleared her throat. "I think I'll just stay here, in case anyone comes in."

"I'm pretty sure everyone's going to the faerie ball," Gray said.

"Doesn't seem like something a wolf pack would want to do," Jessie muttered, forgetting they all had just as good of hearing as she did.

"The faeries call it a ball, but it's really a big party," Gray said, "and we don't ever miss a good party. Right, Jack?"

Jack didn't answer, but banked another shot instead. The red stripe dropped into the pocket.

"I'm not letting it go," Gray persisted. "Everyone will be there. And not everyone's lucky enough to meet the girl of their dreams in the woods like I did. Yours just might be at that party tonight."

Jack leveled him with a glare. "Who says I haven't found my mate already?" he deadpanned.

Jessie's stomach sank at this rhetorical question. She hadn't noticed any of the signs that he'd found his life's mate, and she suspected he was only trying to get Gray off his back, but just the idea of Jack being with anyone else made her queasy. She'd have to accept it at some point, so she could only hope she'd find her own life's mate before he did. She didn't think that very likely, though. As far as her heart was concerned, she'd already found him, even if the idea was not only preposterous but absolutely impossible. She couldn't help what she felt.

Jack, who'd been playing against himself, sank the last of the balls, and took off without so much as a goodbye to anyone. Gray and Rissa were too caught up in each other to notice, and they left shortly after. By seven o'clock, the entire bar had cleared out. Sundae hadn't asked or required it, but Jessie stayed in case anyone did decide to ditch the faerie ball and come to the pack's favorite hangout. The place felt large and lonely, but it was still better than sitting in her little studio apartment in Sundae's basement.

Especially when there was the off chance that Jack may return. After all, he'd said he wasn't going to the ball, hadn't he?

Jessie sighed as she grabbed the mop handle and steered the wheeled bucket out to the front of the bar. She really needed to get a life. She had her own invitation at home, and Sundae had tried to talk her into going to the ball. Instead, here she was, in a big, empty bar all alone with midnight only a few short hours away and pining for a guy she could never have. But a faerie ball? She couldn't fathom herself there, and being surrounded by faeries as a single lady wasn't exactly a bright idea. No, she was better off here, alone. At least she'd have no regrets in the morning.

By the time she finished mopping the floor, she knew Sundae and Gray had been right: Nobody was coming to the bar tonight. She lay on her back on the pool table and stared at the ceiling, debating whether to hang around anyway—they may come in after midnight, looking for something to eat in their drunken state, she thought—or to go home and snuggle up in bed with a good book.

"Aren't you coming to my party?" asked a female voice, making Jessie jump so high, she clung to the ceiling.

Chapter 2

Jessie retracted her claws and dislodged herself from the foam ceiling tiles. She landed on her feet and wiped her hands on her pants as she took in the newcomer. Long purple and black hair, smaller than Jessie who was a petite thing herself, and smelling like faerie. She wore a tight-fitting black dress that barely covered her ass and sheer black tights with stiletto heels. Jessie suddenly felt ugly and underdressed in her t-shirt and torn blue jeans, her chestnut hair pulled into a sloppy ponytail.

"I'm sorry. I wasn't expecting anyone," she said as polite as she could muster.

"Of course you aren't. They're all at my party. And I was wondering why you're not there."

Jessie had been walking toward the bar, but she stopped and looked at the woman whose brown eyes glinted with faerie mischief. Her age was difficult to discern—she was a faerie after all—but she looked to be in her early twenties.

"It's not exactly my kind of thing," Jessie said.

"Oh, please," the faerie scoffed. "It's a *faerie* ball. It's everyone's thing!"

Jessie's hands went to her hips. "If it's your party, why aren't *you* there?"

"It's not just mine, of course. There are lots of faeries there to ensure everything is okay. Don't worry. Nobody will miss me . . . as long as I don't stay too long."

Jessie stared, waiting for her to announce what she needed so she could get back to her party. "Well . . . what can I do for you?"

"You can come to my party."

Jessie rolled her eyes. "I told you. It's not my thing. *Faeries* aren't my thing."

The faerie stuck her bottom lip out and gave Jessie puppy-dog eyes. When Jessie didn't give in, the faerie put on a big smile and held her hand out.

"Let's start over, okay? I'm Becca. It's nice to meet you, Jessie."

"You already know my name?"

"Well, yes, silly. I came here to get you."

Jessie huffed a breath of exasperation then continued her walk behind the bar.

"Why?" she demanded as she turned to face Becca, who had sauntered up to the other side. "Why are you so adamant about me coming to your party? Why do you want someone there who obviously doesn't want to be there?"

Becca giggled. "Trust me, once you get there, you'll definitely be glad you came. Your presence is missed, and not just by me. All the Amadis are there. Including someone . . . special."

Becca's body twisted side to side as she clasped her hands in front of her and batted her inch-long eyelashes. Jessie's eyes narrowed, and she opened her mouth to speak.

"I suggest you reconsider before rejecting this offer," Becca cut in, her voice less sweet and more threatening.

Jessie let out a sarcastic laugh. "The last thing I need is a favor from a faerie."

"Oh, this isn't from a faerie. Yes, it comes from the Otherworld, but not from the faerie realm." Becca tilted her head, her brows raised and her dark eyes challenging.

Jessie's breath caught. If not from the faerie realm but from the Otherworld, the only two options were Heaven and Hell.

Becca smiled when she saw that her message had gotten through to Jessie. "Trust me. It's good. So . . . " The faerie reached over the bar and grabbed Jessie's hand. "We need to get you ready!"

Jessie knew better than to trust a faerie, but she also knew better than to ignore anything sent from Heaven or Hell. If the Demons or the Angels had something for her, they'd find a way to deliver it, and if it did happen to be from Hell, she certainly didn't want to be alone when it came.

"I don't have anything to wear," she muttered.

"Oh, that's not a problem!" Becca appeared in front of her and waved her hands in the air. Jessie's jeans and t-shirt disappeared, replaced by black leather pants and a black tank top decorated with rows upon rows of sequins. Black boots that reached her knees and lifted her five inches on their heels replaced her Converse All-Stars. "You need a little something here, too."

Becca's fingertips brushed Jessie's cheeks, and then her hands flitted over Jessie's hair. After a few minutes, she took a step back and scrutinized Jessie as though analyzing an art project. Then she gave a sharp nod.

"Perfect!" she said with a clap of her hands. "I know you want to see, so go check yourself out."

Jessie hurried for the ladies' room, grateful that Sundae knew the need of hanging a full-length mirror in there. Her breath caught once again. She'd been afraid the faerie would have gone over the top, but Becca had made her up just right. She looked sexy as hell.

"What do you think?" Becca asked, appearing right next to her.

Jessie's eyes cut toward the faerie. "Are . . . are you my . . . faerie godmother?"

Becca's face blanched. "Oh, god, no! Do I look like such a hideous creature?"

Jessie turned to face the faerie fully. "Of course not! I don't know what a faerie godmother looks like."

"They don't even exist except in those Norman fairytales. And those make us faeries look old and grandmotherly." Becca shook herself as though a shudder ran through her.

"Okay, then . . . are you trying to earn your wings or something?"

This time Becca snorted. At least, she made a strange little sound although Jessie didn't think faeries actually snorted.

"I'm a *faerie*, not an Angel. Not that Angels earn their wings like that anyway. What's with all the mythical accusations?"

"Why are you doing this?" Jessie demanded, cutting to the chase this time. She flipped her hands toward the mirror, indicating her new look. "Why do you insist I go to the ball?"

"I told you. It's for your own good. And believe me, you'll be glad you did." Becca grabbed Jessie's hand and held it tightly, indicating she wouldn't let go for anything. "Come on. I'll take you there."

All of the air in Jessie's lungs flew out of her as though a vacuum sucked it out. She'd never flashed before. Were-creatures needed a mage's help, and she'd never needed to do so. In fact, she'd only met a few mages in the short time she'd been a were-panther. Apparently, faeries could help her flash, too, because she no longer stood in the bar. Rather, she was outside and at the bottom of a broad stairway that led to a white, marble mansion towering over her. A heavy bass—all she could hear of the music from this vantage point—throbbed from inside and colorful lights pulsed in the windows and arched doorways. Jessie felt a sudden and dizzying need to be inside, to join the party, to have the time of her life. Everything about the place tugged at her, creating an overwhelming desire to discover all the promises held inside.

"Oh, can't forget this! It's a masquerade ball, after all." Becca waved her hand over Jessie's face, and something immediately covered it. Jessie's fingers touched it gingerly and moved to take it off. "Nuh-uh. It must stay on for the entire time you're here. Otherwise, you'll ruin the magic."

The curiosity of what the mask looked like didn't kill this cat. Needing to know what was inside that mansion just might, though. She pretty much forgot about the mask on her face as the draw to climb the stairs and join the party overcame her.

Chapter 3

As soon as Jessie entered the castle in the sky—at least, that's what the faerie palace felt like—everything changed. Her favorite music (country) played, making her body automatically move to the beat. The scent of her favorite sweets lingered in the air, and when she licked her lips, she tasted cinnamon candy on her tongue. She drifted through a haze of colored lights that made her feel as though she walked on the clouds themselves. Her senses were overcome with everything she loved as the real world slipped away.

"Aren't you glad you came?" Becca, her face now disguised by luscious purple feathers, asked from her side. The faerie took her hand and pulled her deeper into the party, where masked guests danced, their multi-colored drinks sloshing in their glasses.

Three more faeries skipped up to her and grabbed at her arms and hands. They chatted incessantly about the party, two of them with heavy British accents and the other with a southern drawl.

"We're so glad you came!" The one with the purple streaking her white hair finally acknowledged Jessie. "I'm Debbie, and this is Stacey and Lisa, and we've been waiting for you."

Jessie lifted a brow.

"Well, actually, *he's* been waiting for you." Stacey, whose white hair was feathered with bright pink in it, nodded toward a man standing in the shadows in the corner. "He doesn't know it yet, but he will."

Oh, great. They were setting her up. The faeries had brought her on a blind date! What had she done to them? She didn't owe them anything! These irate thoughts left Jessie's mind as soon as they entered, and she found herself nodding and smiling. Somewhere deep inside, she knew they were influencing her, but she couldn't fight it. To be fair, not too many people of the Earthly realm could fight the effects of faeries.

"So you just stay here, and we'll take care of it all," Lisa, the one with green hair and the southern accent, said.

"Just remember—leave the mask on or you'll ruin the magic," Becca added, and then the four of them disappeared.

A minute later, Jessie couldn't even remember speaking with them. She couldn't remember where she was or why she was there. All she knew was the music pulsing through the floor had become a part of her, and all she wanted to do was dance. She twirled in place, and when she stopped, a drink had appeared in her hand. She tossed the whole thing back, then swung around again. Now someone's hand appeared in hers.

A large one. Warm. Strong. Sending electric currents up her arm.

Another hand landed on the small of her back. More jolts of pleasure danced through her body.

Her whole being rose to a new high as she slowly looked up, noticing the broad chest and shoulders, the biceps bulging against the long-sleeve shirt, and the metal face looking down at her. It wasn't a real face, of course. His mask—black, red, and silver metal—completely covered his real features, though. A film over the eye-holes even camouflaged his eyes. But Jessie could *feel* them. Feel the pierce of them as he gazed at her, and she never wanted him to let her go.

Keeping his hold on her, he swept her to the side, spun her in place, dipped and lifted, and pushed and pulled until she was woozy with euphoria.

"I love to hear you laugh," he said as she leaned her back against his arm and giggled while he spun her around.

She didn't know if his voice was really so perfect and lovely or if it was the faerie magic messing with her senses. She didn't know if any guy could smell as good as he did. If anyone could feel so right as he held her, their bodies fitting perfectly together. She did know the only guy who'd ever made her feel this way before was . . . *What is his name?*

Some guy she knew but couldn't remember him now. She could only think of this man in her arms at this very moment, and she did know being with him was too good to be true. But she didn't care.

She relished in the moment. She delighted in his touch. She danced the night away with him, never wanting to be anywhere else but here. He hummed to the music, sometimes even sang to her as the band continued to play all of her favorite songs. He asked her questions about herself, wanting to know all of her favorite things in life. He told her how he loved the outdoors, and that he always felt most like himself when he was in the wild. Just like her. But he also told her that he'd rather be nowhere else this very moment but here with her.

"Your mask is terrific," he said at one point while they danced to a slow ballad.

Jessie laughed. "I don't even know what it looks like."

She reached to take it off to inspect what she hadn't seen yet, but a green-haired faerie flitted over to them and batted at her hand.

"No, no, no," Lisa said. "You don't want to ruin the magic now, do ya?"

Jessie smiled after the faerie danced away.

"Well, I'm glad you like it," she said to her mysterious guy. "That's saying something."

"It's perfect," he murmured, his voice near her ear, and suddenly, Jessie wanted to dispose of the masks. Of their clothes. Of everything between them. She wanted to feel his breath on her ear, taste it on her lips.

"Is it midnight yet?" she asked, her voice thick and breathy. She was excited for the New Year to start so they could leave this place, shed the masks, and truly get to know each other. Hopefully while naked.

He turned them in place, but neither noticed a clock. Once the song ended, however, the music stopped completely. Voices started rising with excitement. Someone—was that Sundae?—started a countdown. Jessie and her gentleman friend counted with them.

"Happy New Year!" they yelled with the crowd.

The band broke out into the melody for Auld Lang Syne, and everyone sang along—or tried to. Most people didn't know the exact lyrics, but the faeries made them all sound like professionals. Jessie turned to the man who had made her feel like a princess all night long and looked up at him.

Again, she couldn't see his eyes, but she could feel his gaze, a piercing all the way into her soul. He tilted his head toward her, and her lips ached for his touch. She couldn't stand it any longer. It was midnight now. Surely they could remove the masks. How else could anyone share a midnight kiss? Jessie raised her hand and gripped the edge of her mask, feeling soft fur against her fingers. She hesitated, hoping he'd remove his mask at the same time—or better, would do it before her so she could see him first. The man closed his hand over hers, though, and shook his head, but then he released it and caressed the tips of his fingers down her neck. Screw it! She would go first.

She leaned up on her toes, pressing her chest against his. Their hearts beat in unison as they tried to gaze into each other's eyes. She once again grabbed the bottom of her mask and lifted. It peeled slowly away, from chin to lips to nose to brow, and as it did, the music faded away. The lights dimmed. The sweet fragrance dissipated. The man whose face she didn't know reached out for her, but his fist closed around nothing. His image wavered and swirled, becoming nothing more than a mist.

Jessie blinked.

Darkness engulfed her. She closed her eyes again, but the darkness remained when she opened them. Her gaze darted around as her mind re-oriented itself to her surroundings.

"Shit!" she groaned.

She was in her own room, wearing the same jeans and t-shirt she'd worn to work that day.

Chapter 4

Had it really been a dream?

"No!" Jessie snapped out loud, although there was no evidence to the contrary. No fancy clothes lay on the floor or hung in the closet. No sexy hair and makeup showed in the mirror when she stopped in the bathroom. No sweet smell lingered on her skin and no taste of cinnamon on her lips or tongue. And definitely no furry mask to be found anywhere in her apartment. She'd already torn it apart, trying to disprove what was so obvious: she'd dreamt the whole thing.

But it had felt so *real*.

She didn't remember leaving the bar and coming home, but apparently she'd done just that. She glanced at the clock on her bedside table: 12:24. She'd slept right through midnight. How lame!

"Well, at least it had been a good dream," she muttered, and she threw herself on the bed, hoping that if she fell asleep, the dream would continue.

No such luck. She did fall back to sleep, but her dreams were fleeting. Snatches of the faerie ball showed, as though her mind tried to grasp the beautiful dream but couldn't bring it back to life. She woke up grumpy the next morning, glad it was a holiday so she could stay home by herself, drink coffee, and lose herself in a good book. She'd just snuggled under the covers with a mug in one hand and her ereader in the other when there was a knock on her door.

"Jessie, someone's here to see you," Sundae called to her.

Jessie considered not responding, pretending like she was still asleep, hoping Sundae—and the visitor—would go away. There was no one she'd want to see right now. Who would come to see her anyway?

Sundae knocked again. "Are you okay?"

"Um—" Jessie cleared her throat. "I don't feel well. I think I've come down with something."

The door burst open then. Jessie mewled with surprise.

"Sorry," Sundae said, "but she wouldn't take 'no' for an answer. You know how they are."

Jessie frowned at her boss and landlady, who stood in the doorway wearing her usual low-cut jeans and a tight sweater that showed off all her curves. Her straight brown, almost black, hair swung against her shoulders as she looked behind her. A small body pushed past her. A petite woman, smaller than even Jessie, with black and purple hair that hung far down her back, strode into Jessie's apartment.

"I'm not the only one looking for you," Becca, the faerie, said.

Jessie blinked. She looked at Sundae. The pack leader shrugged, but then a small smile lifted one corner of her mouth.

"Actually, I did hear something . . . " Sundae said, but she didn't finish.

"What's going on?" Jessie demanded as she placed her mug on the nightstand and dropped her ereader to the bed. "Someone needs to explain!"

She couldn't believe the faerie from her dream was standing in her very room now. She'd never even met Becca before, and here she was! And Sundae wasn't surprised by it at all.

"I'm what's going on," said a familiar male voice that made Jessie's stomach flip over. Sundae had stepped into the apartment and now Jack walked in, too.

Jessie jumped up from bed and immediately regretted it. She hadn't bothered changing out of her purple and hot-pink striped pajama bottoms and tank top. She suddenly felt naked and vulnerable and wished she'd remained under the covers.

"I . . . uh . . . don't understand." She couldn't help the stammer. She may have been in her own home, but she was completely out of her comfort zone. Jack was in her place! In her one-room place! In her *bedroom*, in other words.

"Does this, by chance, belong to you?" Jack asked, and he held up what looked like a dog's head. No, a wolf's, and only its face.

Jessie laughed, and it sounded a bit on the hysterical side. "Why would I have a wolf's face?"

"It's a mask," Jack clarified.

Jessie's brows pushed together. "Okay, a mask. You know what I am, Jack. I'd never—"

Becca, who stood behind Jack still, cleared her throat. "Well, yes, you would."

Jessie looked at the faerie. "Yes, I would what?"

"You'd wear a mask like that. In fact, you did. Last night. At my party?"

The air seemed to suck out of her lungs again, but not because she'd flashed. Her reality was crumbling all around her.

"I . . . didn't go to a party last night."

"Of course you did!" Sundae and Becca said at the same time.

"I saw you there," Sundae said. "At least, now I know it was you. I kind of thought so, but the mask threw me. Never thought I'd see a cat wearing a dog mask."

"Because I wouldn't!"

"But you did," Becca insisted. "I gave it to you, remember? And I told you that taking it off would ruin the magic. So when you removed it, we had to send you back here."

Jessie plopped down on her bed and dropped her head into her hands. "So let me get this straight. I went to the faerie ball."

"Yes. I helped you get ready, remember?"

"And I wore a wolf mask? That *you* gave me?"

"Yes."

"And why on earth would you do that to me?" This last question came through gritted teeth. She was proud to be a cat. The thought of looking like a dog, even a wolf, freaked her out.

"I was told to," Becca said. "Not my decision."

Jessie was about to ask whose it was—if all of this was true and everything that had happened last night wasn't a dream, it must have been Hell after her—but Jack stopped her by taking two steps closer. He stood in front of her now and knelt down to her eye level. He held not only her mask in his hand, but another as well. Red and black and silver metal.

"I think the wolf mask was for me, so I'd know you," he said quietly. He looked down at the masks in his hand as he continued. "I wasn't even going to go, but Gray got me to thinking when he said all the Amadis would be there. There was only one person I would want to see, but I'd been denying my feelings for months now. So I thought maybe if I went, I'd find the one I was really supposed to be with. I even said to myself, 'I'll know her when I see her.'" He paused and looked up at Jessie, and she felt the same pierce into her soul that she'd felt last night. "The only woman I saw was the one I'd wanted all along, and she was dressed specifically for me."

Jessie stared at him for a long moment, blinking back the hope that insisted on rising, a tangible feeling growing in her chest.

"And you're here because . . . " The words came out in a whisper, her throat too dry to manage anything more.

Jack glanced at the masks. "Because it's a New Year. A fresh start. Time for me to stop making excuses and to act on what's right. And you're right for me, Jessie." She began to shake her head, but he pressed his hand against her cheek and stopped her. "I've known how right you are since that day I found you in the woods."

"But I'm . . . I'm a *cat*, Jack. This can never work."

"Do you want it?" Sundae asked from behind Jack. Jessie had forgotten anyone else besides the two of them were still in the room.

"It doesn't matter," Jessie said. "Your pack—"

"My pack wants what's best for each member," Sundae interrupted. "And you and Jack are best for each other. It's been clear to the rest of us for months. We've been waiting on the two of you to realize it."

Jessie sucked in her bottom lip and gnawed on it as she looked at Sundae, then Becca, then Jack. His hand still pressed against her face, and his thumb stroked her cheek. She couldn't believe her dream had come true! That it actually happened. And now the man she'd thought she could never have was on his knees in front of her, practically begging her to take him.

"Can I have that kiss I missed last night now?" he asked as he leaned in closer. He waved a hand behind him, dismissing the onlookers.

"My job here is done," Becca said happily. "And yes, you do owe me. Both of you."

She and Sundae disappeared, closing the door behind them, while Jessie flopped backwards on her bed.

"We owe the faeries now," she groaned.

Jack climbed onto her bed on all fours and placed a hand on each side of her head to hover over her. He lowered himself to only inches above her.

"It will be worth it," he promised before pressing his mouth to hers.

Desire

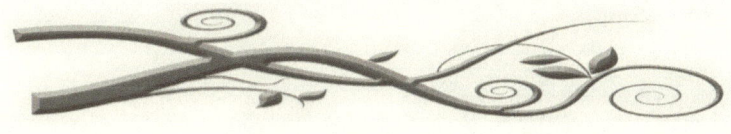

For our final story, we come back to Alexis and Tristan. On Christmas Eve, they promised each other midnight on New Year's. But can they keep that promise? As with all of the stories in this holiday collection, this one doesn't belong anywhere in the main series. It's just a fun escape from your world and from theirs, as rife with war as it is. So read it with no other purpose but the pure enjoyment of it.

Chapter 1

Every inhabitant of the Amadis Island must have been out in the village tonight to ring in the New Year. A crowd of vampires, mages, and various were-creatures mingled together along the main business avenue and leaked onto the side streets, as well. A festive atmosphere surrounded the area with many laughs and cheers ringing through the air. Christmas decorations still adorned the quaint shops and cafes lining the road, and the village tree was brightly lit in front of the council hall at the top end of the cobblestone street.

This was where I stood, near the ginormous tree about halfway up the hill, my gaze sweeping the crowd for the sandy-brown head that usually rose above most others.

"Still can't find him?" Blossom, the blond witch and one of my closest friends, asked from right next to me.

"Nope. Where could he possibly be?"

"You didn't set a place to meet?"

"I didn't expect to lose track of him!" I looked up at the bald man standing next to Blossom. "You're sure you didn't see where he went, Jax?"

The four of us had been walking along the main street together, drinking cider and chatting, when Blossom saw a shop of magical baubles and brews she wanted to check out. The guys stayed outside while we ducked in, and when we emerged, they were nowhere to be seen. We found Jax down the street at the pub, but no Tristan.

"Sorry, Princess," the were-croc said. "Had to take a leak. He said somethin' about needin' to go soon when the clock rang eleven, but we chaps don't need to hold each other's hand like you lasses do. Maybe he meant go as in leave, though, because when I came out, he was gone. He's probably lookin' for you, Princess."

I glanced at the clock on the council hall: 11:19. *That's plenty of time to find him.* But when I reached out mentally to search for his mind signature, I couldn't even find that. *Where the hell could he be?* I blew out a frustrated breath and at the same time, my eyes fell on a blond head, hair the color of straw, about twenty yards away.

Owen, have you seen Tristan? I asked him telepathically.

The warlock cocked his head to the side, then slowly turned until his eyes landed on me. "*He's not with you?*"

He was, but now he's gone.

He shrugged. "*I know he had something crazy planned for the two of you, so I don't know why he'd take off without you.*"

I flashed down to him and put my fists on my hips.

"What do you mean?" I demanded out loud. I knew of no special plans for us, especially crazy ones. "What kinds of plans?"

Owen made an *oops* face. "Was it supposed to be a surprise? He didn't sound like it. Said you two made plans last week. You're sure you're not forgetting something?"

I wracked my brain but came up blank. "Did he say where?"

"Not really. He just said I didn't need to worry about protecting you tonight. He'd take care of it. Which, of course, makes me worry."

I frowned. "Why would I need protection? We're on the Amadis Island."

"Exactly."

My brows pushed together as I tried to mentally find Tristan again while also trying to figure out what he could possibly have planned. Obviously, whatever it was would not be here in the village because he was nowhere to be found.

"I'm going back to the mansion. Maybe there's a note . . . or he's cloaked or something." I flashed away, appearing in the foyer of the matriarch's mansion on the other side of the small island in the middle of the Aegean Sea.

The large, stone house was unusually quiet, everyone back at the village participating in the New Year's celebration. Flames danced in wall sconces, throwing shadows on the walls and grand stairs. Following my nose, I climbed the stairs and hurried down the hall of our wing to the end. Tristan's mouth-watering scent lingered faintly in the air right outside our suite's door. Maybe he'd had it cloaked and muffled so we could spend some alone time without anyone "hearing" me when my orgasms caused my thoughts to broadcast to anyone in telepathic reach. That was the only explanation for why I couldn't detect his mind signature, although it meant the cloak would have to be awfully strong magic. And that meant Owen would have had to put it up. So he was in on this all along?

I threw open the suite door and inhaled. Then frowned. Tristan wasn't here. His tangy-sweet scent of mangos, papayas, lime, sage, and a hint of man remained just as faint as it had been in the hallway. My gaze slid across the dark front room of the suite—empty—and then I moved into the bedroom and bathroom. Empty as well.

"What the hell, Tristan?" I asked out loud. My hand settled on my waist, and my fingers tapped out an impatient rhythm on my hipbone as I once again tried to think if I'd forgotten something. The sheer curtain in the doorway to the balcony blew inward, letting the moonlight shimmer in. The dim light fell on a small, white rectangle on the bed that I hadn't noticed before but now couldn't miss. It practically glowed with the moon's illumination.

An envelope.

I jumped to the bed and snatched it up. My heart leapt with excitement when I saw my name in Tristan's elegant scrawl on the front. A wax seal covered the tip of the flap on the back with a fancy, Old-English-like K pressed into it. My big, bad warrior could be so mushy and romantic. What had he done now?

My finger slid under the flap, and I very carefully broke the seal. Did he create some kind of fancy invitation? Or maybe he drew me something, a beautiful sketch of where he was? I pulled the card out, stared at the writing and frowned.

A single card. Flat. Four words, blood red on the shining white paper.

"Meet me at midnight."

"Well, duh," I muttered. "Of course we'd meet—OH!"

The realization smacked me upside the head. "Meet me at midnight." Those had been his words last week, when we'd had some alone time on a private little island Christmas Eve. We had to come back to the Amadis Island much sooner than either of us wanted to, so we promised we'd meet tonight.

"I'm so stupid!" I shrieked at myself. How had I forgotten so quickly? Of course, the Daemoni attacks hadn't stopped for the holidays—in fact, they'd increased seeing that Christmas was the time of year they hated most. We'd taken a short break to celebrate ourselves, but in the days since, we'd been crazy-busy with reports, debriefings, and strategizing.

Without further thought—midnight was fast approaching—I flashed to the edge of the shield over the Island, appearing in the middle of the sea. Then I flashed again toward Athens, to the tiny private island I'd found for our Christmas celebration. I appeared on the beach, and the island was completely dark. No candles floating in the water or lighting the beach. No light in the house either. Shit. Had I been wrong?

"I began to worry you'd stand me up."

Chapter 2

Tristan's voice filled my head as soon as I touched on his mind signature. I spun around, and my beautiful husband stepped out of the foliage near the French doors that led from the beach to the bedroom. Wearing khaki pants and a light-colored button-down shirt, he looked as sexy as ever. And then his mouth stretched into a smile, a sublime grin that made my heart flip and my knees melt just as much now as the first time he flashed it at me so many years ago.

I rushed to him and threw my arms around his neck. One of his hands clasped my waist while he held up a finger against my lips.

"I couldn't get anyone out here to cloak or shield this island," he whispered. "That's why it's so dark. I don't want to draw the wrong kind of attention to this place."

I nodded. He meant Daemoni attention.

"Yeah, well, as soon as you make my mental wall fall, everyone in a ten-mile radius will know we're here," I teased.

He gave me a sexy smile. "I hope we can get that far. We'll just have to pay attention as long as we can and hope for the best. For now . . . " He leaned in closer and pressed his forehead against mine. The gold in his eyes sparkled brightly, mesmerizing me, as our breaths mingled in the small space between us. His tongue swept over his lips, and my own couldn't help but imitate. "For now, I'd be happy with a kiss at midnight."

I leaned up on my tiptoes and arched myself into his strong body, moving my lips closer to his. His hand tangled in my hair and pulled my head back. Instead of planting his mouth on mine, though, he ducked his head and pressed his lips to my throat.

"It's not midnight yet, my love," he murmured against my skin. A web of electricity spread across my flesh.

I grinned, though, because I saw a spark in the distant sky. Midnight had to be here . . . or at least very close. I didn't hear the church bells in the distance yet. They'd carried over the water on Christmas, so I should be able to hear them tonight. But my eye had caught what would be the first of many fireworks.

Tristan's lips slowly made their way up my neck, along my jawbone, to my ear. He nipped at my lobe before moving closer to my mouth. My body trembled with anticipation just for a kiss. You'd think after being together as long as we'd been, this would get old. Thankfully, it never did.

I heard a church bell in the distance.

I felt Tristan's velvety lips on the corner of my mouth.

I sensed a swarm of Daemoni headed our way.

"Shit!" Tristan muttered as we both jumped to attention.

That hadn't been a firework I'd seen out of the corner of my eye. It must have been a spell, because several evil mages suddenly circled the little island, the colorful lights of their magic zooming through the air.

Tristan and I both ducked and rolled, avoiding any hits. Daemoni witches and wizards surrounded us. Although they were the weakest of the mages—sorcerers being the most powerful and warlocks in between—we still had a difficult time fighting them. They didn't charge in like tanks, engaging in hand-to-hand physical combat. No, they fought from a distance, shooting their magic at us. And we didn't have a mage to back us up, to shield us from their spells. But we did have our own powers, and we had speed.

"*Divide and conquer*," Tristan said.

I rushed for the closest witch while shooting electricity at a nearby wizard with my left hand and reaching for the dagger hidden at my hip—never leave home without it—with my right. I thumbed the amethyst on the hilt and the blade appeared just as I swiped it at the witch. Pink, yellow, blue, and green lights shot through the air, some coming a little too close for comfort, making my skin zing. The sand where I'd just been standing shot into the air like a geyser.

My dagger connected with the witch's torso, and she screamed, then disappeared, flashing away to safety. One down, three to go. I didn't have time to physically check on Tristan, but through my mind I knew he was fine taking down the six mages on his side. I twisted and turned, dodging spells while slashing my blade across flesh and shooting electricity at my enemies. Another one down and gone with a *pop*. Only two more now. The church bells continued ringing in the distance.

I kicked at the wizard who was closest to me and swung my dagger, pushing Amadis power through it before plunging it into his side. He screamed even louder than the witches before, but didn't flash away like a coward. Instead, he magically dislodged my blade, spun in place, and then threw a blast of orange light at me. At the same time, I blasted an electric current, connecting it with his heart. His mouth formed a surprised O, and finally he disappeared.

I tried to turn toward the remaining witch, my final target, but my legs suddenly felt like overcooked noodles. Soft and limp and gummy. As I went down, I pushed a current at her, but my fall made it miss. She cackled a stereotypical witch sound, but she laughed too soon. My body may have been flopping around on the ground like a fish out of water, but she didn't realize Tristan stood behind her. I returned her smile. Or tried to. I couldn't really feel my face anymore, so I wasn't sure what my expression really looked like. What kind of spell had that guy hit me with? Right as she lunged at me, Tristan blasted her away. She landed in the water with a splash, which was followed by a faint *pop* as she flashed away.

Tristan sprang to my side and fell to his knees. He gathered me in his arms, but I could only lay limply. I tried to speak, but my mouth didn't move. My tongue felt like a snake was attached to it.

I got hit, I said silently, the only way I could communicate.

Tristan's mouth twitched as though he fought a smile. "*Yeah. You did.*"

He shook his head, but he looked amused. Needing to know what he saw, I looked at myself through his eyes. If I could have, I would have gasped. My face looked like a basketball—same size, shape, and color. Parts of my body were swollen just as much, but others not at all. As I took this in, however, the scariest part of all began: my tongue really was the size of an anaconda and now my throat closed around it.

Tristan! Can't. Breathe!

His eyes widened with alarm, then his mouth clamped over mine. A kiss? He was going to kiss me now? I was about to die! Although . . . if I was going to go, this would be my chosen way, kissing Mr. Beautiful. We'd missed our midnight kiss—the bells had stopped ringing long ago—but he pushed his tongue into my mouth and made the most of it. I thought that's what he was doing anyway. I could barely feel any of it, and that really sucked. My lungs burned with the need for air. My throat felt like a vice gripped it. My vision was beginning to tunnel. And I couldn't even feel this last damn kiss I would ever get!

Goodbye, my sweet Tristan.

"*No,* ma lykita. *You're not going yet.*" His tongue continued exploring my mouth, reaching deep within. And then I realized I could feel it. Just barely at first. A light tickle. The wetness against my dry tonsils. I gagged. I choked. I gasped for air.

Air! Oh, my god, air! He pulled away as he felt me gulping for glorious air. It burned through my throat and filled my lungs. My chest squeezed, and I coughed. My limbs began to twitch, and feeling slowly returned to my face. Tristan bent over and kissed me again, delivering his healing qualities. When he backed off, I was able to raise my hand to my face. I could feel my chin and cheekbones again.

"Damn wizard," I muttered.

"Are you okay now?" His eyes swept over me from head to toe to check for himself.

"Well, I'm kind of pissed off. We missed our midnight kiss."

His hazel eyes came back to me, and his lips turned up in a slight smile. "That wasn't enough?"

"I couldn't really feel most of it." I frowned. "But it was the midnight part. I've always wanted a kiss right at midnight."

Tristan tilted his head. "I have an idea."

Chapter 3

"Are you sure you're okay?" Tristan asked me before sharing his idea.

I ran a quick physical inventory of myself. All of the swelling seemed to be gone. I felt no other after-effects from the fight with the mages. Damn, I hated fighting mages. I'd take a nest of vampires over them any day . . . at least, unless Owen was nearby. One of his shields around me could have prevented my body's self-suffocation. Of course, there was a reason we were alone, and Tristan and I together had made it through fine.

"Yeah, I'm good," I answered. "So what's this idea of yours?"

He tightened his arms around me and held me close against his chest. I was liking this idea so far.

Then the air whooshed out of my lungs and my vision went blank for a fraction of a second. He'd flashed us away from the island, and now we were in someone's field. He flashed us again, and now we were in a small village. Again and we were in a vineyard. Again and we were in a dark alley, the sounds of a crowd and traffic surrounding us. He took my hand and led me out to the street. And right in front of us stood the Eiffel Tower.

"*Paris?*" I squealed.

"It's not midnight here yet," Tristan said with a smile. "We can still have our kiss."

A crowd filled what looked like a park or green space in front of us as music played, people whooped and hollered, and lights danced up and down the Eiffel Tower itself. Daemoni mind signatures dotted the crowd of Normans', with clusters here and there in the area. I could only imagine what they thought of the prospects for new recruits right now. Alcohol and parties led to poor decisions, such as, "I've never met you before, but you're sexy as hell, so sure, you can bite me." Paris didn't seem quite as rowdy as I'd seen in New York City's Times Square on TV, but people had definitely been celebrating with wine and champagne and midnight hadn't even struck yet.

Tristan stood behind me and wrapped both arms across my shoulders. He leaned his head down and murmured in my ear, "Would you like to see the Eiffel Tower or would you like to be on the Eiffel Tower?"

I sucked in a breath. Who ever got an opportunity like this? When would we ever have it again? My answer was a no-brainer.

"On it!"

He held me tightly again, and we flashed to the top of the tower. Now the crowd was below us, and I was surprised they couldn't see us because the tower was completely lit up. I leaned over our perch on one of the braces and watched the lights travel slowly down the side. The people below chanted in French, and I assumed they were counting down to midnight. I straightened up and turned to face Tristan, a smile breaking out on my face. He returned the grin and pulled me back into his arms.

Light suddenly flooded us. The crowd broke out in loud cheers and whistles. Fireworks began exploding right around us.

"It's midnight," Tristan said, and he grabbed my chin and pulled my face toward his.

And the next thing I knew, I was falling.

Something had plowed into me, knocking me off the beam. What the hell? What could have done that? Or, rather, who? I plummeted toward the earth, my stomach falling faster than the rest of me. After the initial shock disappeared, I regained my senses, just in time as I passed a crossbar close enough that it could have scraped the skin off my nose. I reached out for it instead, grabbed on and swung around. My feet hit a support beam, and I pushed off and up so I could land on a wider, horizontal bar. Just as I checked my balance, another figure joined me.

I recognized her short, blond hair and her perfect little body, though the one and only time I'd seen her was in northern Florida, encouraging Sonya to change her sister Heather into a vampire. I thought this vamp's name was Lesley, and I was able to pick that out of her head to confirm it.

"What are you doing here? In Paris?" I asked, half as a distraction and half because I was seriously curious.

She had such a sweet and innocent face, like the proverbial girl next door—except for the red eyes. And the fangs she'd fully let out so they extended beyond her lip when she smirked at me.

"Florida bored me," she said nonchalantly before she lunged for me.

I jumped up to dodge her and grabbed onto the beam above me, my hands barely grasping the edge. I swung my legs back and forth, building enough momentum to flip over the top of the beam. My feet planted on the bar, but once again, Lesley landed right in front of me.

Tristan? I called out. He was nearby but I sensed him fighting other vampires. Lesley seemed to be the only one focused on me.

"*Be there in a minute, love,*" Tristan deadpanned.

I pulled my dagger out and held it in front of me, jabbing it at the air as a threat to Lesley. She hissed, but took a half-step back. It was only a feign, though, because a second later, she blurred at me.

"What are you trying to prove?" I wondered aloud as I blasted her with my power, effectively pushing her away. Her back and head slammed into a vertical beam. She snarled and came on the attack again.

This time she tricked me. She flipped over me and charged from behind. I spun around, hands up, expecting her to fight me, to beat me down with her unnatural strength, like most vamps tried to do. But not this time. Not this girl. She went straight for the jugular, literally. She flipped once more, so fast her shape blurred, and I didn't even know she came near me, but pain pierced my throat. And then she froze.

Everyone fighting up here at the top of the Eiffel Tower froze. Several pairs of glowing red eyes turned toward me, dotting the shadows in the tower below and above me. I pressed my fingers to the gash in my throat. The flesh was already healing, but blood still gushed. The smell—sweeter and more powerful than anyone else's blood—stopped them all dead-cold.

Except Tristan.

He'd been below me, but now he jumped and pushed off beams and flipped in the air, making his way toward me. But now everyone else was blurring toward me, too, moving as fast as Tristan. And some were so much closer already. A snow-white hand clamped onto my arm and tugged at me, nearly pulling me off balance. More hands grasped my legs. I blasted them with electric current, but they fell back only momentarily. Bone-white hands were reaching over and under the beams all around me. I zapped them while frantically searching for Tristan.

I have to flash, I called out to him. We didn't have a meeting place, though, and if he wasn't close enough to follow my trail, we could be separated by hundreds of miles. I could only hope we'd both make it back to the Amadis Island safely.

"*Let's go then*," he said as his arm snaked around my waist, and he flashed us out of there.

Chapter 4

We appeared on the edge of a forest, the lights of a small village on the other side of the snow-covered field before us. I barely had time to draw in a breath before the Daemoni vampires popped in all around us, apparently having followed our flash trail. The wound in my throat had already sealed and the bleeding had stopped, but the blood on my neck and chest was still fresh and wet. Their eyes glowed brightly, their attention focused completely on me. Lesley's tongue darted out and swiped over her lips.

I looked at Tristan, and he looked at me. His mouth lifted in a smirk, and I rolled my eyes. Then he gave me the signal I was looking for—a quick nod. A confirmation that we were both on the same page. At once, we lifted our hands and blasted the vamps with our powers. His paralyzed them, while mine electrocuted them. I lifted my right hand, too, and added a dose of Amadis power. The vamps snarled and snapped at us anyway, their lust for my blood overcoming any physical pain.

"*Ready*," Tristan said in my head. I shot out a stronger blast of all of my powers, sending the vampires backwards twenty feet—too far for them to follow our trail now—while Tristan wrapped his arms around me and flashed us away again.

We appeared in another field, but this one wasn't covered in snow. I had no idea where we were now, where he'd brought us. Hopefully closer to home.

"How close are we to the Amadis Island?" I asked.

"Far. We're in England," Tristan said.

"England?" I frowned. I just wanted to go home now.

"It's not midnight here yet."

I looked up at him with a raised brow.

"And I know the perfect place for our midnight kiss," he added before pulling me into his arms again and flashing.

We appeared on the top of a tall building overlooking a river with a giant Ferris wheel lit up in blue on the far bank. On our near side, a tall clock tower stood on the other end of our building. I only knew it from pictures, but I recognized Big Ben. The hands showed it was 11:58. We had two minutes to spare.

And eight Daemoni mind signatures right below us.

"You're fucking kidding me," Tristan muttered as they came closer, climbing the side of the building. More vampires. At least the blood on my skin had dried. But they still weren't going to relent.

"I'm freakin' tired of this!" My fists rested on my hips as I stared down at the vamps crawling up the walls like spiders. "You are not ruining it again!" I shouted now.

We weren't supposed to kill, not even our enemies unless absolutely necessary, and I didn't think they'd die from the fall, but I was done being nice. Done running away. Done putting up with their shit tonight. I raised both hands, palms out, and directed a mix of all of my powers at the vamp closest to me. Electricity and Amadis power hit him hardest, sending him into convulsions. His hands released their grips from the wall, and I used my power to push him far from the side of the building. Then I let gravity do its thing. In quick procession, I hit each of the others in the same way, sending them all to the ground far below. Some popped up immediately and jumped to hit the side of the building as far up as they could go in a single bound before trying to climb the remainder to us. I hit them again and again.

The first dong from Big Ben sounded.

"Midnight," I said, distracted from the vamps that continued to pursue us. I looked at Tristan. He looked down at the vamps.

"Are you done playing?" he asked me as the second dong rang through the night. He jerked his head toward Big Ben. I grinned. And we both flashed to the clock tower, appearing on a ledge just below the VI on the side facing the river. No vampires followed us.

Big Ben rang a third time, the sound vibrating all the way through my bones. Bright lights shot up in the air in our direction, sending my heart into a gallop as I thought mages attacked now. But then the lights exploded into showers of lights. Fireworks!

I turned to my husband. He gripped my wrists in each of his hands, lifted my arms above my head, and used his body to press me against the clock. As his mouth clamped down on mine, the clock gonged again and more fireworks exploded. My lips parted with his, our tongues danced together, fireworks popped all around us, and Big Ben continued ringing in the New Year. Our kiss deepened and went on and on with only momentary breaks to suck in air. Tristan's hands slid down my arms and grasped each side of my face and holding me as though he feared I'd pull away too soon. I wrapped my arms around his neck and pulled him closer. I lifted my legs and encircled his waist, and he ground his pelvis against me. I moaned into his mouth as I soaked up every sensation of this glorious kiss that lasted long after the twelfth stroke.

When we finally broke apart, Tristan twisted away to stand beside me. We watched the rest of the fireworks show from our perch on Big Ben, our backs against the clock, our hands clasped together.

An insane giggle rose in my chest as I considered the reality of our night. We'd been in Greece, Paris, and London in a matter of two hours. We'd brought in midnight three times, in three different countries and three time zones. Unfortunately, we only had one midnight kiss. But damn if it hadn't been worth every bit of it.

"Happy New Year, my sweet Tristan," I said between my giggles.

"Happy New Year, *ma lykita.*"

"Fighting the Daemoni sucked, but I don't know if you can top this next year."

He gave me a sublime grin with a hint of cockiness. "Is that a challenge? Because you know how I love a challenge."

"As long as we get another year, I can't wait to see what you do."

He swung his leg around so he faced me again, each of his feet on the outside of mine. "For a kiss like that, I'll do whatever it takes."

I rolled my eyes up to look at him through my lashes. His forehead leaned in to press against mine.

"I think we should practice a lot before then," I whispered.

"Agreed." He bent down and his lips met mine and we picked up where our midnight kiss left off as the crowds below cheered and sang and celebrated the New Year and all of the hope it promised.

Recipes

Christina's More Powerful Than You Know Baked Chicken Wings

Submitted by Christina Silcox

<u>Ingredients:</u>

    1 pkg. frozen chicken wings (I use a 10lb package for parties)
    Non-stick cooking spray
    Buffalo wing sauce (as hot as you can stand it)

1. Preheat oven to 400 degrees.

2. Evenly place chicken wings on foil-lined cookie sheets sprayed lightly with nonstick spray.

3. Bake for 45 minutes from frozen. Remove from oven and pour off excess liquid. Pour Buffalo sauce by spoonful over each wing, taking care not to add too much sauce so the wings aren't soggy.

4. Bake for an additional 15-20 minutes until the wings look slightly dry to the touch. Serve with blue cheese or ranch dressing, and celery sticks.

Tristan's New Year's Good Fortune Pork Tenderloin

Submitted by Char Wilcoxson

This has been a New Year's tradition for a few years now to make. The Chinese believe that eating pork for the first day of the New Year will bring good fortune, and this is a family favorite for pork tenderloin.

Ingredients:
Pork tenderloin
1 ½ cups honey
½ cup brown sugar
½ cup soy sauce
3 Tbsp. maple syrup
1 Tbsp. mustard
2 Tbsp. dried onions
1 Tbsp. chopped garlic
2 Tbsp. butter
½ tsp. Ginger

1. Place Pork tenderloin in a crockpot/slow cooker.

2. Warm ingredients in a saucepan just enough for them to melt and blend together, then pour over the tenderloin.

3. Cook on low for 6 to 8 hours depending on the size of the tenderloin. Occasionally use a ladle to pour some of the sauce on the top of the tenderloin.

Kate's Unforgettable Chinese New Year's Dish

Submitted by Kelly Victorine

This is for Kate and her wanting to have an unforgettable New Year's. This is my dad's Chinese food that is super good!

Ingredients:

    2-6 Tbsp. Sesame Oil (judge accordingly based on desire)

    1 ½ tsp. or 3 Cloves Garlic, minced

    Walnut sized Ginger

    1 tsp. Hot Pepper Seeds (judge accordingly, more = hotter)

    4 Chicken Breasts (bone out)

    ½ Stock Celery

    1 Can Bamboo Shoots

    1 Can Sliced Water Chestnuts

    ½ Onion, white

    1 Green Pepper

    1 Tbsp. Oyster Sauce

    1 Tbsp. Soy Sauce

    ½ cup Wine, White

    1 tsp. Cornstarch (for thickening)

    1 cup Peanuts

1. Heat 2 Tbsp. sesame oil in pan and stir fry garlic, ginger, and hot pepper seeds in pan.

2. Add chicken and cook until done.

3. Remove chicken and set aside.

4. Stir-fry all vegetables in 4 Tbsp. sesame oil.

5. Add chicken back into mixture.

6. Mix oyster and soy sauce with wine and cornstarch, pour over vegetable/chicken mixture.

7. Simmer 5-10 minutes.

8. Add peanuts.

9. Serve over white rice.

Faerie Dill Pickle Dip

Submitted by Michele Luker

Ingredients:
- 8 oz. cream cheese
- 8 oz. sour cream
- Pickles diced up, as many as you want
- Pkg. of dried beef lunchmeat, diced up small

1. Mix this all together and it is like rolled up pickles.

2. Serve with Ritz crackers.

Magic Shrimp Dip

Submitted by Michele Luker

Ingredients:
- 2 8-oz pkgs. cream cheese
- 1 bottle cocktail sauce
- 2 cans mini shrimps

1. With the cream cheese softened, spread it out on a platter, then pour the cocktail sauce over the top and spread it out evenly over the cream cheese.

2. Drain the mini shrimp in the cans, and sprinkle over the top.

3. Chill. Serve with Crackers.

Bewitching Carrot Cookies

Submitted by Jill Cruz

<u>Ingredients:</u>
- 2 cups diced carrots
- ¾ cup butter or margarine, softened
- 1 cup sugar
- 1 egg
- 1 tsp. vanilla
- 2 cup flour
- 2 tsp. baking powder
- ½ tsp. salt

1. Cook carrots until soft, mash them.

2. Cream butter and sugar together, add egg and vanilla. Beat until fluffy. Stir in mashed carrots.

3. Sift together flour, baking powder, and salt. Blend into batter.

4. Drop from teaspoon onto ungreased baking sheet.

5. Bake at 375 degrees for about 12 minutes.

Midnight Kiss Bourbon Drops

Submitted by Jill Cruz

Ingredients:

    1 cup semi-sweet chocolate chips
    2 ½ cups vanilla wafer cookies, crumbled
    ½ cup bourbon
    ½ cup powdered sugar
    3 Tbsp. corn syrup (or simple sugar)
    1 cup chopped pretzels (or nuts)
    Granulated sugar

1. Melt chocolate morsels in microwave or over stove top double boiler until melted.

2. Remove from Heat.

3. In a large bowl, combine powdered sugar, vanilla wafer crumbs, and pretzels (or nuts).

4. Add chocolate and mix until combined.

5. Let stand for about 30 minutes or until cooled.

6. Form into 1-inch balls while chocolate is still pliable.

7. Roll into granulated sugar.

Christina's Magical Caramel Sauce

Submitted by Wendy Jahnke

<u>Ingredients:</u>
- 3 ½ sticks margarine
- 8 cups brown sugar
- 1 ½ pints half-and-half

1. Boil margarine and half-and-half over medium heat.

2. Once boiling, add brown sugar slowly, stir until consistency is smooth.

3. Serve with baked goods or fruit.

Masquerade Crisp

Submitted by Felicia Semmler

Inspired by Jessie and all her were-panther awesomeness.

<u>Ingredients:</u>
- 4 apples peeled and cored
- 1 1/2 cups flour
- 2 snack size apple sauce containers
- 1 tsp. vanilla
- 1/8 tsp. liquid imitation butter
- 1 tbs. sugar
- 1/2 tsp. cinnamon
- 1/4 cup hot water
- 4 Tbsp. brown sugar

1. Preheat oven to 350 degrees.

2. Slice apples about 1/8-inch thick and layer in bottom of 9x9 greased baking pan.

3. In a separate bowl, add the rest of the ingredients except for 2 Tbsp. brown sugar (this is for the topping) and mix until crumbly. Then sprinkle the mixture evenly over the layered apples. Finally, sprinkle the remaining 2 Tbsp. of brown sugar on top and place in oven.

4. Bake until apples are tender - depending on how thick the apples are cut they can take longer than 30 minutes. Just stab them with a fork/toothpick to see if they are at the desired softness.

A Faerie Nutty Chocolate Delight

Submitted by Heather Brandt

Ingredients:

    Butter or cooking spray

    1 pkg. mini marshmallows

    1 12-oz bag regular chocolate chips

    1 cup chunky peanut butter

1. To begin, I first coat a 13x9 pan with butter or cooking spray, whichever I have on hand. Then use the mini marshmallows to fill the entire bottom of the pan with one layer.

2. After that, place bag of chocolate chips and chunky peanut butter into mixing bowl. Microwave on high for 3 minutes. I recommend you stir about halfway through. Add an additional 30 seconds or so if needed to make sure chocolate is melted completely. You will have chunks from the peanut butter, but you shouldn't have any from the chocolate.

3. Once chocolate is melted thoroughly and mixed with chunky peanut butter, pour evenly over marshmallows. Place in fridge until chocolate is hard and then cut to desired sizes.

A Were's Delight Strawberry & Vodka Fritz

Submitted by Zee Hayat

Ingredients:
    Strawberries (mmm)
    Kiwis
    ½ cup sugar
    A shot of martini or vodka (optional)
    1 cup of water

1. Using a small saucepan, add in the water and sugar and boil for 7-10 minutes.

2. Once it has been boiled, put it in the fridge to cool it down a bit.

3. Clean the strawberries and kiwis (ensure you remove all seeds from the kiwis).

4. Put the clean fruit in a blender and blend until smooth.

5. Add the sugar water and blend to ensure, then add the vodka or margarita.

6. Pour mixture into a large casserole dish or a baking dish.

7. Put the casserole pan into the freezer and freeze for an hour or two.

8. Use a fork to scrape the ice that has been formed after the first hour and put back into the freezer. The idea is to make it look like shaved ice, after it is completely frozen.

9. Repeat the above process over and over until it is completely frozen, or you can leave it in the freezer without breaking it the first couple of hours, but that just makes it harder to break once it is completely.

Alexis And Tristan's New Year's Breakfast

Submitted by Sue VanNort and Shelly Fenner

After Tristan and Alexis' fight to be together at midnight on New Year's Eve, traveling around the world in their attempts to have an undisturbed kiss at midnight, they may need something to restore their strength a bit! This has all the ingredients!

<u>Ingredients:</u>
    2 or 3 large potatoes, peeled
    1 medium onion, chopped
    1 lb. ground sausage
    1 red pepper
    1 green pepper
    ½-dozen large eggs
    Sausage gravy

1. Dice potatoes, onion, red and green pepper.

2. Place in warmed frying pan with melted butter.

3. Cover and simmer over low heat.

4. After 10 minutes, mix in sausage and cook over low heat.

5. In a separate frying pan, scramble eggs until done. Mix in sausage gravy and allow to simmer for 5 minutes.

6. Mix both pans together and serve with rye toast and mimosas. Best breakfast ever on New Year's morning!

Around the World Club Sandwich

Submitted by Jessie deSchepper

This is our Dutch version of the Club Sandwich – something Alexis might want after her trip around the world New Year's Eve.

Ingredients:

olive oil for frying
½ cup sliced bacon
4 eggs
½ loaf of brown/wheat bread
Extra virgin olive oil
1/3 cup soft blue cheese
2 Tbsp. mayonnaise
1 bunch radishes
2 beefsteak tomatoes
1 avocado
1 cup watercress
1 head of lettuce trio
4 slices ham

1. Fry the bacon for about 5 minutes in a dry skillet.

2. Beat the eggs in a bowl. Pour the eggs into the pan with the bacon and fry in about 8 minutes on both sides until golden brown.

3. Remove the eggs from the pan and cut into quarters.

4. Preheat the oven to 400 degrees F.

5. Place the bread slices on a lined baking sheet and sprinkle with a dash of olive oil. Bake in the oven for about 6 minutes until crisp,

6. Mash the blue cheese in a bowl, stir through the mayonnaise and season with a little freshly ground pepper.

7. Cut the radishes into slices.

8. Cut the tomatoes into slices.

9. Make the avocado and cut the flesh into slices.

10. Cut the cress loose.

11. Spread 4 slices of bread on the blue cheese dressing, radishes, tomatoes, avocado, cress, lettuce trio, and ham.

12. Divide the fried eggs on 4 slices of bread.

13. Put 2 slices per sandwich bread invested in each other and finish with not invested slices bread.

14. Insert a skewer into all corners and cut the sandwich into 4 triangles.

Hemelse Modder (Heavenly Mud)

Submitted by Jessie deSchepper

Heavenly mud is a solid Chocolate and Dutch dessert. Yummy!

<u>Ingredients:</u>
>½ cup dark chocolate
>2 Tbsp. butter
>1 Tbsp. water
>1 ½ Tbsp. sugar
>2 eggs, separated

1. Break the chocolate into a saucepan and place in a pan of boiling water.

2. Add a spoonful of water while the chocolate melts.

3. Stir the butter and sugar until cream.

4. Add one by one the egg yolks.

5. Beat the egg whites very stiff, add a pinch of salt.

6. Stir the soft chocolate into the butter mixture and place this mixture on the rigid protein.

7. Stir it all together lightly.